The
Beloved
Land

JANETTE OKE
&
T. DAVIS BUNN

The Beloved Land

BETHANY HOUSE PUBLISHERS
MINNEAPOLIS, MINNESOTA 55438

Published by Bethany House Publishers
A Ministry of Bethany Fellowship International
11400 Hampshire Avenue South
Bloomington, Minnesota 55438

Printed in the United States of America

ISBN 0-7642-2723-8

JANETTE OKE was born in Champion, Alberta, during the depression years, to a Canadian prairie farmer and his wife. She is a graduate of Mountain View Bible College in Didsbury, Alberta, where she met her husband, Edward. They were married in May of 1957 and went on to pastor churches in Indiana as well as Calgary and Edmonton, Canada.

The Okes have three sons and one daughter and are enjoying the addition of grandchildren to the family. Edward and Janette have both been active in their local church, serving in various capacities as Sunday school teachers and board members. They make their home near Calgary, Alberta.

T. DAVIS BUNN, a native of North Carolina, is a former international business executive whose career has taken him to over forty countries in Europe, Africa, and the Middle East. With topics as diverse as romance, history, and intrigue, Bunn's books continue to reach readers of all ages and interests. He and his wife, Isabella, reside near Oxford, England.

By T. Davis Bunn

The Book of Hours
One Shenandoah Winter
Tidings of Comfort & Joy
The Music Box
The Messenger
The Quilt

Drummer in the Dark
The Great Divide
To the Ends of the Earth
The Ultimatum
The Warning
The Presence

By Janette Oke & T. Davis Bunn

Return to Harmony

Another Homecoming   •   *Tomorrow's Dream*

SONG OF ACADIA
The Meeting Place   *The Birthright*
The Sacred Shore   *The Distant Beacon*
The Beloved Land

By Janette Oke

Celebrating the Inner Beauty of Woman
*Dana's Valley**
Janette Oke's Reflections on the Christmas Story
The Matchmakers
Nana's Gift
The Red Geranium

CANADIAN WEST

When Calls the Heart　　*When Breaks the Dawn*
When Comes the Spring　　*When Hope Springs New*
Beyond the Gathering Storm
When Tomorrow Comes

LOVE COMES SOFTLY

Love Comes Softly　　*Love's Unending Legacy*
Love's Enduring Promise　　*Love's Unfolding Dream*
Love's Long Journey　　*Love Takes Wing*
Love's Abiding Joy　　*Love Finds a Home*

A PRAIRIE LEGACY

The Tender Years　　*A Quiet Strength*
A Searching Heart　　*Like Gold Refined*

SEASONS OF THE HEART

Once Upon a Summer　　*Winter Is Not Forever*
The Winds of Autumn　　*Spring's Gentle Promise*

WOMEN OF THE WEST

The Calling of Emily Evans　　*A Bride for Donnigan*
Julia's Last Hope　　*Heart of the Wilderness*
Roses for Mama　　*Too Long a Stranger*
A Woman Named Damaris　　*The Bluebird and the Sparrow*
They Called Her Mrs. Doc　　*A Gown of Spanish Lace*
The Measure of a Heart　　*Drums of Change*

Janette Oke: A Heart for the Prairie
Biography of Janette Oke by Laurel Oke Logan

*with Laurel Oke Logan

"These are the times that try men's souls."

—Thomas Paine, 1776

Prologue

Once when Catherine was a little girl, her father had taken her to a concert in Halifax. A visiting admiral had gathered together a group of musicians from his fleet. A flute, two violins, a cello, a bass fiddle, and a miniature concertina had played Handel and Purcell. Strange that she would remember those details from a night when she had been scarcely nine years old. But Catherine recalled everything about that evening. The garrison had entertained the admiral with a fine dinner, one which included all the officers' wives and families. To Catherine's eager young eyes, the hall had seemed nearly on fire with all the candles in the chandeliers, on tables, and in wall sconces around the room. And the music had transported her away across the seas, to a place she knew only in books—a world of fine palaces and grand dames, with scores of servants and nights to enjoy such fine meals and wonderful music.

"What are you thinking about, daughter?"

Catherine smiled at her father in the doorway. "I am writing to Anne and Nicole." She was back in her true Georgetown setting. Nova Scotia had been her lifelong home, its frontier simplicity far from the world she had glimpsed that night so long ago.

Her father had come from his back bedroom. She could tell his legs and hips were bothering him. He kept his hands extended to grip and support. The path was well known, the stanchions familiar. He released the doorframe to hold the back of the settee by the fire. Then his other hand reached for the side wall's middle beam. Then the high-backed rocker, then the cabinet separating their sitting area from the cooking area, then the long bench with the water pitcher and basin, then the window above the alcove, where she was writing. Catherine resisted the urge to help him move about. Father John was seldom cross these days, but he thoroughly disliked anyone putting themselves out on his account. He was determined not only to make his own way but help as he could around the house as well. Which, given his health just six months earlier, was nothing short of a miracle.

John Price took a long breath at the open window, clearing away the remnants of his afternoon nap. "How is Andrew?"

"Resting comfortably." In truth, that was more hope than fact. Now it was Andrew who had not been doing well at all. "That is, at least he is reclining." Catherine could feel her father's eyes searching her face at the rueful tone.

He turned away eventually to pluck a pewter cup off the wall shelf and pour from the pitcher of well water. "I don't see much progress being made on your letter," he observed.

Catherine had to smile. "I was thinking about the concert you brought me to when I was nine."

"No, lass, you were eight. Two weeks shy of your birthday." He drank and sighed satisfaction. "They played Handel."

"I am astonished that you remember it at all."

"Those days seem far closer to me than last week." He drained his cup and set it by the window. "You looked like a tiny angel, you did. You in your lovely new dress and your hair all shining and your eyes trying to take it all in." He patted her shoulder and lowered himself into a chair across from her.

Catherine used the conversation as a reason to put down her pen. It was a remarkable boon in these later years of his life for her father to be revealing this side she had never known. Truth be told, she sincerely doubted that it had even existed in the past. She turned in her chair so she could study him.

John Price had always been a strong man. Even now, with time's biting winds etched deeply into his features, and mobility restricted, he still held himself erect in the manner of the officer he once had been. Yet now there was a light to his eyes, a depth of awareness and care that belonged to one whose youth had been renewed like the eagle's, as the Psalmist said.

"Why are you inspecting me, daughter?" her father asked in a bemused tone.

Catherine reached across the table to grasp his hand. "I was thinking," she replied, "that I have never felt so close to you as now."

"Families are meant to stand together when difficulties come."

"I was not speaking of Andrew, Father."

"No." He seemed content to sit and return her gaze. There was no need to speak of the new person now housed within his aging frame. Nor to describe again for her how he had come to relinquish his harsh military grip on life, even upon religion, and instead see faith with changed eyes.

"Since you are not making much progress on your missive," John Price quipped, looking at the single line, "March 10, 1778," at the top of the page, "I was wondering if you might help me for a moment with something out in the back."

"Certainly. Just let me fetch my shawl."

Chapter 1

Since Andrew's latest ailment, Father John had grown increasingly determined to not only move about unaided, but also serve around the place in whatever way he could. When Catherine put some task aside, planning to take it up at a later time, Father John might try his hand at it. She had caught him darning a pair of socks one recent day. This had given rise to much hilarity, since the old man had such a large amount of woolen thread over the hole, it probably would not have fit in his boot.

Catherine now followed her father outside, staying close in case he stumbled. He walked with one hand trailing along the rough planks of their cottage, picking his way carefully along the uneven path. "I've always thought of this as the between-times," Father John told her over his shoulder. "Neither one nor the other. Not winter, not spring, not much of anything save waiting."

"Yes," Catherine replied slowly, thinking about the symbolism of his words. The last snow had been only four days past, and the gathering clouds suggested they might have yet more. But the in-between days were warm enough for them to walk over bare earth, brown and thawing. Like the weather, her father was waiting too for spring, the one in a far better place.

Catherine blinked quickly against the tears and said as evenly as she could, "I have decided to alert Anne and Nicole to their father's condition."

Father John rounded the corner of the cottage and carefully aimed toward the shed by the rear fence. Formerly this had been where Andrew had carried on his leather working, but his poor health had kept him away for over a year.

John now leaned against the shed door to catch his breath. He eyed the clouds, the patches of snow upon the northern hills, the tangle of bare branches in the forest to the west. Anywhere but into his daughter's face. "It is a thing that needs doing," he finally said.

"I hate to worry them over nothing," Catherine argued, more with herself than her father's statement.

"You'd never forgive yourself if you left it until too late." He now did look directly into her eyes, and she could see the truth she did not want to acknowledge.

She opened her mouth to object, to say that Andrew was certainly not as bad as all that. But Father John's gaze held the calm of one who himself was approaching that final door with confidence about what awaited him on the other side.

He repeated softly, "It needs doing. The young women need to hear this from you. And hear it now, not after . . ."

He let her finish the hard statement herself. She used her apron's edge to wipe her eyes and took a deep, shaky breath. The fact was, she had not wanted to write her daughters because it would mean putting the truth into words she had long attempted to avoid.

Andrew's tools stood in careful array along the side wall. It seemed as though he had been there only yesterday and not left them untouched these many months. Only a strip of leather upon the workbench, curling and drying with age, indicated how long it had been.

Catherine helped her father pry open the back shutters. She had no need of palaces nor fancy frocks, not even for a life where music and fine dinners were a part of her days. All she wanted was what she had here, she reflected as she gazed out the open window. Her cottage, her God, her life—and her husband. Her heart was gripped with a fear like none she had ever known. Andrew might indeed be taken from her. And

16

soon. And she must write those letters.

"Help me here, would you, daughter?" John Price waited for her to join him before shifting a saddle off a pile of ancient army blankets. They both coughed as the blankets were lifted and folded and set aside. When they arrived at the bottom item, her father cried, "Just where I thought it was! After all this time!"

It took Catherine a moment to recognize his old campaign chest.

"Yes, daughter. Not seen these many years, left here when you and Andrew and I first moved to Georgetown. I have not touched it since." John Price fiddled in his waistcoat and extracted a rusty key. "But I found the key and the chest both without a moment's hesitation. There's a bit of life in this old codger yet."

Catherine smiled and shook her head at him. She turned again to the chest. The seal of her father's old regiment and his final rank of major were stamped in chipped gold leaf upon the top. John Price required both hands to turn the key, but it finally gave, and together they cracked open the top. Inside were things she had last seen when packing for the move that had brought them here. Normally the memories associated with that tragic time—the remembered shame of Andrew having been drummed out of his regiment for aiding the French during the Acadian expulsion—would have been something else to avoid. But Catherine now dove eagerly into the past. "I had forgotten how many medals you had, Father."

"Never mind that old rubbish." He lifted the slender shelf that had been fitted across the top. His fingers trembled in anticipation as he lifted out a formal uniform and cocked hat in their wrappings of rice paper. A frayed battalion standard was next, then spurs and a ceremonial dagger. All were impatiently set aside as of no consequence. No matter that for Catherine's entire growing-up years her father's military career defined his very existence.

Once again Catherine saw him as he was now. Far more than years had made him not just a beloved father but also a source of solace in the midst of uncertain and anxious times. "You have changed so much," she said quietly as she held the small dagger for a moment before adding it to the pile. "I would be hard pressed to even list the ways."

He lifted his gaze, revealing a dusty streak across his forehead and that same illumination in his eyes. "There is only one change that bears mentioning," he replied. "And for that I have my Maker to thank. And Andrew for introducing me to Him."

The present swooped back, and Catherine's fear gripped her throat and turned her voice husky. "I am so desperately afraid." She sank onto a small step stool, her arms wrapped around herself.

John Price's response offered neither empty solace nor false hope. "God willing, I shall be here to aid and comfort you throughout whatever comes." He laid his hand on her shoulder, then leaned on it as he pulled forward a chair and eased onto it.

They sat as they were, two generations bound by history, by love, and by Andrew's current crisis. Finally Catherine was able to ask, "What are you seeking?"

"This." John Price lifted out the last item, a small packet wrapped in burlap. "I had this strange notion . . ." he began, then shifted the thought to say, "I had no idea I would live to be such an old man."

There was a strange expression on his face that Catherine could not understand. Her intuition told her that whatever was in the package held a significance beyond simply another symbol of her father's past.

He unfolded the burlap to reveal a pair of leather-bound books. The top one was so ancient the locking clasp fell off at his touch. He set it gingerly to one side and offered her the second. "This is your mother's diary. I should have given this to you years ago."

"Mother's?" Catherine's own voice was little more than a whisper. Other than a chipped china figurine that rested on the mantel, she'd had no idea there was anything else. Her mother's face and form were only imagined—she had been motherless all her life.

"It was what you said the other night when Andrew was struggling to breathe. About needing someone to lean on. About longing for your mother, wishing you had even a memory. You were so tiny when she . . ." Unashamedly he wiped at his eyes. "I should have given this to you when you were still a child. But I couldn't bring myself to share it, not then. Then I felt it would be something for your later years, but over time I forgot I even had it." He dropped his eyes to what she now held. "Useless old man that I am."

Catherine leaned forward and placed a hand on the sallow cheek. "You are anything but useless. I don't know what I would do without you, especially now that Andrew is so ill. I would have given up had you not been here to help bear the load."

He kept his gaze upon the book in her lap. "I could not bring myself to ever read it. At first it was too painful. Then I went through, well, a time of great anger. For a while I blamed her for leaving us. I know you can't understand that. I don't myself anymore. I suppose I thought she should have fought harder and not given in to death. Then I simply put it out of my mind. I was afraid, you see. What if . . . what if I read something that told me she had found me to be troublesome or did not love me?" Reluctantly he lifted his gaze and revealed the old pain. "I knew myself well enough to know there was much she could have complained about in those pages. I was cocky and rigid and selfish. It is a wonder she could love me at all."

"Oh, Father. You are none of these things."

"If I am not now, it is only by the grace of God. For that is surely how I lived the majority of my life." He sighed and reached for the older volume. "And this is my own father's journal—another generation beyond the one you hold."

She watched him cautiously open the cover, only to have this too come off in his hands.

"I should have told you before now—"

19

"Told me what?"

John Price was carefully turning each fragile page as he spoke. "I have read these pages only once. It was in the days after your mother died bringing you into this world. Those were dark times. Had it not been for you, I don't know what would have come of me."

Catherine could feel the cold radiate up through her dress from the hard-packed earthen floor. But she simply tucked her skirt about her legs as she focused her full attention on her father.

"You never knew your grandfather. Old Edwin Price was as stern and unbending a figure as any I have ever met. Like an admiral he was, hard as old iron and full of pride. Never knew a man who could rage worse than my father. Like facing a firestorm, he was, when crossed. He was a military man himself, a colonel. You know we come from a long line of officers in the royal corps."

"I know. But—"

"He passed on close to the same time as your mother. They shipped his gear to me at the outpost. It took months to arrive, along with word that he had gone. Which was not altogether a bad thing, the distance and the time, don't you see. Because when his things did arrive, in the midst of all my grief over losing your mother, I discovered this diary. And what I read, what I read—"

He stopped abruptly and slapped an open page with one hand. "Found it! After all these years, it was right where I thought."

"Found what, Father?"

But his eyes remained focused upon the page. After a moment he said, "And it's just as I recall reading it all those many years back." He looked at Catherine. "So shocking then I almost burned the thing. Can't understand what it was that made me keep this book. A small token of the old man, I suppose." He turned away then and spoke as though to himself. "Of course, it was God's hand all along. I see that now. Yes. Here it is before me once again."

Catherine reached over and placed a hand upon her father's arm. "Father, speak to me."

He looked at her again. "My father was married twice."

"What—?"

"Never knew it, of course. He had never spoken to anyone about his early days. What a shock it was to see the words written here in his diary. You can't imagine."

"I don't understand—"

"No, of course not." John Price took a long breath. "My father fought against the French in one of our many wars. He was captured and imprisoned. He shared his cell with an elderly Frenchman, who had been incarcerated over some minor matter. His granddaughter came to visit him daily, bringing him what she could in the way of food and clothing. Over time Edwin came to know and . . . and admire her."

"Your father fell in love with a Frenchwoman?" Years of antagonism between two great nations were captured in her question.

"Hard to imagine even now, I agree. You can see what a blow that would have been, reading it those many years back. What with me carrying such a load of hatred over the wars and my wounds. But there it was. The old Frenchie who was my father's cellmate died, but still the young lady kept coming. They talked of marriage and a future together, though it all seemed so bleak in that wartorn time. But young love was not to be denied."

He turned the page, all without taking his eyes from his daughter's face. "One of the young French guards was infatuated with her, and she led him on a bit until she had won his confidence. One night she served him full of wine and used his key to release Edwin.

"They married in secret and hid themselves in a remote fishing village. They began making plans to escape to England. Then word came through one of the fishermen that the police were scouting the region, looking for an escaped English officer."

"A Frenchwoman." Catherine shook her head in wonderment, recalling her father's previous hatred for the French and all the pain it had caused them both.

"She had become ill and was too sick to travel. She insisted Edwin flee for his life, promising she would follow as soon as he sent word. Celeste's brother, a fisherman, risked his life to take Edwin across the Channel. He could see, as did the entire village, that Edwin and the Frenchwoman were bound by a love more vast than any nation or war. Those were the words my father used in his diary."

John Price stopped then. But Catherine could see from the expression on his face that there was more. "Tell me the rest, Father."

John Price studied her face for a long moment.

The realization struck her very hard indeed. "She was pregnant?"

"Indeed so." His eyes dropped to the page. "What hit me even harder than the news that I had a half sister was that my father eventually learned his first wife had died in childbirth."

"You didn't know?"

"All my life I thought I was my father's only heir. Here in these pages, just after you were born, I learned how he had spent years searching. But our two countries remained at war— at least as near as breath to that state. And there was no concern for a young orphan lass."

"A daughter," Catherine murmured. "A half sister. My aunt."

John Price suddenly raised his head. "I have thought of something." He reached a trembling hand to grasp Catherine's. "I wonder if Andrew's brother, Charles—"

"Oh yes, I will write to him," Catherine said, her thoughts leaping ahead in the conversation. "I'm sure he would want to take up the search for some news, maybe even to be able to find her." She squeezed her father's hand. "It will be wonderful to have something like this to add to my letter. Something with a measure of hope." Excitement filled her heart and her voice. "He knows many influential people, both in England and in France. If there is news to be had, Charles will discover it," she finished confidently.

Chapter 2

" 'Although Father John is getting on in years,' " Anne read aloud to the small group gathered by the fire in the sitting room, " 'he continues to help me as he is able.' " Catherine's letter included the little story about the unwearable darned socks, and they all chuckled. Anne picked up where she had stopped. " 'I fear all this only adds additional strain to his frail body, but there is no stopping him. He feels a responsibility, especially now that Andrew is unwell.' " Anne tried to swallow over the lump in her throat.

"His heart," Charles murmured, his hand against his chest. "What a family trait to share with my dear brother."

Catherine's next words appeared and vanished on the page through the film of tears in Anne's eyes. " 'Andrew has good days and bad. The bad, I am sorry to say, are coming more often and are far more severe.' "

Anne could go no further. The letter dropped to the floor as her hands covered her eyes.

"Anne, my dear."

Anne heard the rustle of skirts as Judith, Charles's wife, rose from her place beside her husband. She was a woman well versed with sorrow, having lost both her husband and her oldest son, Anne's own first husband, in scarcely the space of a year. She would know that words had little effect at such a time, and she only knelt beside Anne and put gentle arms around her.

Charles asked softly, "Shall I finish reading for you?"

Anne nodded mutely.

From the other side of the fireplace, where Anne's Thomas sat holding the child, her boy John observed softly, "Mommy's sad."

Anne pressed a small square of cambric to her eyes and drew as steady a breath as she could manage. Small John now stood on the settee alongside Thomas. His round arms circled her husband's neck, cheeks touching, dark hair burnished and intermingled in the firelight. Two sets of eyes regarded her with loving concern. John's little chin quivered with effort to not cry also. "I'm fine, darling," Anne managed to say, though forming a smile seemed beyond her. "It's just . . . it's the news that your grandfather isn't well."

Thomas held the little boy closer.

John released his grip on Thomas's neck long enough to wipe his own eyes. "I'm a big boy now."

Charles had crossed the room to retrieve the letter at Anne's feet.

Anne had thought she would never feel as separated from her parents as she had at her wedding to Thomas. But now . . . The tears returned, this time nearly blocking out Charles's voice as he found the place and began to read.

Anne found herself surrounded again by the scent of the bright English morning on the day of her marriage to Thomas. They originally had planned for a small double ceremony in the largest parlor of Charles's manor. It was, after all, a second marriage for both her and Judith. Charles had become less than welcome in London society since his vocal opposition to the war against the American colonies. The family had not returned to the city for over a year. No, the ceremony was to be a private family event.

But when they spoke to the vicar about their plans, he had counseled them to make it more public. Not for the society folk from London, he urged, but rather for the villagers who cared so deeply for them. Was it not right, said the vicar, that local families who in recent years had been so blessed by the

Harrow estate and the benevolent outreach of the family should witness this wedding?

Thomas had joined Anne in forming schools and nursing care, and had with Charles's blessing begun organizing private ownership of what formerly had been commons land. Whereas so many of England's villages and small landholders were desperately impoverished, those within Charles's domain were not only protected but even prospering. And so it was decided that it would be a church wedding.

When Charles and Judith, Anne and Thomas and John had arrived in the village at the time arranged with the vicar, they found the entire community decked out in garlands and bunting. The children, dressed in their best, sprinkled petals from the season's first blooms on the path up to the church doors.

Inside the ancient Norman structure, flowers and candles filled the air with light and color and scent. As Anne had walked up the aisle with her husband-to-be on one side and her son on the other, joining Charles and Judith before the vicar, her heart sang with the rightness of the day.

If only her parents, Catherine and Andrew, and yes, Louise and Henri, had been with them, the moment would have been perfect indeed. . . .

She returned to the present with Charles's voice reading the final lines of the letter. " '. . . not asking you to come, Anne. It is exceedingly distant and with the war on and no end in sight, it is no doubt impossible. But I feel you should know the truth. Hopefully, by the time you receive this, Andrew will be much improved. With love, your mother, Catherine.' "

The entire manor seemed to have awakened early the next morning. When Anne went downstairs to have what she hoped would be an hour of quiet reflection after a rather restless night, she found her son and husband already seated at the servants' table in the kitchen. Maisy was busy at the stove.

"I remember it clear as day," the bighearted woman was proclaiming as Anne entered. "Fifteen musicians gathered upon the upstairs balcony makin' more noise than the Second Coming. Half a hundred people thunderin' up and down the grand hall, doing a dance like I've never seen before in all my days."

"It was a polka if I recall," Thomas supplied, tying a napkin around John's neck. "All the rage at the time."

"Sounded like elephants on parade if you ask me." Maisy turned and pointed at John with her ladle. "Then what do I find but young lordship here curled up on top of a laundry basket full of my best damask tablecloths, fast asleep."

"I was sleepy," John announced confidently.

Maisy advanced upon him, the wooden spoon held like a weapon, her face a mock scowl. "Then why is it," she demanded, "that you have insisted upon waking the whole household from useful slumber a'fore the sun's even crested yon ridge?"

John shrieked with glee and hid his eyes at Maisy's approach. The woman had cared for the child since his arrival, and they loved each other dearly. Maisy grumbled and ruffled the child's hair, kissed the top of his head, then retreated to her stove. "Whatever should we feed such an impossible young man?"

"Porridge!"

"No lad who robs me of my sleep deserves a fine bowl of porridge. I think maybe dried husks with a bit of water will do you this day."

John began waving his spoon in the air. "Porridge—with cream!"

"Quietly, now we must let the others have their rest." Thomas gently wrested the spoon from John's grip, then turned to his wife standing in the doorway. "Forgive us, my dear. He awoke me with his singing."

Maisy smiled a greeting as she stirred the cooking oats. "Shall I fix you a tea, ma'am?"

"I hoped to bring him down and feed him a bit of toast,"

Thomas continued before she could answer, "but Maisy heard him as well."

"It's all right, ma'am." Maisy ladled out a steaming bowl, brought it over to the smiling child, and plied the cream pitcher. "There's no finer way to start a morning in my book than feedin' a happy child."

"More cream!"

"And how do we ask, John?" Anne put in.

"Oh yes, please, more cream," John sang out.

"That'll do for now, lad. Else I'll be mopping up your mess from now 'til the Sabbath."

Judith chose that moment to enter behind Anne. "Good morning, all. Please grind us some of those fine coffee beans that came in the other day, would you, Maisy," she said, still working on the neck catch of her housedress.

"Of course, ma'am."

"Excellent. Bring coffee for us both when it's ready, thank you. Anne, why don't you and I retire to the front room."

Anne followed her down the connecting hallway and into the small dining alcove where she often had her morning time of quiet meditation. Judith went straight to the tall doors to the garden and levered them open. The air was brisk but not unpleasant. "I do so love these early spring mornings, when all the world seems ready to burst into bloom."

"Yes," Anne agreed somewhat distractedly. "Did you want—do you want to see me about something?"

"Indeed so." Judith motioned her toward two chairs, and they moved to sit down. "I awoke this morning with certainty that you had reached your decision," Judith declared.

Anne was caught midway in the process of seating herself. "Yes?"

"I have been through my own share of shocks and sorrow, as you well know." Judith was dressed in a cotton morning frock in colors as bright as the growing dawn. Since marrying Charles she had cast aside her widow's black and embraced her new life with a vigorous determination to cheer Charles's world in every way possible. "And I know that sometimes the

27

hardest moment is not in deciding, but rather in finding peace with what you know must be done."

The woman's brisk no-nonsense tone made it possible for Anne to speak what she had scarcely admitted to herself. "I am going to Nova Scotia."

"Of course you are. You simply must go to your father—and mother—at this time!"

"But how is it possible, dear Judith? What with the war, a ship's crossing that is dangerous in the best of times . . ." Her voice caught, and she looked helplessly down at her hands.

Judith leaned toward Anne. "Now let us move to the heart of what troubles you most about this decision."

Anne took a deep breath and turned to look into the loving eyes of the woman gazing into hers. "John," was all she said.

Judith nodded. Then the rear door opened and Maisy entered, bearing a well-stocked tray.

"I toasted a bit of fresh bread in case you grew peckish," she announced, setting it on a small table between them.

"That was most thoughtful, Maisy," Judith said as she began pouring coffee for each of them.

Through the open doorway there came the sound of a child's delightful laughter. Maisy smiled in response. "That lad is the light to my days, I don't mind tellin' you."

Judith waited until the door had shut behind Maisy. "Yes," she said, "I can imagine that he presents the greatest dilemma in thinking through your decision."

"I have wrestled with this all night long," Anne murmured. "One moment I am determined that John must go with us, that I could not bear to be separated from my child. The next, I am full of anguish over the thought of putting John through the risks and dangers of a sea voyage at wartime."

"Have you spoken with Thomas?"

"Not yet."

Judith put down her cup. "This is what I suggest you do, my dear. First, you will have breakfast. Then you shall leave the child in my care and go for a walk with your husband. You will talk over with him your desires and your fears."

"And then?"

"And then," Judith replied, "you will wait. You will begin to make your preparations, and you will talk further with us, and you will pray. We will all pray. And I am certain the proper answer will come to you. In due time."

The truth of Judith's words rang with hope. Anne reached over and took the woman's hands. "How could I ever face this without you?"

Judith gave her a look of love and concern. "That is the key you must always remember, dear Anne. You need not be alone through any of this. We will aid you in whatever way we can. All of us."

The door again pushed open. "Ah, there you are!" Charles stomped in, struggling to get his right foot into his house slippers. "Where is that letter? And I can't find my reading spectacles anywhere!"

"That's because you left them on the floor by your chair last night," Judith replied, calmly reaching into her pocket. "And I had to rescue them from John."

"Ah, I see. Thank you, my dear." Charles settled the earpieces into place. He turned to Anne, and smiling, she pulled the letter from her pocket and handed it to him. He peered at the pages through his spectacles, then exclaimed, "Here it is! I knew I wasn't mistaken!"

"What is it?"

"The orphanage where Edwin Price's daughter was taken. It's in La Rochelle, my dear."

"Yes?"

"La Rochelle!" His enthusiasm lit the room. "Where our last remaining merchant contact resides. Our dear friend . . . my heavens, now I can't recall the bounder's name!"

"Do you mean Monsieur Duchat, my husband?"

"Duchat! Duchat! I've known him all these twenty years and now couldn't remember . . . Never mind." He turned again to Anne. "When you've finished with your breakfast, would you do me the great kindness of penning a letter?"

"Of course, Uncle."

"My handwriting is somewhat less than legible, you know. Duchat speaks perfect English, but he claims to find my script as unfathomable as Arabic. I want to send young Fred down to the coast this very morning and have this letter sent with the next barker aimed at the French coast."

"You're going to make inquiries about the woman?" Judith asked.

"Where else am I to start? I must have some news to send along with Anne when she departs."

In her sorrow, Anne had missed the news of her grandfather's first wife and offspring during the original reading of Catherine's letter. But she had discovered it for herself when she and Thomas retired for the night and she read the letter over again. "So our French connection, Nicole's and mine," she murmured to Thomas, "is more than simply our mothers' bond of friendship. . . ."

"It will be most interesting," Thomas had replied, "to see what Charles's investigation uncovers."

Chapter 3

It was difficult to say which hit Nicole harder, the fact that her father was so ill or that the letter was sent not directly to her but to Reverend Collins.

The old vicar clearly could see that she was distressed. "I do hope you understand why I opened the letter."

Nicole did not know how to respond.

"With the war and all, your mother of course did not know your whereabouts and thus addressed it to me. I felt your mother would want me to know its contents in case there was anything immediate I could do." At Nicole's brief nod, he added, "Goodness only knows how many letters she sent for this one to actually arrive."

Nicole stared at the single sheet in her lap. It was hard to call this a letter at all. Fourteen lines, merely a quick note to be sent with friends, just in case. By now, her mother wrote, Nicole would most likely have received Catherine's previous letters, the ones that gave greater detail of Andrew's decline. But just in case the conflict had delayed them, Catherine thought it wise to send one further note via church channels. Actually, this had been Grandfather John's idea, she explained to Nicole. The old gentleman had become a great aid and comfort in these dark times.

"Dark times," Nicole repeated, scarcely aware she had spoken at all.

Pastor Collins must have assumed she was speaking of the

here and now. "At least the war is elsewhere," he noted consolingly.

Nicole said quietly, "I must go to him."

Instead of replying, Pastor Collins roamed about his office, straightening papers on his cluttered desk, lining up the painting on his stone wall, stroking the back of his armchair. "Shall I make us tea?"

"You are thinking I should not go?" Nicole lifted the letter. "My father is deathly ill." She could hardly say the last word.

"My dearest Nicole, I am well aware of your distress. I taught Andrew for four years. He and I became such friends, such soul mates, I consider your parents my family also. It grieves me deeply to know he is unwell." Pastor Collins seated himself in the high-backed chair with its cracked leather cushion. "But, my dear, you have seen how difficult it has been even for this one letter to make it through the battle lines."

Nicole rose and crossed to the narrow peaked window behind the vicar's desk. She unlatched the lead-paned window and pushed it open. Sounds of the Boston harbor's market rose in the distance. She recalled her first day here, when another ship had brought her upon yet another unlikely voyage. "I have found passage before when none thought it possible," she said softly.

"True, true."

"And now there is Gordon to help me."

The pastor's tone remained gentle. "Do not forget, he is a man in uniform, and this is a world at war."

The war. It was everywhere, and yet nowhere to be seen. Although New York and much of the Pennsylvania colonies remained under British control, by that spring Massachusetts had become firmly American. For those fortunate enough to call Boston home, it had been a calm winter and spring. Most of the fighting had remained far to the south. In fact, that winter's greatest drama had not been a battle at all, but rather how General Washington had utilized the frigid hardship of Valley Forge.

Most had predicted that America would not have a northern

army to speak of after this long and terrible winter. Instead, General Washington had given the American colonists their first real military training. Over the space of five frozen and miserable months, Washington had taken a motley band of colonial farmers and villagers and craftsmen and turned them into the first genuine army of the United States.

The town's talk was of little besides where the summer conflict would take place. A reckoning, they called it. A birth of a nation. A casting off of chains. Yet there she stood, her father's heart giving away. "I must try."

"Of course you must. But be aware that there is a difference between a vague hope and a real opportunity. Do not allow yourself to be taken in by false promises and those opportunists after deceitful gain."

"What should I do, Pastor Collins?"

"Talk with Gordon. The more I come to know your young man, the greater is my regard."

A flicker of hope came to life in Nicole's heart. Yes, Gordon would help her get to the bedside of her father.

Truly that was how she thought of Andrew now. No matter that she had spent nearly her first two decades of life an entire world away from him and Catherine. Nor did it concern her that Louise and Henri Robichaud were also recognized by both her mind and heart as bearing the same titles. She had two mothers and two fathers. The laws of nature played no role here.

"I must go," Nicole said, rising to her feet.

"Please, not quite yet." Pastor Collins indicated a chair closer to him. "Before you embark on this perilous journey, let us pray together—for Andrew's health, and for our heavenly Father's direction and blessing to you and Gordon."

As Nicole moved to the chair, the vicar reached a hand toward her. "And for His protection on you, my child," he said. "You too have become part of my beloved family."

When Nicole left the seminary refuge and returned to the bustling world of Boston Harbor, she found it desperately hard to hold on to either calm or hope.

Although they were two weeks into April, the late afternoon was wrapped in a wintry blanket of gray, still mist. From unseen waters stretching to her left came shouts of sailors calling down from the shrouds, and the halloos of others casting sounding stones as their ships were rowed toward a safe anchorage.

From out of nowhere Nicole found herself almost overtaken by six horses. Their flanks steamed as they pulled a wagonload of hogsheads, those great iron-strapped barrels used for stowing water and supplies on board. She drew back in alarm as the drover's whip cracked near her face. A few steps farther on and a pair of young apprentices came sweating toward her, each bearing a load of canvas upon his back. She recoiled, only to collide with a woman carrying a crate of shriveled winter roots. Nicole apologized and hurried away from the stallholder's invectives, only to strike the stone wall marking the harbor's main entrance.

At least she knew now where she was. The central cobblestone way led down to the series of docks, from which rose the cries of men and animals. Nicole moved off to one side and began making her way along the rougher side track. She continued parallel to the water until the harbormaster's cottage emerged from the fog.

She stepped through the door to find Gordon behind his desk. He rose to his feet, delight in his face. "Dearest Nicole, you have brought sunshine to an otherwise gloomy day."

A bearded man in the salt-encrusted uniform of a seagoing captain stood to one side of Gordon's worktable. After a quick glance her way, his eyes remained fastened on Gordon.

"I hope I'm not disturbing," Nicole said.

"On the contrary, you have saved me the trouble of sending a man off to find you. If he indeed could do so in this fog." Gordon offered a wave of introduction. "Captain Saunders, may I have the pleasure of introducing my fiancée, Nicole Robichaud."

"Your servant, I'm sure." But the captain did not spare her a further glance. "I am telling you, sir, that I could use this weather to slip right through the British lines. Why, I could be clean away and making sail for Charleston before they find their true north."

"You might," Gordon agreed mildly. "Only there are two problems with your assessment, Captain."

"And they are?"

"First, there is no wind."

"I shall launch my longboats and row us."

"The tide is running hard against you."

"I am empty laden and running light."

"The last word we had was their line was in two rows, one five miles farther to sea. I remind you, Captain, the British are the world's finest sailors when it comes to blockades. They'll have their own longboats launched and hunting with guns primed. A single cough from one of your sailors, a squeak from the oarlocks, and you will be consigning your crew to seaborne graves."

The captain's features above his gray-flecked beard began to color. "I am unaccustomed, sir, to being crossed. Particularly from a landlocked sailor whose own guns are most certainly not primed."

Gordon gave no indication that he had heard the man. "There is also the fact that the wind could well be on the rise."

"Wind? *Wind?*" the captain roared. "There hasn't been a breath in nigh on four days! I lost my way twice just finding this hut of yours!"

"Nonetheless, Captain, my sea sense tells me there will be a south wind blowing solid by the start of the night's watch."

"Your sea sense, is it?"

"I've been stationed here for three seasons now, long enough to study the winds and currents. I would urge you to give it until the tide's turning."

"That would put me outbound after midnight and lessen

my hours of stealth and darkness by half!"

"If the wind does rise, sir, you'll know by then and be best waiting until the morrow, when it will blow hard enough to scatter—"

"Are you intending to deny me the right of departure?" The captain's sea-scarred hands curled.

"That is not my place, Captain."

"Indeed it is not." The captain rammed his hat down with such force he crumpled the crown. "I have wasted all the time I care to. Be informed, sir, that my ship raises anchor within the quarter hour."

"I do hope—and pray—that you are not gambling with the lives of your men."

The man wheeled about and stomped from the cottage, slamming the door.

Gordon seemed not to notice. Instead, he turned and stared out the window at the gray nothingness which was gradually giving way to dusk. "I do hope I am wrong," he murmured.

Nicole stepped toward him and settled a tentative hand on the arm of her betrothed. *And it's very likely my letters have not gotten through either. My parents must not know of my engagement to this man.* She stared up at Gordon's face in profile, noting the set of his features as he wrestled inwardly. She knew the responsibilities he carried for men and mission, and the serious contemplation he brought to every decision, large and small.

Gordon soon turned from the window, his gaze and features softening as he laid his hand on hers. "We have a damp and chilly eve before us. I shall start us a fire."

"Thank you, but a fire will not warm my spirit."

He turned to look into her face. "You have heard something?"

"I have. But I do not wish to add—"

"Thank you, Nicole, but there is nothing more I can do for the captain and his vessel, save pray. What is troubling you?"

Nicole withdrew the sheet of paper from her pocket and quickly read it aloud. The reading took only a few minutes. She described how dismayed she had been at the realization that neither Catherine's longer letters nor her own had made it through the blockade. She yielded finally to tears over her desperate longing to see her father once more. "I feel I have only just come to know them. I can't lose him now, Gordon. Not like this, without being able to . . ."

She eventually stopped because she had to. Outside the small hut came the sounds of men busy with the affairs of danger and motion. Though none yet approached, their presence was enough to keep Nicole's emotions in check. She wiped her eyes and attempted a tremulous smile. Gordon squeezed her hand on his arm.

"Let me pour you some tea," he offered, moving to the corner woodstove and the kettle.

Gordon soon fitted a steaming mug into her hand. "Have you eaten?"

"This morning."

"Nothing at midday?"

"The seminary's supplies did not arrive today. I was planning to scour the market when the letter arrived and Pastor Collins called me in."

"There is scarce little to be found at any price. I broke up a fight this morning between sailors and stallholders taking only silver for the last of their winter carrots." He held up a beribboned document from his desk. "Requisition orders I can't hope to fill. The city's larders are almost empty."

"What does this mean?"

"Drink your tea, my dear." He waited while she sipped, then said, "The war can't continue much longer. It is not just our city. All the colonies are so burdened. And the British forces as well, from what news I have gathered."

"Then the war is ending?"

"Not ending, but waning. Perhaps. Or reaching a crescendo. One or the other is my guess. Either there will be a loosening of the grip or an all-out push for victory. Neither side can go on with conditions as they now are."

"How long—?"

"We shall know by summer's end, of that I am certain. By

the end of this battle season, things will have altered. And drastically if my guess is correct."

"But I can't wait—Father might not . . ." But she could not say the words.

Gordon slowly took a pair of new logs and set them upon the dwindling fire, then gathered up the bellows and began priming the flames.

"Gordon, did you understand? My father's condition may not allow me the time until autumn."

Carefully he replaced the bellows, brushed ashes from the front of his uniform, straightened, and turned with obvious reluctance.

In his eyes Nicole saw the same bleak reality after the exchange with the sea captain—that matters might not permit her to do as she wanted, as she felt she had to. And to force it would cast herself and others into danger.

"Oh, Gordon, I don't know how much—"

The sound of footsteps scraped across the cottage's front porch. A knock at the door, and Gordon said, "Enter."

The young officer would have been fresh faced, save for the saber scar across his forehead. "Commandant's compliments to the harbormaster, sir. He requests your company for dinner."

"When?"

"This very hour, if you please."

"My thanks to the commandant. My fiancée and I shall await his pleasure before the watch changes."

"Very good, sir. Ma'am." He bowed out the door.

"Gordon, I can't—"

"Think of it this way, dear Nicole. At least there will be chance of a decent meal. And news that has a hope of being true."

She did not object further, drawn as she was by both prospects. As she wrapped her shawl more closely about her and permitted Gordon to usher her from the cottage, she could not say which held the greater appeal.

Chapter 4

Boston had always seemed a stern and hardfisted city to Nicole. She would have vastly preferred to reside across the river in Cambridge and held a quiet hope of one day owning a small home there. But as Gordon was apt to say whenever the village was mentioned, Cambridge held neither an adequate harbor nor an easily defensible position. Which was why, once the British had retreated south to New York, the American garrison had moved across the river and encamped.

Another reason, of course, was the public triumph of retaking the city in this most public of manners. The papers smuggled in from England, four months old and full of more dismal news from the south, had declared the city's fall a tragedy. Which had given the American colonists great reason for celebration in the midst of the bleakest winter in their short history.

One bright spot of an otherwise difficult season had been Gordon's appointment as the Boston harbormaster. Up to that point, Nicole had known weeks of silent anxiety. Gordon had proven his worth to the garrison officers, and there had been several small coastal vessels lacking experienced commanders. She knew his yearning to be seaborne once again, doing his part for the effort, yet she dreaded the thought of seeing him depart. Still she had said nothing, for they remained surrounded by the tensions of war. She had been nearly afraid to pray, for there remained the question of what God intended.

She wanted to believe the dear Lord would not tear

them—and her heart—asunder. Yet she only needed to observe her beloved's face whenever he walked along the harbor quayside as he studied the wind and the tide and the set of ships upon the waters, or see the way his features worked when discussing the seaborne world with other officers, to know how much it cost him to be landlocked. Especially now.

Gordon's appointment as harbormaster had been one enormous relief to Nicole. And she secretly hoped that the proximity to the sea would be of at least some satisfaction to Gordon.

The hillside leading up to the commandant's private quarters was lined with tightly packed row houses. Most were of timber and wattle, but some of the stodgier neighbors were dressed with close-cut stone. The candlelight from their windows gleamed wet upon the cobblestone and the surrounding wrought-iron fencing. In the night's rising chill, in what seemed a stubborn and endless winter, the warm colors burning ruddy against the windowpanes left her with the faint promise of something beyond the woes of war. She glanced into the passing windows and imagined that one day there would be for her as well a home and family and comfort. She held more tightly on to Gordon's arm. Would that it indeed come, and soon.

As they approached the hill's crest there came the sound of rolling thunder. "A storm? Now?" Nicole wondered.

Gordon responded with a noncommittal murmur and raised his chin, as though sniffing the mist and damp for signals.

The fog clamped about them made the sound seem to come from everywhere, great rolling booms more in tune with high summer. "Can it truly be thunder?"

She could feel Gordon's tension through his arm. He kept his face turned toward the houses on the seaward side. All Gordon said was, "I fear not."

She wanted to question him further, but they were nearly at the commandant's home. The road had leveled off as they approached the hilltop. Now the wind struck hard, rising out of the south as Gordon had forecast and dispersing the clinging fog.

The house was of red brick with granite cornerstones and window frames. The formal gardens before and behind had been transformed into picket lines of tents and soldiers. Their campfires created sparks now caught by the wind and flung carelessly into her face. Nicole squinted against their sting and saw that every man in the company was on his feet. At the portico clustered another dozen or so officers. All of them, every face she saw, was directed seaward. As was Gordon's.

She knew what she would see.

The city hill dropped down from where she stood in a series of stairlike rooftops. The garden's crest was fronted by a stout iron fence, high metal stakes with arrow points directed at the newly revealed sky. Beyond the slope and the roofs spread the narrow peninsula separating the safe waters of Boston Harbor from the north Atlantic. And out there, upon the inky wash of sea, the battle raged in fire and thunder.

Nicole saw great blasts of flame spurt from guns on ships she could glimpse through the curling smoke. There in the garden, not a man spoke, not a sound rose save the wind, the crackling campfires, and the distant boom of cannon. Then one central vessel caught fire, glowing ruddy as a torch of pure terror.

She did not realize she had cried out until Gordon gripped her shoulders and turned her from the seaborne calamity. His hand under her arm gave her strength to move toward the house. Her heart felt squeezed by grief as she thought of those fathers and sons now lost forever to their families.

Gordon guided her to the brick path and up the front stairs. The commandant greeted her with a formal bow, then looked searchingly into her face. "It is a good sign, my lady, to find one who still has the sensibility to mourn."

"I begged the captain not to take to sea," Gordon said from behind her. "If only I had had the power to forbid him—"

"But you did not. And nor did I." The commandant raised

his head and looked at the sky. "If only I had forecast the changing weather."

Nicole gathered herself together enough to murmur, "Gordon did."

"Ah."

"Not with any certainty, General. I merely mentioned it as a possibility," Gordon acknowledged.

"That and more. Gordon all but stated it as definite," Nicole put in quietly.

The general turned to face Gordon, eyebrows raised.

"A lucky guess, sir. Nothing more."

The wind rose to a new pitch, causing several of the tents to billow. The soldiers shouted warnings and leaped to hold down their gear and dampen the fires. At that same moment another thunderous explosion rolled across the harbor. Nicole's was the only face that did not turn seaward.

"The powder room has gone," Gordon noted soberly. "Broken her back, I warrant."

"Those men," the commandant said. "I hope they had time to put out their boats and . . ."

Nicole pushed through the group and entered a side room. Three officers were gathered by the open front window. The wind had blown out the candles, and Nicole used the shadows for cover as she attempted to gain control.

Gordon came into the room, soon discovered her in the corner, and walked over to take her arm. "Shall I take you back?" he whispered.

"No, but thank you."

He tilted his head to catch a glimmer of light on her face. "Yes, well, the officers are waiting."

"Then let us join them." She used her kerchief to wipe her eyes, and the two moved across the hall toward the parlor.

The garrison commandant chose not to notice the shadows

of Nicole's distress, and his collection of officers took their cues from him. The general held out his arm to Nicole and offered to escort her in to dinner.

As they walked through the side parlor, now given over to maps and charts and paper-strewn worktables, the general said, "Upon my word, do my senses deceive me, or is that goose roasting?"

Nicole nodded appreciatively. "I cannot remember when I last tasted goose," she acknowledged.

The general made a small ceremony of pulling out a chair for Nicole. Gordon seated himself to her left, remarking, "If I did not know better, sir, I would say you had something in mind beyond entertaining us with a fine meal."

The general was caught midway in the process of seating himself to Nicole's right. "How so, Goodwind?"

Gordon turned so as to rest one hand upon the back of Nicole's chair. He pressed firmly against her shoulder. "Roast goose in the midst of the direst spring I have ever seen. I can't even recall the last time I tasted a mouthful of fresh meat," he said to the general.

Nicole understood then. The exchange was not for the general, but Gordon sought to draw her to full alert. She turned to face him and found in his features a warning born out of a lifetime of skirmishes and danger. "Surely you remember," she said, attempting with her tone to say that she not only understood but was ready. "Easter Sunday. We shared that haunch of venison with those at the seminary."

"Ah, so we did." Gordon eased back in his chair. "How could I forget?"

Nicole turned to the general. From beneath bushy, silver-tinted eyebrows, he studied her with piercing alertness. She gave him as unrevealing a smile as she could manage. "But that meal was weeks ago. I am so grateful for this invitation and the opportunity to enjoy this meal with you."

Dinner was brief and rather silent. Nicole did not mind. The goose was tough and had been cooked over a too-hot fire. Even so, her hunger proved a savory spice, and she concentrated on chewing each leathery bite.

Eventually the general set his cutlery aside and declared, "I fear we saved the poor birds from their last remaining days."

Nicole and Gordon both murmured polite rejoinders. "I found it to be most excellent, General," she added. "Particularly during this time of scant provisions."

"Well, then, I too am delighted." A brief gesture drew his officers to their feet. "Gentlemen, perhaps you would retire and grant me a moment alone with our guests." To his aide he added, "Ask Cook to leave the table as is."

"Very good, sir."

Only when the door closed behind the last departing officer did the general lean toward Gordon. "Captain Goodwind, you will be pleased to hear that our American Revolutionary Forces have recently extended our hold of coastal territories to include two of the harbors between here and New York."

Gordon also leaned forward. "Well done, sir."

"Thank you." The man reached to the sideboard behind him and hefted a silver box. "A runner brought a selection of cigars. This year's crop. Virginia's best. Do take your pleasure."

"Thank you, sir. But the delights of tobacco escape me."

The general took his time selecting a cigar and lighting it with a candle. "You have heard of our newest vessel, the *Constitution*?"

"Rumors only. She is said to be a mighty ship."

"Mighty indeed. She was fashioned from sheaves of the hardest wood known to man, live oak timber from southern Georgia. She saw duty in these recent battles. I have it on good report that English cannonballs bounced off her side."

"I would like to have seen that, sir," Gordon said, obviously intrigued.

"Fired well within range, yet they bounced off and fell back into the sea." The general's tone held the satisfied air of knowing he had hooked his prey. "We've heard rumors the English sailors have renamed the vessel *Ironsides*. Well put, I would say. Our own sailors have adopted the name as their own."

"I hope I have opportunity to view the vessel myself,"

The Beloved Land

Gordon said. Nicole leaned farther back in her chair so the two men could converse more freely. She had no desire to see any ship called *Ironsides*.

The general harrumphed quietly. "Indeed. But there is a purpose behind this little tale. In the second harbor, Captain, we captured your old vessel."

Gordon smiled. "That is good news indeed, General. Her owners will be most delighted. . . ." The general's finger-waving denial stopped him. "Of course," Gordon quickly said. "The spoils of war. Forgive me."

"Your allegiance to distant obligations and owners is commendable, Captain. And your loyalty to America is not questioned." The general puffed upon his cigar, eyeing Gordon through the smoke. "As a matter of fact, I am quite willing to return the vessel to your command."

Nicole stirred, and Gordon looked at her before asking, "And in exchange?"

"Let me review for you the situation we face. This has been the longest and harshest winter on record. Our supplies are dwindling fast. Unless we can convince General Washington to send the fleet north, the British blockade will continue to keep us trapped. I wrote Washington about this very fact. The runner who brought this fine tobacco also brought his response."

He paused to roll his cigar about the ashtray. "Washington has informed me that we have been promised provisions from the French government of Louisiana. But the battles in Georgia and the Carolinas have cut off all land routes."

Nicole was beginning to realize where the conversation was headed. A dangerous mission through the blockade to Louisiana . . . She shut her eyes in an attempt to work through the tumult within her mind and heart. Behind closed lids she was once more deep within the bayou country of her growing-up years.

She opened her eyes to find both gentlemen watching her. She understood this as well. Nicole was both surprised and assured by her own calm tone. "You require my presence on the mission."

45

"I confess, it would help matters greatly," the general nodded. "There is no doubt that Captain Goodwind will need an intermediary with the French. We are seeking not only one vessel's worth of supplies, you see. We would like to have the captain establish a regular trade route for supplies."

Gordon said, "Such a venture in wartime will be expensive."

"If you agree to this assignment, we will send with you letters of credit drawn upon banks that operate in both territories."

"I see you have thought this through."

The general put his cigar down and leaned forward even farther. "I cannot overstress the gravity of our situation. Our supplies are so depleted we shall be forced to send you away with virtually nothing in the way of provisions."

Gordon could not hide his astonishment. "But we are facing a voyage of several weeks! And foraging on the way will be impossible with the British on the ground."

"I am well aware of that. But the fact is, sir, my men are starving." He waved an angry hand. "I have heard the rumors around Boston and Cambridge—that the army is hoarding all foodstuffs for the push against Cornwallis and his men down York way. That is simply not true."

"Things are that bad?"

"Things could not be worse. I have learned that some of my men garrisoned farther out have taken to boiling down their belts for soup."

Nicole knew what had to be done. There was no question. She said, "We will not require provisions from here, General."

Gordon's shock was on his face.

"My fiancé and I shall need to discuss this. But if he agrees to take on this task, we can make do with whatever provisions you are able to spare." Nicole turned to Gordon. "Before we travel south, we shall first go north."

"North?" queried the general.

"To Nova Scotia."

"But, ma'am, forgive me, the Canadian colonies are firmly within British hands."

"That may well be, sir." She rose to her feet and offered the general her hand. "But I can assure you, we will be well received in Nova Scotia."

Chapter 5

The days since Catherine's letter arrived had taken on a subtle undercurrent of energy and preparation. Little was said. But in fact the household could sense that decisions had been made. Charles's brother in far-off Nova Scotia was ill. Anne would soon travel to work her healing skills upon the man who had raised her as his own. Of course her new husband, Thomas, would accompany her on this perilous journey.

But what of their precious John?

Anne knew the matter of her son was discussed by all. She observed conversations trail off as she entered the kitchen or rear workrooms. She saw how the servants gathered about Thomas when they thought she was elsewhere.

But nothing was said to her. Not directly. Not even Thomas pressed her. The two occasions when she had attempted to lay out the issues, he had heard her out, then merely commented, "Whatever you decide, dearest Anne, I shall accept as the right course to take."

"But I want you to help!"

"This is the aid I feel I should give," he responded, stepping closer and taking her hand.

"But this is no help at all!"

"He is your son, Anne," he said, looking at her face.

"He is yours now as well."

He did not disagree. "You know I love little John. I never dreamed it would be possible to love anyone so totally as I do you. And now I find it is not you only but John as well."

"Then why won't you tell me what I should do?"

"You have just answered your question. What *you* should do." Thomas turned her hand over and kissed the center of her palm. "In this situation, Anne, you are the only one who can decide." He led her over to a settee and they sat down together.

"You are the child's mother," he continued, still holding her hand. "I would like to think that even were John my own flesh and blood, I would be able to remain objective about this. This is a decision for his mother."

She lowered her face and began rubbing her forehead with her hand. "I don't understand—"

"No. And it is difficult for me to explain. But I shall try. Should John remain here, I will miss him terribly. But you are his *mother*. I can scarcely imagine what it could cost you to take such a step." Gently he stroked her bowed head. "This is one decision you must make yourself. Only know that whatever it is, I shall second it and have full confidence it is the right decision."

This is England in spring, Anne mused as she prepared to accompany Charles and Thomas to London for a few days in preparation for the journey to Nova Scotia. All the world seemed poised to burst into birdsong and blossoms. But just as she put the final item in her valise, then came the clouds outside her bedroom window. Very soon the dark was so thorough it seemed to fill the bedroom with its gloom. Anne fastened the straps on her case and listened to Thomas play with little John in the sitting room of their private quarters. The large Harrow manor was indeed gracious and lovely, but Anne felt truly at home when she and Thomas and John were behind the apartment's door.

She heard a knock on the large double door and Thomas's voice greeting Charles.

"My apologies for rushing you, but we really must try to beat this storm," Charles explained.

"I am ready," Anne called, opening the bedroom door. She let Charles come in and take her leather case. She walked into the sitting room and stooped down to hug her son. "Now, promise me you will be a good little lad and do everything Nanny tells you," she whispered in his ear.

John shook his head, his face drawn into a frown.

"We will be back so very soon you won't even know we are gone," Anne said, hugging the child again, then setting him down. "All right, then."

"Let's be off, then," Thomas said.

John's face began to cloud like the sky outside their home. "Mama and Papa stay!" he cried.

"Come, child, let's go see if Maisy can't find you a little gingerbread man." Ignoring his tears, the big woman scooped up the child and headed for the back stairway.

Anne stood in the doorway, listening to John's wails recede in the distance. Her heart felt as if it were held in place only by the stays of her corset. If it was this painful—for both John and her—to depart for just a few days, how on earth could she bear leaving him for an entire season?

"I must say, every time I read Catherine's account of her father's revelations, I grow all the more astonished." The letter lay open in Charles's lap, held in place by a hand as the carriage rocked and swayed over the winter's ruts.

The three travelers had joined the Great Trunk Road running the entire way from Bristol to London. The battered carriage itself, a far cry from the polished brougham Charles had used before the war, resembled the local postal carriages to avoid unwelcome attention. The driver was accompanied up top by two stout and well-armed footmen, for the roads were increasingly unsafe from highwaymen and other vagabonds taking advantage of the unsettled times.

Charles had no interest in calling attention by raising questions about his movements. Now that the tides of war were turning in the Americans' favor, Charles's previous declarations of support for their independence drew suspicion and malice from those allied to the king. The Harrow position and holdings were kept safe by only two factors. First, the merchant class and the religious among the commoners were growing increasingly strident in their call for an end to the conflict, and Charles was seen as their representative within the landed gentry. Second, Charles did not flaunt himself or his perspectives. Thus he managed to avoid becoming a target. Thus the last thing he would do would be to travel the main roads in a shining carriage with the family crests emblazoned upon both doors.

Thomas leaned forward in his seat. "Please read again the portion about the grandfather's search, will you?"

"Let me see, where does that begin? Ah yes, here we are." He looked up before reading. "The letter speaks of Celeste," Charles explained, "the name by which Edwin referred to his first wife in the diary. Shortly after returning to England, though, he never used her name again, simply stating 'my dear' or 'my love.' " Charles adjusted his half-moon spectacles and began to read. " 'Celeste's brother, a fisherman, risked his life to take Edwin across the Channel to England and safety.' "

"I still can't fathom his leaving his wife behind," Thomas remarked.

"Pray you never have to make such a decision," Charles said without lifting his eyes from the page. "But Catherine explains here that the gendarmes were onto his presence and were about to arrest him again. Which would have meant a hanging. Celeste was ill, probably related to her pregnancy, but no doubt neither of them were aware of it at that time. John's father had no choice, as far as I can see."

Anne stared distractedly out the window of the jouncing carriage. The letter had been read and discussed so often she supposed any of them could have recited its contents by heart.

Normally she would have found such discussions fascinating. But this trip to London merely brought their eventual departure for the transatlantic crossing that much closer. Charles took the opportunity to accompany them to London; then he would travel on to Southampton. His connections—and wealth—would help to arrange berths on a vessel to transport them to Nova Scotia. He also would meet with the man he had assigned the task of hunting down evidence of John Price's family in France.

Anne and Thomas would remain in London for the better part of a week. She was planning to make the rounds of the apothecaries, searching out the elements known to aid in easing the strain upon an ailing heart. There were garlic and alfalfa, of course, and others far more difficult to obtain—hawthorn and turmeric and ginger and gingko and perhaps some of the oriental herbs she had heard of but never used. She would also need to find the components for a strong emetic. There was nothing like a thorough purging of the body, followed by a carefully measured bleeding, to ease the heart's labor. All these items were best obtained before they embarked on their mission.

Then there were the items required for the voyage itself. All passengers were expected to bring their own victuals—which meant organizing at least a month's worth of salt beef and apples in brine and tea and sugar and salt and smoked fish and cider and chickens, perhaps a few goats for milk, and a barrel or two of the unleavened sea bread known as hardtack. Articles of clothing were needed as well—a good heavy cloak for herself and an all-weather for Thomas. And, of course, clothes for the child if he was coming. Here again she was consumed by the lack of decision. Anne clasped her hands together and stared unseeing out the side window. What on earth was she to do about John?

" 'After agonizing months of trying to make contact with his wife' "—Charles's voice broke through her anxiety—" 'Edwin discovered that she had died in childbirth. Along with the anguish of his loss, he learned he was father to a baby girl. Frantic for more news, he found out that on the return trip after delivering Edwin to England, his wife's only brother had been lost at sea. But that was all he learned till much later. Edwin spent years trying to locate his daughter, to no avail. He could not get back into France himself, as the war dragged on and on.' "

The war. Anne knotted her handkerchief in despair. Were it not for the war, she would without question be taking John with them. Andrew and Catherine would be thrilled to see their only grandchild. With Andrew's illness, the young boy's energy and boundless joy would bring its own healing. But how could she risk taking him in such conditions as they were facing? What if the ship were to be attacked and—? But Anne shook her head against such a thought and concentrated once more on the letter.

" 'Every effort to discover the whereabouts of his child only led to more despair,' " Catherine's letter explained. " 'In the meantime, Edwin Price married a fine English girl who was very understanding of his sorrow and predicament. She in fact supported his efforts to find the child. But the search remained unfruitful. They had a son after a few years of marriage, and though the inquiries continued, John Price, my father, was never told of his half sister.' "

"And then comes the triumph," Thomas interjected.

"I should say 'triumph' is too strong a word," Charles countered. "Perhaps a faint gift of hope, too late received." He shuffled the pages and picked up the story from Catherine's letter. " 'Edwin's last entry in the diary relates that he had finally found a faint trail. The baby girl had been turned over to a Catholic orphanage in La Rochelle. He immediately arranged for someone to follow the new lead, sure that this was the one piece of information that would unite him with his daughter.' "

"Only it was too late," Thomas said, shaking his head. "And all came to naught."

" 'The next diary entry was made in a woman's script,' " Charles read. " 'Tearstains still show upon the page. Edwin was killed in a hunting accident. The matter of the child's whereabouts was lost in the sorrowing widow's grief and her efforts to cope with raising their son.' "

Charles peered at the page a long moment, then said, "I fear the carriage and my poor eyesight make this next portion illegible."

"That is where John writes in his own hand, is it not? Here, let me see the page." Thomas took the letter, squinted, and read, " 'My dear Charles, I am asking your help. Forgive an old man and his musings. I do fully understand if you care not to involve yourself in such a futile undertaking.' "

"On the contrary," Charles said, looking from Thomas to Anne, "nothing could give me more pleasure. I count it an honor and a duty to aid the gentleman in any way I can. You will tell him that, will you not?"

"Indeed so." Thomas kept his eyes on the page to read. " 'Strange as it may sound, I feel God's hand upon this undertaking. I doubt you will understand this, but the words need saying. Much of my life was ruled by rancor and bitterness. God has changed my heart, and I need to accept my ties to the land and people who were long my enemy. Perhaps my request to you is part of this healing of my soul. I wish you well, sir, and close with prayers that God will guide you if you should decide to accept this task. Your servant, John Price.' "

Charles murmured, "What worthy sentiments this man has penned. Tell him that as well, I fervently request. He has touched my heart. I count it an honor to know him. An honor. Please pass that along to him when you see him."

———— ✑ ————

The leaden clouds finally released their burdens. Rain pelted the carriage with such force all conversation ceased mid-sentence. The deluge swiftly transformed the road to muck, and the horses slowed to a laborious gait.

It was then that the brigands attacked.

Anne heard the sound of drumming hooves, at first assuming merely a change in the rain's tempo. She then heard the wheezing huff of horses driven hard through the wet and clinging earth. She was about to question why someone chose to ride so close to their coach, when from above came the first cries of alarm.

The highwaymen had chosen well. The driver cracked his whip and shrilled a loud "Hyah!" But the horses could respond with little more than high-pitched whinnies. The carriage wheels, gripped by fetters of wet clay, refused to spin faster.

A wet-gloved hand gripping the stanchion by the right door, followed by a bearded face streaked with rain and mud, appeared in the open window. The man roared words lost in the tumult as he kept his hold on the carriage with one hand and struggled to free the pistol in his belt with the other.

But Thomas was faster. He slid down far into his seat and hammered the gloved hand with his heel. A cry of rage and pain marked the man's disappearance. Thomas hurled himself over Anne, pressing her into the corner of the seat. He yelled at Charles, "Guard the other side!"

The two bully-boys riding on top proved to be such ferocious fighters the next wave of attackers could not mount the running boards. Anne cowered beneath Thomas, flinching with each shout and blow. A blunderbuss boomed just outside her side of the coach, splintering the wood above her head, and to her terrified ear it sounded like a cannonade. Thomas pressed her even closer into the cushions.

A pair of flintlock pistols fired from either side, and the stench of burning sulfur poured through the carriage window.

A voice from above then shouted, "They're climbing up the rear!"

In time to the warning, Anne felt as much as heard the scrape and pounding of boots clambering over the rope netting that tied their luggage to the rear of the coach. Overhead came shouts and thunderous clubbing as the drovers rushed to their defense.

Sounds of rage and struggle came from every side. Hoofbeats drummed alongside, a pistol shot from behind, the driver yelled and cracked his whip and urged the horses to greater speed.

The road's turning caught them all unawares. The horses wheeled the carriage about so sharply, they could feel two of the mud-clad wheels lift off the earth. A roar of surprise sounded from directly above Anne's head as a body was flung off the roof into the rain and the mud.

Two great booming crashes, then a clatter and rumble. Charles cried, "The luggage! They've chopped the catch ropes!"

In response, the carriage instantly caught speed as the weight of their baggage was released. A second figure leapt past the side window, tumbling in a practiced manner as he hit the mud. The men overhead shouted words lost in the rain and the thunder of boots. The driver cracked his whip once more, urging the steeds to fly down the long straightaway.

After some moments of silence, Anne was able to draw in a deep breath. It was over. The rain lessened a notch just as the coach wheeled through another broad turn, finally slowing to a halt.

The driver shouted down, "We must give the horses a breather, sir."

"Of course." Charles was already working at the door latch. "Who's hurt up top?"

"Young Harry caught a bullet through his greatcoat, milord. Barely missed his heart."

"Felt the tug on me like a claw reachin' out of the sky!" The young man's voice broke with the excitement of danger now passed. "Look here, sir! Went clean through."

"Good thing it didn't stray an inch to your right," Charles said grimly. "I'd not want the duty of taking such news back to your dear mother."

Thomas helped Anne straighten in her seat. "Tell me you are all right, my love."

"I'm . . . I'm not injured," she stammered. But her limbs felt like water and her heart pounded with both fear of what they had lived through and relief that it was over.

"Highwaymen attacking on the Great Trunk Road. And in broad daylight." Charles walked around front to inspect the horses. "What a sorry state of affairs."

The elder of the two guards said, "Sorry about the baggage, milord. There were too many for us to guard the coach and the gear both."

"Never you mind. We're safe and that's what matters most." But Charles continued to stomp around the carriage, outrage in his demeanor and voice. "With every able-bodied man off fighting the conflict, it's no surprise the brigands feel free to attack at will."

Anne leaned back in her seat, weakened by the realization that the decision had been granted to her. Strange that she would think of her son when she had barely escaped with her life. But there was no question to her mind now. She could not risk putting her young child in harm's way. This was not merely a matter of the sea voyage and the danger. She would risk her life for her father's sake, and go for the sake of offering help to her mother. But she could not risk young John.

She leaned out the door to share the news with her husband and Charles. But the two men stood alongside the lathered flanks of the nearside horse, deep in somber discussion. Anne settled herself back into the seat. She would wait. Let them put this latest crisis behind them. Then she would tell them of her decision.

Chapter 6

Anne had assumed that once the decision was made, her calm would be restored. But she was shocked and dismayed to find herself even more distraught than before.

The eight days they spent in London proved agonizingly long. Charles sent word twice, first to say no berths were yet available for the voyage, then that news might be arriving from France and he felt it necessary to delay his return until he heard what had been discovered. Thomas was busy with a multitude of legal and business affairs, put off since their last visit to London many months before. Which left Anne with more time than was healthy to pine over her son. She knew that though John would miss them, he would be well cared for with enormous love and attention from Charles, Judith, and the entire household. But herself and Thomas . . . She could not imagine how they would cope with the separation.

Because Charles's London house had been rented out, they stayed with friends of Thomas belonging to a church in the fields beyond Shepherd's Market. In medieval times, when London's mighty walls had ended some five miles farther east, drovers had brought their flocks to Shepherd's Market. Now it was a den of licentiousness, anchoring the farther end of the new, elegant road called Piccadilly. From the Circus at one end to the Market at the other, Piccadilly had become home to London's emerging young society. The pastor of the Farm Street Church made heroic attempts to turn the attention of the local revelers to spiritual matters.

By English law, King George III was also the head of the Church of England. This had Christians up and down the country seeking either a change to the law or a change to the monarchy.

Twenty miles across the Dover Straits, France was in political and cultural turmoil. The cry of *Liberté, Egalité, Fraternité* was on everyone's lips, and revolution was in the air. All of this news was very troubling to the English monarchy. French cities were in flames. The rule of law was in tatters. The masses were breaking free of their fetters.

So long as Anne had remained in their small village in the north, it had been possible to ignore most of this upsetting news. But now it came at her from every direction. The English rulers' response to these threats, both from within and without, was to outlaw public protests, and any criticizing the king or the prince regent were declared criminals and imprisoned.

The result was that churches such as the Farm Street Church became one of the few places where people who disagreed with the nation's current course could safely gather. Members did their best to draw no attention to themselves. They dressed plainly. They spoke quietly. They avoided contact with a society they considered depraved. But their presence remained a thorn in the king's side. As a result, these churchgoers had been given a new name. They were called Dissenters.

The Dissenters constantly lived under the threat of oppression and worse. They decided, as the Quakers and Mennonites and Anabaptists before them, to leave England forever.

Anne could tell the longer Thomas remained in London, the more troubled he became. It was difficult for Anne and him to talk freely, however, for the house where they stayed was always full. Since many Dissenters refused to stay in the uptown establishments where the society's looser ways were on full display, several homes like this one had been transformed into unofficial inns. Only when Thomas and Anne huddled in their tiny room, the scrape of boots heard overhead and the din of conversation below, could they have any privacy.

"I fear I am doing Charles and his estate no good whatsoever," Thomas quietly confessed.

"Why is that, Thomas?" Anne asked. "Who else does he have to whom he can trust his affairs?"

"Doors are closed to me everywhere. I am classed as a Dissenter, which means I cannot even speak to many officials." Thomas looked as worried as Anne had ever seen him. "There are scores of pressing matters. The new Land Enclosure Acts, the village taxes, the state of our roads, our crops, permits for our markets—the list is endless."

"Surely you can—"

"I tell you, Anne, I can do nothing. I have spent days going hat in hand from one place to another, scarcely receiving so much as a by-your-leave. I am unable to even approach the officials, much less request a private appointment."

The murmuring voices below their room increased in volume, and Anne paused till it was quieter, then said, "What will you do?"

"The only thing I can, given the circumstances. I have sought out another to represent Charles here in London. Someone well removed from the Dissenters and their foment."

Anne started to protest, but realized Thomas would not have taken such actions lightly. "I am sure you did what you had to."

"It was agony just the same. All my life I have sought to give my clients my best. To represent them fairly and uphold their interests as though they were my own. I have not just failed Charles. I have failed myself."

Anne sat up in bed and said, "Thomas, hear me out."

The face he turned toward her was grim.

"Thomas, you are the most honorable man I know. You have a servant's heart, a leader's mind, and a prophet's will. But sometimes you are too hard on yourself. You expect too much. You want all you do to be faultless."

Thomas pushed himself higher against the headboard, his gaze glimmering in the room's single candlelight.

When he did not speak, Anne continued, "Life is not like that. Christ calls us to be willing servants. He commands us to accept our humanness and the thorns which this world presses into our flesh. . . ."

Anne stopped. For the first time since Catherine's letter had arrived, she came face-to-face with her answer. She could feel the impact of this realization and the sense of peace which accompanied it. Both together rolled through her soul.

"Please, Anne. I pray that you continue."

She took a breath. "We are called to accept the imperfections life casts upon us and look to Him for strength and wisdom. We must accept that we cannot arrange the world as we would like, and that at times logic will not supply the proper course, nor will our deepest desires be entirely met. This is life in a fallen world, where wars come and go, where nations rage and people cry in torment. We must be strong, not in ourselves, but in Him. And trust that His love and His wisdom and His light will see us through."

He nodded slowly. "You are right." Thomas reached over and took her hand. "I sense that you have reached a decision of your own."

"I have."

"About John?"

"Yes." She gripped his fingers. "I cannot risk his life in such a voyage."

"No." Thomas's voice was low. "You cannot."

"You have known this?"

"I have hoped and prayed you would come to this decision. But I meant what I told you before we departed. If you had decided otherwise, I would have accepted it."

She raised his hand to her cheek. "You are such a good, dear man."

"I must be," he replied softly, "to deserve you."

Chapter 7

Gordon went through the laborious process of handing over his post to the new harbormaster, then sorted through his charts and papers to determine those that would be of value upon open waters. But the entire time, he occupied two spaces. His exterior world held to military precision. He ordered out a longboat and rowed the new master through the anchorage, talking of tides and currents and ships and the blockade. He signed the required documents, bid farewell to the harbor pilots, and invited one lieutenant pilot and a few of the best landlocked sailors on harbor duty to join his new crew.

The majority of his thoughts, though, remained hidden away behind the stern mask of a busy officer. Inside, down deep where none save Nicole and God might detect, he remained in turmoil.

Gordon was marrying a noblewoman. She might eschew the title, but Nicole Robichaud Harrow was a woman of wealth and holdings. Yet by giving her allegiance with him to the American colonies, Nicole was cutting herself off from her position and inheritance. The land in western Massachusetts was hers because it had been granted by the Continental Congress to Charles and he had deeded it to her. But the house had been burned to the ground during one of the battles that had raged through the colony. She had no funds with which to rebuild. All British holdings of colonials, including their bank accounts, had been taken over by the British crown. She was penniless. Despite her best efforts to convince Gordon that she would have it no other way, he could not help but question his own unwitting involvement in this loss of Nicole's wealth.

Gordon saluted the final cadre of harbor soldiers, thanked them in his best quarterdeck voice, then turned his face directly into the rain-drenched wind. His papers and instruments had already been sent back to his quarters. Scheduled to leave at dawn, his own men were busy with last-minute duties. Soon he would be standing upon the heaving deck of a ship under sail. He was engaged to the love of his life. He had every reason to be happy.

Gordon was expected at the seminary for a last meal with Nicole and Pastor Collins. But his feet took him in the opposite direction. Gordon pulled the gold chain attached to his pocket watch. As soon as he opened the latch the face was spattered by the whipping rain. He wiped the face clean and shut the case without taking note of the time. In truth, he was not going to take his present anxiety to dinner with Nicole. If need be, he would make his apologies on the morn.

His thoughts drummed out a dirge in time to his footsteps. *She is losing everything—because of me.* He had fought all his life to rise from humble beginnings and live according to a code of honor. It did not matter to him that Nicole was willingly giving it all up. Were it not for him, what reason would she have for giving herself to the American cause? None. It was that simple.

Gordon found himself standing near the same point they had passed that morning on the way to Merchant's Row. But now something else snagged his attention. Across the North Square from where he stood rose Christ Church, renamed by its parishioners the Old North Church. It was from this white-capped steeple that the sexton had placed two lanterns to warn the Charlestown garrison that the British were marching on Lexington and Concord.

Gordon crossed in front of Paul Revere's silversmith shop and climbed the church's steps. To his great relief, the doors were unlocked. He entered the sanctuary and seated himself midway down the central aisle. A number of others were there, scattered about the hall in silent communion. He studied a few of the faces and wondered at what struggles might be hidden behind closed eyes.

He found it not enough to sit. Gordon slipped to his knees on the scratched wooden floor. He rested his forehead upon the pew before him and closed his eyes. Suddenly he found himself sensing a clarity of thought, and words formed of their own accord.

I beg you, Lord, give me the vision to properly understand. Strengthen me so that I might see with the wisdom of heaven and not of men. Hold me to the passage of your choosing. Chart my course through the storms and torment of this life, and let neither pride nor my past come between me and your divine plan.

Gordon went on with his prayer, asking for direction concerning his marriage to Nicole and their future together.

He lifted his eyes to the cross hanging above the nave and said aloud, "Amen."

He knelt there for a time longer, though there seemed no need for further words. A deep sense of harmony filled the silence within and without.

Eventually he pulled out his pocket watch and now made careful note of the time. If he hurried, he might still make the evening meal.

As he rose to his feet and started back down the aisle, he spotted a familiar figure kneeling in the back pew. The face was so unexpected in this place and time it was not until the man rose to his feet that Gordon recognized him. "My good fellow!" Gordon exclaimed. When a score of faces turned their way, Gordon raised his own hand to his lips and ushered the man from the sanctuary. Once they stood upon the front steps, Gordon wrung the man's hand with both of his own. "John Jackson, as I live and breathe. What a delight! What a genuine delight."

"It is good to see you again, Captain." Clearly the man did not expect such a welcome.

"Don't let's stand upon formalities, man. I insist you call me

Gordon." He pointed at the brevets sewn into the man's great-coat. "Besides which, I see you have been promoted to first lieutenant."

"Yes, despite my best efforts to the contrary," he responded with a wry grin.

"Nonsense. Both Nicole and I found you to be a man of great potential. It is good to see you have finally been recognized as such." He could not help but notice the gaunt features, the pale skin above the man's unkempt beard, the sunken eyes. "You have been ill?"

"Consumption, I'm afraid."

"I am indeed sorry to hear this." Gordon looked more closely at this sergeant who had helped Nicole enter the garrison at Cambridge, then rescued Gordon and his men from the British stockade. But the man's former ebullience was not to be seen. "Are you recovering?" he asked.

"Slowly." A pause, then he added, "I wintered with General Washington at Valley Forge."

The twilight wind gripped Gordon harder still. "My poor man. I have heard it was most terrible."

"Good and bad both, sir. Good and bad. The conditions were fierce, as you have heard. But General Washington took us raw colonial recruits and whipped us into a true fighting force."

Gordon leaned closer still. "What brings you to Boston?" he asked.

"My family left Philadelphia during the battles, intending to come here and stay with relatives. My father learned only at the last minute he was slated for arrest as a traitor."

"A patriot," Gordon corrected quietly.

"My family has left for the West. I have neither the funds nor the strength to follow."

"See here now. You must come and let me arrange quarters. And a meal."

Jackson drew himself up as straight as he could. "I did not come seeking charity, sir."

"Look here, Jackson. I owe you a debt I can never repay.

Were it not for you, I would have swung from a British yard-arm and been buried in a paupers' field. You know this is truth."

"The debt is due to Miss Nicole, not I." He coughed, wracking his entire frame. "Forgive me. The lady, she is well?"

"She is residing at the seminary guesthouse. The lady will be as delighted as I to see you again."

"I should not visit Miss Nicole in this sorry state."

"Nonsense, she will not mind in the least."

But Jackson merely shook his head. "I would ask a boon of you."

"Anything, my man. But let us first see to your well-being."

"This will not wait. Follow me, please."

The tenuous hold Jackson maintained upon strength and resolve was evident in the way he moved. The slightest cough seemed ready to topple him. But Gordon knew better than to offer aid. "How did you find me?" he questioned his guide.

"I asked about and learned you were the new harbor-master."

"Today was my last day."

Jackson stumbled on the rough cobblestones but kept himself erect. "I was headed down to find you when I saw you entering the church."

John Jackson now turned down a murky alley. Other than the torch marking the entrance, there was no light. Gordon hesitated a moment, peering into the gloom. "Where are we going?"

"This way," Jackson urged.

Gordon eased his sword in his scabbard and followed. The way was so narrow he could reach out and touch both walls. Rain dripped and puddled, and wind gusts blew foul odors into his face. Jackson halted before a door and banged loudly.

"All right, all right," shouted a voice. "I'm coming. No need to wake the dead with your racket." The door opened and a gray-bearded face poked through. He held a candle up to inspect the visitors. "Oh, it's you, is it? Well, you're too late. We're closed for the night."

Jackson shoved his way past the old man and entered the shop.

"See here! This is no way—"

Jackson took the candle from the old man and began searching the walls. Gordon stepped through the doorway and stood alongside the old man. The entire shop was scarcely the size of a closet and was lined floor to ceiling with glass-fronted shelves. The candle's flickering light illuminated piles of every imaginable item. Faded medals were stacked like coins along with pistols and silverware and watches and figurines. There were clocks and goblets and stuffed birds and toys. In the corners, muskets and swords were stacked like so much firewood.

"Here." Jackson stabbed a finger at a dusty glass. "This is what I saw. Tell me this is what I think it is."

Gordon moved quickly across the room to stand alongside Jackson. In the uppermost cabinet, directly behind the shopkeeper's table, was a tray of jewelry. The centerpiece was an emerald pendant surrounded by diamonds. "Let me have the light," Gordon said, keeping his tone even, though his heart had lurched a recognition.

"You're a buyer, are you? Well, that changes things, it does." The shopkeeper shut and locked the door. "Let me get a better light going."

He scrambled around the back rooms, where he no doubt lived, and emerged with a whale-oil lamp. He turned the wick up high. "You'll walk a score of miles and more to come across an item as fine as that!" he said.

There was no denying the truth of those words. Even coated with dust, the emerald shone with brilliance.

John Jackson moved up alongside. "It is Miss Nicole's?" he whispered.

"There is no doubt," Gordon returned. The stone had been a gift from Charles Harrow and had been his mother's favorite. Nicole had exchanged it for Gordon's freedom. "None whatsoever."

Jackson coughed again. "I am glad."

"Ah, a special lady's, was it? A friend of the officer's?" The shopkeeper held the lamp higher still. "No question about it, good sirs, the lady has fine taste. Either that or she kept good company."

Gordon turned to the shopkeeper and demanded, "What are you saying?"

The shopkeeper cringed in the face of Gordon's ire. "No offense intended, good sir. None at all. You'd think it was the real thing, that's all I meant."

Gordon realized with a start that the man thought the stone was fake. And why not? How else would the item land in such a place as this? He demanded, "How much for the necklace?"

The hand holding the lamp trembled slightly. "A great amount, good sir. A great and vast amount. I suppose you'll be wanting the chain as well as the pendant."

"Of course the chain. And don't beat about the bush, man, or I'll take my business elsewhere."

"The gentleman was the one who roused me from my bed." Despite his nervousness, the shopkeeper studied Gordon with a shrewd eye. "Most officers who darken my door come seeking coins for their next meal."

"Which you are no doubt reluctant to give," Gordon shot back.

"No need for such a tone. No, my good sir, no need at all."

"The price!"

"Ah, well, the price." He gave a theatrical sigh. "I could hardly set a price on such a piece as this."

Gordon laughed shortly. "Then I bid you good night."

He turned for the door, motioning John Jackson ahead of him.

"Wait a moment now, good sirs." The shopkeeper hastened toward the two. "Wait a moment. I might have been too hasty—"

"You and I both know," Gordon said in measured tones, "that in such times you could hold this item for a hundred years and not find a buyer."

The old man attempted indignation. "I'll have you know a fine lady was in here not two days hence—"

"Hear me out." Gordon unbuckled his belt and laid its sword upon the counter between them. "Do you know what it is I have here?"

The gleam in the shopkeeper's eye said it all. Before him lay a ceremonial sword, presented to Gordon by grateful shipowners when he had returned from a journey laden with spices and profits. The scabbard was chased with silver, as was the twined guard to the pommel. Gordon had imagined he might be buried with this at his side.

When the shopkeeper hesitated, Gordon laid a silver-sheathed dagger and a powder horn decorated in the same ornate style beside the sword.

Gordon did not speak again. He merely pointed to the locked shelf. The shopkeeper misunderstood his silence as a threat and withdrew the pendant with a trembling hand.

Gordon gathered up the goods, waited for John Jackson to unlock the door, and wordlessly stepped into the night.

Though the wind remained damp and biting, the rain had ceased. As the two men stepped to the end of the narrow lane, the moon emerged from behind a cloud.

Gordon stopped in the square and faced the newly discovered cohort. "I had entered the church where you found me seeking answers from God. And you, my friend, are the clearest evidence of a miracle I have seen in many a day. I feel in my bones that your coming here was ordained by our Lord."

Slowly Jackson lifted his gaze to meet Gordon's. "You are speaking as your lady does, about—" he struggled for words— "about matters of faith."

"Yes, I am learning to listen to the voice of God." Gordon clapped the man's shoulder. "And I believe you are the answer to our prayer. Nicole has a piece of land west of here, granted to her by her uncle. Armies from both sides have swept through, razed the house, burned the fields, driven off everyone who once called the place home. I am wondering if you would be willing to go there and make a start of refashioning a homestead." When Jackson did not respond, Gordon added, "This is not charity, my man! Who else might Nicole and I entrust with the responsibility? You can go and work at your own pace until your strength returns. The place should not be left alone through another planting season."

John Jackson studied the cobblestones at his feet, then raised his head and nodded slowly. "I am your man."

Chapter 8

Anne was seated in the small corner garden below the library window when Thomas and Charles came around the house together. She smiled at them and said, "England never ceases to amaze me. One day, all is midwinter bleak, and the sky so gray I feel certain the sun will never dare show its face again." She waved her hand about her. "The next, and all the world is alive and green with the joy of new awakenings."

Neither Thomas nor Charles seemed to know how to respond. The older gentleman tugged on his embroidered waistcoat. Her husband finally asked, "What are you reading?"

"The Psalter. King David reminds us to take shelter under the shadow of God's wings. What a descriptive thought that is!" Anne moved to one end of the bench and motioned to them. "Why do you not join me? We can read aloud together."

But neither man made any move to accept her invitation. Anne looked into her husband's face, and she knew then why they had sought her out, and why they had come together.

But she held to her inner calm, the peace that had been a gift from God. "This was the last book I studied with Nicole," she continued, "and this bench was where we had many wonderful discussions. It was here in this garden that I truly came to know my sister." She smiled up at Charles. "I have never properly thanked you, Uncle. How wonderful it was to have this time and this place to know Nicole as both sister and dearest friend."

Charles lowered himself into the bench. "I used to look out upon the two of you from my library." He indicated the window directly overhead. "I often have marveled at how different you two were, and yet how alike."

Anne moved closer to Charles, making space on her other side. She patted the bench. "Come, my husband, sit yourself down and tell me the news of our departure—information that requires two strong men to deliver."

The gentlemen exchanged looks of astonishment.

"Here, I will make it easier for you." When Thomas still did not move, Anne held his hand and pulled him down. "You have found berths for us, and you have the date of our departure for Nova Scotia."

Thomas inspected her face. "You . . . you are accepting this with great calm."

Anne did not answer immediately, gazing out over the garden.

"I should have thought, well, with John—"

"John is staying," she confirmed. She took a long breath and Thomas squeezed her hand. She needed to know if she could state the facts and retain her composure. To her great relief, the peace remained. "John is staying here at Harrow Hall. I know the Lord who is making it possible for me to go to my father will also be with John. . . ." She slowed to a stop, but her voice did not break.

Charles took her other hand. "I can only assure you that we shall care for him as though he were our own son."

Anne turned to look into Charles's face. "I was blessed with two fathers," she said. "Why should John not have the same gift?"

"My dear . . ." Charles stopped to clear his throat. "Forgive me," he said, his voice still husky. "Thank you, Anne, for the gift of your trust. Judith and I . . ." But he could not continue.

"John loves you both," she assured her uncle. "I could not find more devoted care. Of that I am certain."

Judith and Anne were making a tour of the local villages. Numerous projects—agricultural reform, schools, sanitation, medical care, classes for Scripture studies—were now well under way, and Anne was turning over their supervision to Judith during the time she was gone. "It is wonderful to know, dear Judith, I can leave these efforts in your hands," she said to the older woman beside her in the open brougham.

"The seeds are planted," Judith replied. "I shall see the crops remain well tended."

Judith handled the reins with ease. Harry Day, Maisy's youngest lad, rode a dappled gray and acted as their official escort. Two villagers also accompanied them on horseback, one riding ahead and the other behind. Even this close to the estate, even surrounded as they were by neighbors and friends, there was still risk of attack by highwaymen in these uncertain times. The villagers had worked out the system themselves, trading off once they knew who would escort the two women onward.

The afternoon was sliding into dusk. Anne looked around at the pleasant shadows and confessed, "It is difficult to leave England at such a time as this."

"It is difficult to leave one's home at any time," Judith replied. "Much less saying good-bye to your own son."

Anne swallowed down the sudden lump in her throat over the coming separation. "I meant—I was talking about spring coming and the world so beautiful. . . ." She fought against the fear and dread trying to steal away her peace.

Judith kept her gaze fastened upon the leather reins in her gloved hands. "I simply am wondering if you are able and ready to hear me out."

"I am desperately sorry to be leaving John." Anne turned to look at Judith. She tried to match the older woman's matter-of-fact tone. "And yet I feel at peace with the decision."

Judith grasped the reins in one hand and reached for Anne's with her other. "I have watched you come to your decision, and I believe it is the right one, the only course of action in the situation you face."

Judith again took the reins in both hands. "Anne, my dearest, I care for you as I would my own daughter."

Anne only nodded. Finally she said, "But you are worried about something—"

"It is nothing, I hope. But yes, I am concerned." She looked at Anne. "I feel that you and Thomas must give thought to your own safety."

"Safety—in what way? Do you mean safety if our ship should be attacked?"

"No, my worry has to do with enemies of Charles. You know he has them in high places. Besides, the Dissenters are becoming an increasing irritation to those in power. It is only natural they should have spies among them. People who will buy news for gold." Judith cast her a tense glance. "News that the parents of Charles's official heir are taking to the high seas."

"What are you saying?"

"It is public knowledge that Dissenters have hired this vessel and more than three hundred of their community are moving to Nova Scotia."

"Yes." The London broadsheets had reported how these Dissenters had become so disgusted with their rulers and the war that they were renouncing their citizenship and moving away. Starting anew in an area where common decency and faith in God still had a place. "But what does that have to do with us?"

"Imagine for a moment. French warships and privateers scour the waters off our coast, looking for prey."

Anne's hand moved to her throat. "You don't think—"

"I don't *know*. But what if news of your departure was intentionally passed to these brigands? Out to sea, who is to know what happened, and by whom?" Now that the worries were spoken, Judith's obvious distress tightened her voice. "I have had the most dreadful nightmares, both asleep and awake. Charles felt I should not add to your cares, but I could not bear to not at least tell you this much in the event the Lord would want you to take precautions."

Anne struggled to sort through the sudden torrent of tumbling thoughts. "But it took weeks to find this passage. And there is only the one vessel."

"There is only one from Portsmouth."

"What are you saying?"

Judith reined in the horse, then raised one hand to keep their escorts at a distance. "Only one Dissenter vessel is leaving from Portsmouth," she repeated, her voice low. "All the firebrands who have so vocally opposed the king are traveling on this one. But there are two others departing from Plymouth."

"Three vessels?"

"The two from Plymouth are not leaving for another week, which would delay your departure. But these other two are departing in relative secrecy. I learned of them only after I confided my torment to the vicar. He has two relatives who journey on the Plymouth boats. May I tell you what I have thought might be a course of action?"

"Please!"

"Here it is, then. Make a public pronouncement of canceling your berths. If there is anything intended against you, and I do so hope I am wrong, that may save others on the Portsmouth vessel from danger. Then secretly buy two new berths upon a vessel departing from Plymouth. There are spaces available. I have checked. This time though . . ." Judith hesitated, then confessed, "I fear it will sound overly cautious."

"You think," Anne supplied for her, "we should travel under assumed names."

"Only until you are at sea." The remaining words tumbled out in a rush. "I know it must sound like foolish prattle from a meddling old woman, Anne. But I could not just let you go without speaking. My conscience would not let me rest."

"Thank you, Judith. Thank you."

Judith's grip on the reins slackened, and the horse took that as a signal and began trotting on. "What will you do?" she asked.

"The only thing I can, given the circumstances," Anne replied. "Discuss it with Thomas."

That evening, in the bedroom with Thomas, Anne outlined Judith's conversation, then ended feebly, "I have done a poor job of conveying both her concerns and my own. But there you are."

Thomas was facing toward the night-shrouded window. In the firelight his features held a grave air. Finally she could stand his silence no longer. "It's all right. You may tell me that I am being foolish and unduly concerned."

"You are many things," he replied, not turning back. "But never that. Never."

"Then what are you thinking?"

"I have long feared Britain's rulers are being pressed at the wrong time. The troubles in France, the war with America, the trade woes, Parliament in foment—everything is in turmoil and striking them at once from all sides. I have worried mightily at what impact these confrontations with the Dissenters might have. They are the loudest voice and the weakest force, and thus easily attacked."

Thomas stared grimly out at the dark, peering intently at something only he could see. "Twice I have written the London churches, beseeching them to cease with this fiery clamor. I have begged them to do so for the sake of their wives and children. For my efforts I have been called a fool, a coward, and a king's man. Their utter failure to understand my concerns has caused me to question my own judgment."

"Why have you not told me of this?"

"You have had other things to contend with, my dearest."

"You are saying Judith is right?"

"Perhaps." He nodded slowly toward the night. "And perhaps it is something I should have thought of myself. It did not even occur to me that there might be other ships leaving from more distant ports. And the idea of traveling under aliases is most wise. Yes, yes . . ."

Anne's sense of relief was unexpected, as were the tears. She dabbed at her eyes. "Forgive me. It has been a very long day."

"You are quite worn out. And it is not just the work you and Judith have been doing in the villages." Thomas came over to her chair and laid his hand on her shoulder. "You are preparing for a long and arduous journey. You are leaving your son behind. The war stands in your way. And all you have to look forward to at the other end is an ailing father."

Hearing Thomas give names to all her concerns only made it harder to hold back the tears. She leaned her face against his hand and wiped at her eyes.

"You are a good and strong woman who is bearing a great deal just now," Thomas said. He stroked her shoulder for a moment, then said, "Now you must excuse me for a moment."

"Where are you going?"

"First to see if Maisy can make a cup of tea for you." Thomas turned to the door as he shrugged into his housecoat. "Then to find Judith and thank her for suggesting what is in truth the only reasonable and prudent course of action."

Chapter 9

Nicole watched from her perch on the lead wagon as Gordon guided the horses onto the river ferry and secured the wheels. There was no sign of the tension in his expression that in recent days had furrowed his brow and made him distracted, even distant. She had not known how to reach him, though she had tried. In fact, if she were to put any name upon Gordon's outlook, it was hope.

He had not appeared for dinner at the seminary their last night with Pastor Collins. The next morning she had received a message delivered by John Jackson, of all people, a most unexpected messenger. He explained that the general had suddenly instructed Gordon to travel to the southern depot for horses and wagons and what supplies and crew might be found, and he handed her a short note. She was to be ready to depart the morning of the fourth day. Nothing more, save a declaration of his care for her. Of course it had been penned in haste—the stationery bore the general's official crest. But she had puzzled over what it could be that remained unsaid between them for some days now.

John Jackson's surprise appearance was a distraction from further worry. The man's health had clearly suffered, and Pastor Collins took up with the ministrations Nicole had begun. But simply regular meals were doing him the most good. Gordon's idea to send him west to oversee work on the farm was a stroke of genius.

Now Nicole sat and observed the man she was soon to wed. No doubt he was thoroughly engaged with this return to his world of ships and sails and sea. Yet this alone did not explain the light in his eyes, the confidence seen in his movements.

Finally the third wagon was loaded and the wheels secured. Gordon waved to the ferrymaster and shouted, "Let's be off!"

The master and his two mates strained to push the ferry across the river's current. All three plied great wooden paddles, like long spoons, hooked to three of the ferry's corners. Like most river people, they were men of very few words, calling tight little instructions to one another. They held the ferry's nose pointed straight at the opposite shoreline with a skill that under other circumstances Nicole would have found fascinating. But today her concentration was on what was happening in Gordon's mind and heart.

Gordon climbed easily onto the seat beside her. "What do you think, my dear, should we head farther up the coast or find berths for the night in Cambridge?"

She studied her man. "I don't know what to think."

He glanced at her, then at the sun, pulled out his watch and flicked open the cover. "My inclination is to strike north. The coastal roads are all firm in American hands, by what I hear. We should cover a good number of miles before dark and still find an inn without too much difficulty."

There were any number of questions she wished to put to him, but not while a dozen pairs of ears were within listening range. Gordon's vessel awaited them up the coast in Marble Harbor, a smaller port not so well patrolled by the British blockade as Boston. She answered quietly, "As you wish."

He cast her another glance, then sprang down and walked over to Carter's wagon. The bosun's horses were scrawny nags, but Nicole knew they were the best that could be had. The only reason Gordon was not more worried about these tired and hungry horses making the journey, he had told her, was that they had so little to carry.

Gordon had selected ten of the best men he could find, all

of them well salted—the term used to describe men with experience before the mast, he explained. He had no idea what sort of crew he would find or how many men might be available in Marblehead. But the war had made seasoned men of good health very scarce, and he was worried about taking to sea without a full bevy. But Nicole noted not even that seemed to affect him this morning. He said something in his dry captain's tone that set all the men to laughing, then turned to Nicole with his smile. "All right, lads," he called. "Let's unleash the wagons and be ready to move out soon as the ferry touches ground."

The off-loading was far swifter, as the horses were nervously eager to leave their watercraft behind. Gordon placed their own wagon first in line. He flicked the reins, turned to ensure that the others followed, then pointed the horses north. When they arrived at the first fork, where the road stone indicated the turning for Cambridge, he said, "Unless you object, my dear, I should prefer to journey onward."

Nicole smiled and nodded her agreement.

He flicked the reins and headed along the coastal road. "It was truly miraculous, coming upon Jackson after all this time."

"He improved noticeably while you were gone." She waited, hoping he might say something more. "Your enlisting him to begin work for us was quite extraordinary."

Gordon took a moment before responding. "I would call it one of the most remarkable events that has come my way."

"I was—I was concerned about you, Gordon. I was worried."

"I apologize once more for missing our dinner."

"It's not that." She gathered the folds of her cloak about her. "I thought I knew you, Gordon. But lately I've wondered if you might be reconsidering our marriage." Her voice dropped nearly to a whisper, then she quickly added, "But this . . . this new outlook I see in you has me further baffled."

He cast her a swift look, then turned his face toward the westering sun. "Yes, Nicole, I can imagine that you have had questions. First, though, let me assure you of my love for you."

One hand dropped its hold on the reins to grasp hers.

Nicole glanced behind her, ensuring that the next wagon in line was sufficiently far away, then gave a tremulous smile to Gordon, who was watching her intently. "I am both relieved and reassured to hear you say that," she said, "but I still don't understand . . ." She could not finish the thought.

"Because," Gordon said, then stopped himself. She feared the one word would be all the answer he was prepared to give. Finally he said, "I had myself the most remarkable conversation with God."

"I beg your pardon?"

"I talked with Him, and He with me. The essence of prayer, I suppose. The reality of the experience is rather foreign to me. I know not how else to describe it. But I went to God with a dilemma. And He in His eternal wisdom gave me an answer, the only answer there is." He squeezed her hand, then turned his attention forward. "The simple but profound truth is that I must place my trust in Him," he said as he flipped the reins.

"Gordon, I don't know what to say." She clasped her hands tightly together.

"Yes, I would imagine so." He flicked the reins once more. As the horses pulled the wagon a trifle farther away from the others, he went on, "Do you know, we have never spoken of the date."

Instantly she knew what he meant. The sudden change of direction, though, and the ease with which he turned away from the previous discussion left her with only "What?" as her response.

"I know we have thought to wait until we could see the war's end. Either that or be certain I would not be called again to sea. But I have spent these past few days reflecting." He stared out over the horses' backs. "God willing, I shall make this my final sea voyage. It was on the sea that we first met, don't you know. How better could I bid this portion of my life farewell than to share one final journey with you on the water."

Nicole felt her hands loosen their grip as she took a long breath.

"It also occurred to me that we should ask your father to marry us while we are with your parents. I should be honored to stand before such a fine gentleman and join my life to yours."

"Gordon," was all she could manage right then. But he seemed to understand her joy as he reached again for her hand.

Chapter 10

Of all the departures Anne might have imagined, this had not been among them.

Harrow Hall was silent, and the last hour before the dawn was draped in a mist so thick Anne could not see the lead horses from her place by the carriage door. Only Maisy's presence by the front doorway signaled any normality. The housekeeper twisted her apron and murmured a final plea. "At least let me light the fire and prepare a bit of nourishment."

"We have been through this before," Charles replied but without impatience as he scouted the darkness. "No lights, no indication of any kind that the house is awake."

"But what of some breakfast for the poor little bairn?"

"Young John is where you deposited him on the carriage seat, wrapped in your warmest quilting and still sound asleep. He will be fed later when he awakens. You have heard the same news as the rest of us. Secrecy is our strongest weapon." Charles called softly into the gloom. "I say, Harry!"

"Here, sir."

"Are your outriders ready?"

"Just finishing with watering their horses, sir."

"And the provisions?"

"Stowed as your lordship ordered."

"Then let's be off."

Judith hugged the distressed housekeeper. "You are a dear woman, Maisy, and we shall all be fine."

Anne ran back up the steps to hug Maisy a final time. "Thank you again. For everything."

"Oh, to see you go off like this just rips my poor heart in two." The woman was doing her best to keep from weeping as she crushed Anne to her warm bosom. "I won't cease praying 'til I see your lovely face before me again."

"I know you will take good care of John." Anne whispered the words over the lump in her throat.

"Like he was my own flesh and blood." Maisy released her and waved a sorrowful farewell to Anne's husband. "Fare thee well, Master Thomas."

He lifted a hand in silent response, and she buried her face in her apron and turned away.

"Come, Anne. The night is dripping wet and you mustn't catch a chill." Thomas helped her into the carriage by the sleeping child, and the others clambered on board. The driver gave a quiet click, and the carriage moved forward, its sounds cushioned by the night mist. Anne pushed down the window and peered behind them through the gloom and the fog. The beautiful manor that had become home to her was already out of sight. She could not allow herself to wonder when she would see it again.

Harry Day and two other footmen rode with the driver, while two villagers on horses led the way, another two behind. All carried pistols and stout staves. The carriage showed no light whatsoever. The villagers ahead of them were chosen from those who knew the roads best, for the intention was to ride hard so that by daybreak the travelers were beyond the borders of Charles's land, beyond any who might know their identity.

Three days after the Portsmouth vessel had set sail, word came from the south of England that the night after the Dissenters' vessel had left port, a flotilla of ships had attacked. The Dissenters had been saved by what could only be called a miracle. Just as the attackers had opened fire, four British troopships returning from the colonies had appeared from nowhere and counterattacked. The Dissenters' ship had turned and fled back to port. They had lost a mast and much rigging, and seven passengers had been wounded by flying debris from the first cannonade, though none had perished.

Accompanying the news were rumors that one of the attacking vessels had carried English men on the captain's foredeck. It being well known that noise carries far across open water, and no voices are louder than officers on the verge of battle, this rumor had all the elements of fact. When questioned about British guns turned on a British ship, the palace was reported to have quickly replied that pirates were drawn from every quarter and nation. They were a scourge, and the king and his prince were most grateful for the ship's safe return. The palace spokesman, a permanent sneer in place, had finished with, "Perhaps the Dissenters would now see the error of their ways and swear fealty to their king."

As a result of the rumors and the resulting fears, the two Plymouth vessels had set sail early, without their passengers. They had secretly docked in a small fishing harbor on the wild North Devon coast.

By first light they were midway to Bristol. They breakfasted on the move, halting only once at mid-morning to water the horses and stretch their own legs. The day turned out to be perfect for travel, for even after the sun burned away the early mist, a light northerly breeze cooled the carriage.

Anne had debated over taking John along to shipside and those final farewells. But finally she could not bear the thought of giving up any precious moments with her son, and no one chose to contradict her. She simply could not imagine herself kissing her slumbering son and stealing away. And John proved to be a delightful traveling companion for all of them. Even as the afternoon began waning, and they stopped to exchange their weary steeds for fresh ones, John's innate curiosity and childish prattle kept their spirits high.

They watered the second set of horses at a spring-fed trough on the crest of the southern downs. Steep-sided hills rose to flat plateaus stretching as far as the eye could see. The outriders were gone now, having turned back when the teams had been changed, leaving just one who now rode on top with the others. They came to a roadside inn, and the nine of them, driver and guards and travelers together, sat at a long table in the back of the low-ceilinged room. They ate in silence, quieted by the knowledge of a long night still ahead of them. Only John and Charles appeared free of fatigue. Once they had completed their bowls of stew and cups of tea, the two resumed a game they had played on and off all day.

"All right, then," Charles said, frowning mightily. "Here's a test for you, my little man. Fail it and I shall be obliged to tie you to the back of the carriage and make you run along behind."

John laughed gleefully.

"Who makes this sound—*coo, coo, coo?*" asked Uncle Charles.

"A robin!"

"No, you silly fellow, a dove. How many times must I tell you that?"

"Dove!"

"That's it. What a brilliant lad you are."

"Another!"

"Very well. Who says *caw, caw, caw?*"

"A robin!"

"Do you know, I am almost certain you are having me on." Uncle Charles shook his head from side to side while John chortled again. "Do you seek to try my patience?"

"Another!"

"You haven't answered this one yet. Who says *caw, caw, caw?*"

"Robin!"

Charles narrowed his eyes. "And who, pray tell, says *bow-wow, bow-wow?*"

"Robin!"

"No, you tricky little fellow. It's a puppy dog, as you well know. One that will come and nibble on the fingers of little boys who try to play their elders like fools. Like this, you see." He grabbed John's small hand and made a show of dining upon his fingers while the boy shrieked with delight. "My, my. I had no idea little fingers could be quite so delicious. Do you know, I think I shall have a few more."

As they were leaving the inn Judith drew Anne to one side. "I fear there may be no chance once we are at the dock to say this. And I cannot let you depart without thanking you once more, from the bottom of my heart."

Anne did not need to ask what the older woman meant. She forced herself to hold her composure and reply, "There is no doubt in my mind that this is the best course to take."

"For all of us, save you." Judith's arms circled Anne in a warm embrace. "Charles and I both will shed years and worries while we attempt to keep up with John," she added with a smile. But her expression turned serious again when she said, "Anne, we could not love him more if he were our own son."

And then both women wept.

Chapter 11

The difference from Boston was evident within a few moments of the three wagons' arrival in Marble Harbor, also known as Marblehead. The village rose alongside a well-sheltered deepwater harbor. By no means as large as Boston's port, the encircling arms still offered ideal protection from the open sea. Four large vessels occupied prominent positions about the anchorage. Gordon pointed out to Nicole the *Hannah*, a vessel that had gained its reputation as a blockade-runner.

They noticed they were surrounded by villagers relatively untouched by the war. There was little sign of deprivation here, of the desperate want so prevalent on the streets of Boston.

"Look at that woman's gown!" Nicole said to Gordon. The lady's yellow silk, with parasol to match, was as fashionable as any she had seen. "It might as well have come straight from London!" she marveled.

"Paris, more like, given the present state of affairs. This is a smugglers' port. Home to any number of swift blockade-runners and privateers. They make a living of sneaking under the nose of the British."

"Why don't they bring their supplies down to Boston?"

"They do, for a price." Gordon angled his hat to block the late afternoon sun. "But enough of their wares are kept close to home, as you can see."

Gordon gestured over the rooftops to where the ships sat at

anchor. "Do you see that ship anchored closest to the northern rocks? That is a British man-of-war, or I'll eat my hat. Take note of the dark smudges about its bow. Smugglers fought hand to hand with the finest of the British fleet and captured their vessel."

Nicole felt no need to study the ship. Her mind still held a too-vivid image of another vessel caught by night and a British blockade, wrapped by flames and the shrieks of dying men.

Gordon's attention remained upon the ship at anchor. "The men of Marblehead did not sink her, which of course is easier than capture. They strike for profit. Which means they had to take her intact. They might be smugglers, but they are also fine seamen and warriors both."

She shivered. "I want nothing to do with them."

"You no doubt shall have your wish, though we could well do with more experienced hands." He gestured to where some sailors loitered outside a tavern. "These men sail for profit, as I said. There will be precious little gain from taking us upon a voyage where speed and stealth are what we require—and all we can offer."

As they rounded the harbor entrance Gordon stood up in the wagon. "I say, that is my ship!" he exclaimed. "They've repaired all sign of her capture. See the new wood along the portside? That's as fine a bit of joinery as I've ever seen. Why, she might as well have been repaired in Portsmouth!"

Nicole hid her smile at his boyish excitement. Then she noticed several places where bright new wood signaled repairs, and she imagined the thunder of cannons as they crashed through the hull, the fire and terror and death. . . . She shook her head quickly to clear away those awful scenes.

The quayside was a spit of land extending out from the village like an arrowhead. Gordon called to an officer standing watch over a group of scurrying laborers. "I say, good sir. Could you tell me where I might find the harbormaster?"

"You are addressing him now."

Gordon leaped lightly out of the wagon to the rocks. "Captain Gordon Goodwind at your service, sir."

"Goodwind, as in master of yon vessel?"

"The same."

The man growled. "You are three days late in arriving, sir."

"And well I know it. But the roads and arranging last-minute details delayed our departure. I hope I have not added to the difficulties of your job."

"Not you, sir. Not you. But the work commissioned by the general—I declare it has almost been the death of me."

Gordon looked over his ship. "They have done a fine piece of work on the repairs nonetheless."

"Only because I have stood over them with musket and threats both!" He shook his head in ire. "The only way I could get cooperation was by refusing them permission to even board their own vessels until the work was under way. A more avaricious and spiteful clan I have never encountered!"

"They work for profit."

"They work for themselves and none other!" the officer shouted, his face red with anger. "I have begged and pleaded to be freed of this posting. The war is waning and I am trapped in a backwater filled with smugglers and thieves!"

Gordon stripped off his glove and held out his hand. "I am most grateful for your work and for requiring theirs."

"Randolf Nettleton. Forgive me, Captain. But it has been a harsh and loathsome duty your commandant laid upon me."

"I will be writing the general a note, bringing him up-to-date concerning my departure. Perhaps you would be so kind as to deliver it in person. I could then make mention of your desires and ask his help for your transfer as a personal favor."

"You would do that? For a perfect stranger?"

Gordon waved his hand toward the ship as he said, "I have difficulty just now seeing anything other than a job well done. The fact that you have endured much to complete this task only places me further in your debt."

"I am quite—"

"Say nothing further on the subject, my friend. But please suggest where we might find a berth for the night, and supplies for the coming journey."

"A berth is no problem. All three of the inns you see facing the harbor are clean and commodious, at least for those with money." He dropped his voice. "As for supplies, they are here, but precious dear."

"I must secure food and other essentials for the voyage."

Nettleton still looked doubtful. "We are too far removed from Boston for the commandant's paper to carry much weight. It will require gold, or they will not unlock their stores, you mark my words."

Nicole was still sitting in the wagon, too far to hear much of the exchange. She could not have said why the man who appeared on deck now caught her attention. His unkempt beard fell almost to his chest, his sailor's pigtail was untarred and ragged, and his features were roughened, no doubt by sun and salt and hard wear. His clothes hung in tatters on his thin frame, and one ankle was marked by old scars—the signs of a jail rat's heavy iron fetters. But there was something about the way he stood and stared at her, something about the set of those once-massive shoulders, that drew her from her seat and down the side steps.

"The commandant has given me what gold he could. . . ." she heard Gordon say. But then he turned to ask her as she moved up the gangplank, "Nicole, what is it?"

"Lady Harrow!" the disheveled figure called.

She halted at the midpoint on the gangplank. Her hand on the railing, she peered at him in disbelief. "Samuel?"

The man's voice trembled. "I feared I was dreaming."

The last time they had seen Gordon's second mate was the day they had left by longboat for the shoreline down from Boston Harbor—the previous summer, when they had set off for the Harrow holdings. "Samuel, it is you, isn't it?"

Gordon was behind her in an instant. "Samuel, indeed," he exclaimed.

"Sir, never in all my born days did I ever think to set eyes upon you again," the man said.

"But what have they done to you?" Nicole asked.

Gordon turned on the officer in charge standing at dockside. The officer instantly said, "It was none of my doing, Captain."

Samuel spoke up. "He's right, sir. All about here have treated us fair and square."

"Then who—?"

"Our very own officers, sir. When they seized the ship, they demoted us all to common sailors. They set all of us before the mast and kept us on punishment watch."

"For how long?" Gordon's anger was clear.

"'Til the Yanks attacked." He used his rag of a sleeve to wipe his brow. "It's been a terrible long winter, sir." He looked around at his shipmates, many in worse condition than he.

The harbormaster climbed the gangplank to stand alongside Gordon. "They're some of the finest workers I've ever set my eyes on, I'll give you that."

"But look at the state of them!"

"We've fed them as we could from our supplies, I assure you. They haven't been here long enough for that to show. But as for clothes—" Nettleton shrugged—"I told you. The army's paper carries no weight here."

"He's right, sir," Samuel nodded. "We've been treated fair. And left to berth here on board like proper jack-tars."

"Two of these men were injured in the attack," the officer explained. "They're in the squadron's sickbay and coming around well. When these men heard you'd been given the vessel's commission, they begged to remain on board. Every one of them. Such loyalty is to be commended, sir."

Gordon asked, "How many are left?"

"All but Williams, sir. He caught a bad chest and went down hard."

"God rest his soul." He raised his voice. "You all need to know I've changed sides, lads. Carter and the others you see dockside are with me. We're off on a mission for the Yanks. Any who want to hold to the new course are welcome. Those who prefer shore duty will have your papers and my best wishes to see them off. You men take a moment to talk among yourselves."

"We don't need a moment, sir." Samuel's words raised the motley group to stand at attention. "We'll follow you to the ends of the earth and beyond."

Four days of almost constant effort yielded few supplies. There were two distinct faces shown them by the Marblehead merchants. When it came to business and bargaining on their goods, they were ruthless. But by the third day, the entire waterfront seemed to know of Gordon and Nicole—how his vessel had been seized and used in the British blockade, how the British had then arrested Gordon as a spy, how he had escaped through the endeavors of an American army sergeant and this woman rumored to be a titled lady. Whenever Nicole walked their meandering lanes and stopped in merchants' shops, people offered the sober greetings of those who shared the strain of sea-bound lives and the privations of war.

Finally toward the end of the fourth day, she and Gordon took a walk around the dockside and up into the surrounding hills. They felt they had done all they could in preparation for embarking on the morrow. It was a warm afternoon and a welcome escape from the ship's cramped quarters. Nicole slipped her hand through Gordon's arm. "I will be overjoyed to be on our way come morning," she murmured.

Gordon tipped his hat to a pair of ladies and waited until they had passed. "The thought of how I have bartered over supplies these past few days leaves me no end of weary."

An older gentleman veered off the other sidewalk to make his way across the lane toward them. "A word, if you please, Captain," he called.

Bearded and shaped like a seasoned barrel, he wore a greatcoat puffed out over a vast chest. "The name's Darren, Captain Goodwind. I skipper yon vessel *Hannah*."

Gordon gave a proper bow. "At your service, Captain Darren."

"Word's been passed about concerning your troubles and your journey ahead." He bit hard on a long clay pipe, sending aromatic puffs skyward with each word. "Left a good impression around these parts, you and your crew."

"It has not hindered your traders from squeezing every farthing from our meager purse," Gordon answered sardonically.

"Aye, they're a rapacious lot," he replied with good humor. "Now then. We're expecting you to be setting sail soon. How do you aim to set yourselves beyond the reach of yon Redcoats?"

"I would be grateful for any advice you could give, sir."

This was clearly the response Captain Darren had been seeking. "Come moonrise in two nights, our fishing vessels will be making their way home. They will be taking a southerly course and no doubt will be meeting up with the blockade. The Brits don't sink the fishermen. But they do have a mind to rid them of a goodly portion of their catch. Blockade duty being what it is, they're as eager for fresh food as any."

"I don't understand," Nicole said. "Your fishermen know they will be caught?"

Gordon nodded slowly. "They are a decoy."

Darren's keen pleasure at Gordon's perception showed in his smile. "Myself and another vessel, we'll be charting a northerly course outbound. You'd be welcome to tag along 'til we're safely away."

"I am indeed obliged, Captain," Gordon said. "We shall delay our departure and be ready to sail with the midnight tide two nights hence."

Chapter 12

Anne awoke as the carriage swayed around a bend in the road. She leaned forward to peer out the window. The sea stretched before her in the early morning light. Its expanse only reminded her of the coming farewell.

Anne looked around the passenger coach at the sleeping travelers. Judith leaned upon Charles, who rested against the opposite side, steady snores escaping with every breath. Anne smiled in spite of herself.

The farther they had traveled through the night, the closer they had come to the ship and separation. When Anne could hold her eyes open no longer, her last sight had been of Thomas sleeping directly across from her, with John sprawled across the remainder of the seat, his head in Thomas's lap. Now her son and husband lay curled up together. Sometime during the night Thomas had stretched out, and the boy had crawled up to lie across his chest. They lay in the comforting closeness of parent and child as the rising sun painted them in the softest hues. Anne turned again to look out the window and struggled to keep her sobs silent.

She did not turn back until she had regained control. Then she gazed at her two most precious people until the carriage lurched over a particularly deep crevice, throwing them all about.

Charles snorted awake, rubbed his face, then stuck his head out the window and called softly, "I say, have a care, George."

"It's Harry what's driving, sir. George is asleep up top." Harry's perpetual smile could be heard in his tone. "Can't help the rocking, I'm afraid. There's hardly more'n a country lane to follow."

Charles poked his head out farther still. "So I see. And there is the sea."

"Yes, and a beautiful morning to you, sir. We've made right good time."

"Pull up, will you, and let us all stretch our legs."

"Right you are, milord. I see a lay-by just ahead."

When the coach halted, the four adults climbed down to walk about, stretching complaining joints and limbs. Harry woke the driver and the other two guards, and they made great difficulty of clambering to earth.

Anne handed around mugs of watered cider. She then took the breakfast sack from Harry and laid out their morning meal.

"What a sight," Charles remarked. "I say, where's the lad?" he added, looking around.

"Still asleep." Thomas moved up alongside the older man, and together they stood gazing out over the green-blue vista.

It was indeed a wonderful view. Beyond the lay-by, the lane took a series of steeply winding turns down a cliff of heather and stone. Below them, a village of gray stone cottages lay nestled within the cove's circling arms. The coast here curved back upon itself, and the village faced almost directly north. The rising sun formed a sharp line of light and shadow where it struck the high cliff. They could hear voices rising from the quayside where two tall-masted ships lay within the harbor. A line of people and produce plodded across the gangplanks.

"There is no place on earth quite so lovely as north Devon on a fine day," Judith said as she joined the two men. "Alas, there are very few fine days in these parts."

"Aye, I have heard of dangerously high seas in this region."

Thomas kept his voice low to spare Anne.

"The sailors call this the Wild Coast," Judith confirmed. Thomas knew her family had been Welsh merchants and traders for generations. The ways of the British seas were a vital part of her heritage. "My father used to prize the Devon and Cornish fishermen above all others, both as sailors and officers. But there are precious few who are willing to leave behind their beloved homeland. On such a day as this, I can well understand why."

From the dockside came an officer's shout, and in response the shrill song of a bosun's pipe. "No doubt the captain seeks to make way while the weather is with him," Charles said. "We should be under way shortly."

Just then Anne called that their breakfast was ready, and they soon had eaten their bread and cheese. John had by this time awakened in high good cheer at the adventure of sleeping in the carriage and picnicking for breakfast.

As the carriage turned about and began the descent, a convoy of wagons and coaches appeared behind them. The men called a halloo and waved. Through her open window, Anne thought the women among them seemed both wan and stricken. When one of them offered her a tentative wave, Anne replied with as solemn a gesture. The men thought of the challenge, the adventure of the crossing, and a new life. But the women were leaving family and friends—the only life they had known.

When the carriage pulled up at dockside, Charles and Thomas hurried about, helping the other travelers unload their bundles and chests and barrels.

With Judith nearby, Anne stood watching, holding John's hand and trying not to squeeze it too tightly.

"Excuse me, Lady Harrow?"

Both women turned as one at the address. None here was

to have known their identity, save a single individual. They found themselves facing a young man wearing a vicar's white collar beneath his black Dissenter cloak. Anne said, "You must be Pastor Fields."

"Just so." He removed his hat and bowed over Anne's hand.

"And I am traveling as Anne Malvern with my husband, Thomas," she said, keeping her voice low.

"Yes. Of course. Forgive me. I have the name here on my list."

"Malvern," Anne repeated as he searched for the name. They had decided upon the maiden name of Thomas's grandmother. Judith took John's hand and led him over to watch the loading of the ship, out of earshot of the exchange.

"Yes, here it is. None save myself and my wife know your identity."

"Once we are safely out to sea, we would be happy to be known by our true names," Anne told him. "We seek to disguise our identity for their sakes as much as our own."

"This is perfectly understood. You are not the only ones who are departing today under assumed names, I assure you." He held his hat in front of him. "Actually, I wished merely to thank you for your most generous gifts."

Anne smiled and said, "I'm glad we had the wherewithal to do so, Pastor. Good stewardship, I believe you would call it."

"My lady—"

"Mrs. Malvern, if you please, Reverend."

"Ma'am, I cannot thank you enough. As a result of your most kind donations, our entire congregation is making this journey. And even the poorest family among us shall travel with fresh produce and bedding and medicines and tools for the home that awaits them."

"My only request is that the gift remain a secret between ourselves and God."

"As you wish, ma'am. But I could not possibly let your goodness go without a word of thanks." He backed away. "I must go see to my family. After we are safely away, my wife and I shall assist with the introductions to the others in our group."

Anne sat on a trunk, her little boy on her lap. She tried not to hold him too tightly. He chattered away, pointing out all the fascinating things that were happening.

"Look, Mama!" He pointed to a crate of cackling chickens being carried on board. Fortunately she was not required to answer very often. It took heroic effort to hold back her tears.

Too soon the loading of the ship was completed . . . too soon. The sun was high, the day warm, the sea kind, the wind a southerly breath of invitation. The captain's cries turned impatient, and finally Charles came and stood by her to murmur, "I fear the moment has come, my dear."

John turned to look up into his mother's face. "Are you going away now?"

"Yes, my dearest one. You remember I told you that Grandfather Andrew is ill—"

"And you are going to help make him well again," he finished for her. "And Papa is going too?"

"Someone must come and take care of me, isn't that right?"

John nodded somberly. "Are you sad?"

"Yes, because I shall miss you very much. But I shall think of you every day, and pray for you, and look forward with all my heart to seeing you again as soon as I can." It both surprised and comforted her how she held to such calm. She felt a great distance between herself and the moment, a sense of watching herself speak. The same amazing peace kept her eyes dry and her voice steady. "You must promise me to be good and obey—"

"Uncle Charles and Aunt Judith," he said, repeating the familiar exchange they had gone over several times in recent days.

"That's right, my dearest."

"And Maisy."

"They all love you very much and will cherish you and keep you well. Now give me a hug and a kiss and tell me you love me."

"I love you, Mama." He looked at her with clear-eyed innocence.

She kissed his cheek and the silken hair upon his forehead. She breathed in the warm fragrance of her son. Then she did the most difficult thing she had ever done. She let him go.

Anne found it only mildly surprising that her face remained dry. She watched her husband lean forward to bid the boy good-bye and realized Thomas was weeping so he could scarcely speak. She let Judith stroke his shaking back. There would be time on board to hold one another.

They gathered together and prayed, including John's small frame in their little circle. They hugged and they spoke final words, or at least all did save Anne. She let herself be moved from one moment to the next, coming fully alert only when her son was guided into the carriage. She heard Charles say something and knew he wanted to give her the letter he had prepared for Andrew. But just then her hands would not function, nor her mind make room for anything save the boy. John's face emerged through the open window, and the sunlight lit his hair. She fought to keep her eyes utterly clear, for this was the vision she wished to find every time she shut her eyes during the weeks and months ahead. This was the sight that would sustain her.

"Come, my dear. It's time."

Anne allowed her husband to lead her away. She did not wave so much as reach out, openhanded, toward her son. "Good-bye, my dearest!"

Up the plank she walked. She released Thomas's hand and moved to the side of the vessel, from where she could stand and see the sunlit tableau below. She felt Thomas move up behind her and was grateful for his comforting strength. She heard him shout their farewells and let him speak for them both. As the sailors drew in the gangplank and tossed the ropes on board and raised sails and canted the vessel seaward, it was all she could do to hold to her calm. So long as her boy was visible, she was determined to remain composed.

But finally the harbor became merely a flat pan at the base of curving cliffs, the village a stony speck upon an emerald hill. Then the sunlight played upon the rolling waves, and the golden reflection gentled away her vision entirely. She turned then, as did several other women gathered there upon the railing. Anne buried her head in Thomas's chest and gave herself over to sorrow's flood.

Chapter 13

The entire voyage was unlike anything Anne had ever before experienced.

Her first sea voyage had been in the hold of a ship wallowing in the storms of winter. She had been mourning the loss of her first husband, Cyril, and traveling to England because of Nicole's fervently expressed invitation. Her days had been defined by cold and howling gales and crashing waves and moaning passengers and her own dismal grief. Only her tiny baby, her dear little John, stood between her and the darkness threatening to engulf her soul.

Now, in the first hours and days of this next journey, her son's absence threatened to be her undoing. Anne found herself wracked with sorrow. Within the sleepless hours of night, surrounded by the cramped berths of other passengers wrenched by their own farewells, Anne experienced a small measure of her mothers' pain—yes, both of her mothers.

She had known the facts of this all her life, how her French birth mother had allowed her friend Catherine to take her to an English doctor to try to save her frail life. And that while Catherine was in Halifax, the English had expelled the Acadians to the four corners of the globe. Raised by the English family, her beloved Andrew and Catherine, Anne's double heritage was as much a part of her as her name, her hair, her eyes, her own breath.

She had never *lived* it, though, until now.

But I will see John again. We will be reunited soon, she told herself over and over. And sometimes, *Oh, Mama Louise, how did you bear the sorrow, the not knowing. . . ?* She at least knew where John was, that he was being lovingly cared for in a place that was his home.

———— ✣ ————

Sabbath fell upon the third day of their journey. Anne had not slept more than a few hours in the two nights since their departure. She ate because Thomas placed food in front of her and urged her to do so. She moved about the deck only when he grasped her hand and led her. That Sabbath morning began with the dawn, when Thomas drew her from bed with a bowl of the hot black tea called sailor's broth. He directed her toward the chamber where the other women had gathered to wash and dress for the morning service.

By that time all the ship knew of Anne and Thomas, both who they were and how they had left their son behind. Anne had heard others tell their own tragic tales, but she had tried to close her ears to the words and the tears, unable to bear anything further. But this morning was different. As she returned to the main hold and gathered about the central table for a breakfast of ship's bread and brine-soaked apples and more tea, Anne sensed a soft whisper within her heart.

For the journey they had taken the Dissenters' style of dress, homespun frocks of black and gray. Thomas wore a long black overcoat and stiff-brimmed hat. Anne smoothed back her hair and settled upon her head a starched white bonnet and tied it beneath her chin. As soon as the bosun had piped the morning crew on deck and the others to their breakfast, the passengers made their way from their quarters.

The captain greeted them, doffing his hat and bowing to the elder of the two pastors. "It is my habit at sea to offer the men a Sabbath reading. But I'd be grateful for a proper vicar to bless this day."

"It would be an honor for you and your men to join us."

They began with a song, and another, and another still. One of the men drew out a concertina, another a mouth organ, and one more a set of bagpipes. There were no hymnals, nor any needed. This was a group bound together through years of shared worship and common faith. They greeted the rising sun in four-part harmony, causing the sailors to cast astonished glances among themselves.

At the beginning of the fourth song, Anne lifted her head far enough to study the sky above her. Every sail was out, a great billowing mass of canvas that filled the blue left empty by an absence of clouds. The sun rose behind her, burnishing the sails overhead. The timbers creaked, and the deck beneath her feet was never still. A pair of great black-headed seabirds with wingspans broader than her own outstretched arms flew along-side the starboard railing, their heads tilted as though to better hear the hymns.

The younger pastor, the gentleman who had greeted them at quayside, opened the Bible to the book of John and began the day's reading. Anne listened, marveling that the words were coming to her understanding in their proper order. Her thoughts were clearing, her vision, her awareness.

She inhaled deeply, and it seemed as though it was the first true breath she had taken since their departure. She breathed again and found herself taking stock as one would when arising from a sickbed, making sure that all was finally back in working order. A third breath, and she realized that her sorrow was no longer the dominating force. The absence of her beloved John was still there and would be with her for as long as they were apart. Yet she held it with acceptance, a place that permitted her to look forward as well as behind.

"Thank God."

For a brief instant she thought it was she herself who spoke the words. For that was exactly how she felt. Then she realized it was her husband who had murmured the thanksgiving. Anne turned to him and found the intelligent eyes inspecting her with love and concern. He whispered, "You have returned."

Anne reached for his hand. She did not care if it was not proper in this time and place. "I have."

Chapter 14

"We need to make plum puddin', Nana."

"Plum pudding? I thought you were not particularly fond of plum pudding." Judith previously had assumed that every child loved the treat. But her grandson had proved an exception. He had taken a few bites, then pushed back his bowl. "That's quite enough," he had announced in grown-up fashion. "I do not want to thicken my waist."

Judith had hidden her smile behind a hand, casting a curious gaze toward John's nurse. Had the child heard her make such a remark? She would caution the woman again to guard her speech in front of the impressionable young master.

John was speaking again, leaning up comfortably—and comfortingly—against her knee. "Mama likes it," he was saying, returning to the call for plum pudding, though he sounded a bit forlorn. "We should make it today in case she comes."

Judith felt a mist gather in her eyes. She knew John longed for his mother. In spite of their efforts to keep his days full and interesting, there was no way she and Charles could keep the boy from missing the most important person in his life.

"I'll speak to Cook," she said now as her hand gently stroked the brown curls. She simply could not bring herself to say to the child that his mother would not be returning on this day, nor on any day in the near future.

He smiled up at her, seeming content that the matter was settled. Then he darted away to the shelves that held his books and toys, calling over his shoulder as he ran, "Would you read to me, Nana?"

Judith loved to read to him. She wasn't sure what was the nicest part of it—sharing the mystery and adventure of his childish story or having him tucked up close by her side. So close that she could smell the freshness of his morning bath, feel the warmth of the small body, and sense the complete trust that he placed in her as his grandmother. There was one other part that she kept tucked away in her heart—the bittersweet memory of the boy's father, her son Cyril, now gone from this earth for most of John's short life.

There was no need for her to answer his question in words. She moved to make room for him in the chair beside her as he took time to select just the right story.

It was one of her favorite times of the day. Though a bit early—John was an early riser—Judith did not mind slipping from her room to make her way to John's nursery just as the sun began to lift itself over the lip of the eastern horizon. She and Nurse had worked out the arrangement. Nurse would bathe and dress the boy, then leave for the kitchen. Judith would savor the time with the child, secretly hoping the woman would not be too efficient and bring back their breakfast too quickly.

When they had taken over John's care when Anne and Thomas had left, Charles had spoken firmly. "We must not spoil the lad. He must not be allowed to run freely and undisciplined through the house. It would be easy to let him set his own boundaries, given his sweetness and my gullibility. But for his sake, we must maintain order and discipline. We do not wish Anne to return to an obstinate son."

Judith had nodded her agreement. Charles was right, of course—but, oh, it would have been so enjoyable to have the delightful little boy with her every hour of the day.

A routine had been established and Charles strictly adhered to it, though Judith sensed there often were times when he would have liked to break his own rules. But Charles's approach was the correct one. They could not allow the young master to become chief of the entire household. Judith was allotted the early morning hours and some time again in the late afternoon while Nurse took her tea. Charles assigned himself the late morning. Together the man and boy would walk through the gardens or down to the stream, or they would ride out, John proudly seated in front of Charles on the saddle. Other children in his situation were often given their own pony led by a groom, but Charles held to this intimate time to which he had laid claim. "He will have a lifetime to ride on his own," he had confided to Judith. "I have only a short time to hold him close and listen to his chatter."

In the evening, just before Judith and Charles had their dinner together, they would make one last trip to the nursery to tuck John in and share in a prayer time. This was a special time for all of them, though Judith often brushed at tears as she listened to the pleas from childish lips for God to take extra care in looking out for his mama and papa. His second petition was just as earnest. That God would please make Grandpa Andrew all better again so Mama could come home.

Judith's reverie was interrupted when John scrambled up beside her. She placed one arm about him as she drew him close. "What is this story about, my boy?"

"It's about a man. He plays a . . . a thing . . . see . . . that makes music."

"Music? Why yes, he does. The instrument is called a pianoforte."

"What does it do?" John's eyes were wide with questions.

"Well . . . like you said. It makes music."

"I wish I had a pian-fortay."

"Well . . . we do. Down in the front parlor."

"We do?" The face lifted to hers was full of surprise and delight. "Can I hear it?"

"I . . . I do not suppose there is anyone here who can play it. I cannot."

"Can Nurse?"

"Oh, I'm quite sure she cannot."

"Can Uncle?" John had been schooled to call his mother's

uncle "Uncle Charles," but when he became excited he sometimes shortened the address.

"I do not believe your uncle Charles has ever played the pianoforte, but I shall ask him."

"Someone needs to play it," insisted the child.

Judith smiled. "I will discuss it with your uncle Charles at supper this evening."

John nodded slowly. Judith could see he longed to have the issue resolved immediately.

"Now we had better read the story before Nurse gets back with your porridge."

His eyes turned from her face to the pages of the book. One small hand reached out and gently stroked the illustration of the instrument. Judith decided she would speak to Charles immediately. It was unusual for a child to feel so drawn toward something to which he had not yet been exposed. Could it be possible that he had an innate aptitude for music? If so, they needed to discover and nurture this gift.

"Good morning, my dear," Charles greeted Judith with a smile as she entered the library. "Did you sleep well?" He laid aside his London newspaper.

Judith smiled in return and nodded. "I have just come from the nursery," she began as she moved across the carpet.

"How is our boy?"

"Fine. Doing well, I believe. He had a bit of a surprise for me." She pressed against the rich mahogany of Charles's desk as she spoke.

Charles leaned forward, watching her intently.

"He has a new storybook—one of those you ordered up from London. Nurse said that she has already been asked to read it many times. It is the story of the young prodigy Mozart. John is—well, to say the least—quite taken with it. Especially the pianoforte. He said that he would like to have one. When

I told him we already do have one in the parlor, he asked to hear it played."

Judith now had Charles's full attention. He seemed to understand where this conversation was heading. "He is only a child," he said.

"So was Mozart when he began to play," she answered quietly.

He nodded.

He leaned back, the leather chair squeaking under the shifting of weight, and cleared his throat. But he did not speak. His eyes held a faraway gaze, as if he were reaching for some memory that was eluding him. Or else causing pain. "My mother used to play it," he finally said, his voice a bit husky. "I used to sneak out of bed to hide behind the draperies and listen. Once I fell asleep, and there was no end of commotion in the household until I was discovered." He chuckled for a moment, then added, "I was sure I would be scolded and sent off to my room, but instead my mother lifted me up to the bench beside her and played one more song before sending me off with my nurse. From then on she invited me to the parlor in the evening and let me listen to her play. I treasured every moment. After she died . . ." He hesitated, and Judith saw him working to swallow. "No one has played it since," he finished. She could see the sorrow in his eyes.

Judith waited until she felt Charles was more composed. She eased around the corner of the desk and let her hand fall gently on his shoulder. He reached up and accepted the hand into his, giving it a squeeze.

"Would you mind if someone played it again?"

"No, not at all." His answer came more quickly than she would have expected. "I think I should quite enjoy it."

"I think our John would enjoy it also."

"We've one problem," Charles said, leaning back so he could look up at her. "We have no one who plays—unless you have kept a secret from me, my dear."

"No secret," said Judith with a smile quickly followed by a sigh. "I have never had the pleasure of music instruction."

"I do not suppose Nurse—"

"I have already asked her. She does not appear to have any interest, let alone any knowledge."

The chair squeaked again as Charles moved forward, his arms outstretched to lean on the desk. "There must be a solution. If the boy wishes music, he should have music."

Judith smiled. Charles would do whatever needed to be done. "I will see you at breakfast," she whispered and placed a kiss on his cheek.

Chapter 15

Five days at sea was but a brief passage, a swift run in the eyes of well-salted sailors. Yet when they started their final tack in the Bay of Fundy for their sunset run down Cobequid Bay, Nicole and Gordon and all the men bore the strain of those seemingly endless days.

As the headlands at the Georgetown point rose high and emerald green to her right, Nicole felt a stirring within at the sight of her beloved cliffs. She leaned against the starboard railing as Gordon called in the controlled voice he had used ever since they had passed the British fleet anchored in the Halifax harbor. Sailors rushed about her, climbed the nettings, and unfurled the remaining sails. Nicole kept her gaze fastened upon the point where she and Anne had spent so many wonderful hours.

Three times during the voyage they had heard the pounding thunder of seaborne war. Once it had begun in the evening, and she had hoped the reddish glow on the horizon was somehow a second sunset. Gordon had ordered all lights doused and all sails made taut, and she knew the truth of it.

The second day of their voyage, Gordon had broken out the British flag to fly from his signal halyard. Nicole knew this tactic was known as flying under false colors. She also knew the reason, sailing as they were directly toward the massed power of the British fleet. She had said nothing. But Gordon must have felt her concern and crossed the quarterdeck to stand beside her and explain that he would do everything in his power to return this vessel to its rightful owners. That, in his eyes, it indeed remained a British vessel. Nicole did not voice the fact that a British-owned ship sailed by a captain and crew whose loyalties were with the American Revolutionaries made for a dangerous situation. If they fell into the hands of either side . . . She did not allow herself to finish the thought.

Perhaps because they sailed so boldly and directly toward the British might, in a British vessel, they were never challenged. Twice sails were spotted just over the horizon, and the passing vessels boomed out cannonades of greeting. Gordon replied in kind, saluting with a smart raising and lowering of their colors. North they continued, sailing as far outside the reach of Halifax as they could manage before turning and running straight up the Bay of Fundy.

"Well do I remember that point." Gordon's voice surprised her after his unannounced approach. He came over to stand alongside her. "The day we walked out there together, I had every intention of declaring my affections."

"I know," Nicole responded quietly, moving close enough to graze his arm with her shoulder. It was all the familiarity she dared upon the ship. A captain was to be seen in public as a solitary figure, Gordon had once told her. She had never understood just how true these words were before this voyage. "I knew your heart then. But I could not determine my own heart and so could not permit you to speak."

"Yes, you knew," Gordon agreed. "You knew your heart and you knew mine as well. You also saw the absence of faith in my life, my lack of the divine compass."

She brushed windswept hair from her face and looked up at her betrothed.

"I have never thanked you for your strength of purpose, for your commitment to God. Here in this stolen moment, I wish to speak now what has gone too long unspoken." Gordon kept his tone quiet and steady. "Your refusal to give in to what we both were feeling is what my overproud heart required. Thank you, my dear, for bringing me to the point where I can speak these words."

"Gordon . . ." She fought to maintain control.

They exchanged a lingering glance, nothing more. Yet it was enough to fill her heart with calm. "This is the most at rest I have felt since we set off from Marblehead."

"There is nothing quite as difficult for peace of mind," Gordon agreed, "than a threat—known or imagined—just over the horizon."

"If I had realized, I would not have made the request."

"Were we doing it only for you, I would have needed to decline. Much as I love you, much as I know your yearning to see your father once more, I could not have agreed."

He was interrupted from further discussion of their broader mission when Carter called from his place by the wheel, "Ready to come about, Captain."

"Very well." Gordon turned around, studied that all was in place, then called, "Hard about."

"Hard about it is, sir. Look lively there, lads."

Carter spun the wheel. The ship pointed its nose into the wind, then swung about so the wind blew over its opposite rail. The sails snapped full, the sailors pulled hard on the lines, the ship heeled over sharply. Soon enough the cliff disappeared into the distance.

To the west, the setting sun reflected upon the shimmering waters of Cobequid Bay. To the east, the expanse reached out to approaching night from deep blue to slate gray. As the bay narrowed about the ship, the wind filtered through the surrounding hills in fits and gusts, yet scarcely ruffled the water's surface. Nicole remained where she was as the first stars came alight, full of the promise of the homecoming.

Their plan was to berth in secret far enough down the bay to avoid confrontation with any British vessel. Many of the surrounding French villages remained hostile to British soldiers and ships. Since the waters were most decidedly British, it was hoped they could berth, continue up to Georgetown, and return without challenge.

Carter joined Gordon by the starboard railing and watched as they scouted the banks. She knew they would search for likely anchorage and landfall in the last light of day, then would load the travelers into boats and finish their trek under cover of dark. They would ride to Georgetown, to Andrew and Catherine Harrow. Nicole's parents had helped both French and loyalists from the southern colonies resettle in these former Acadian lands. It was Gordon's hope that their connections to the Harrows would help to seal the villagers' loyalty and keep their presence a secret from the British.

Both Gordon and Carter studied the bank through telescopes, conferring quietly back and forth. A nearly full moon emerged over the forested hilltop just as the day's last light faded. The two men seemed to reach some agreement.

Glimmers from lamps could be seen both to their right and left from villages nearby. But directly ahead of them all was dark and silent. Gordon moved to the wheel and directed the steersman toward land as the men hurried aloft and began gathering in sail. Two sailors stood at either side of the bow and cast leaded lines up ahead, chanting softly the rising depth as they pulled them back up to count the measurements. Gordon soon gave the order to drop anchor and lower the longboat.

Gordon cast a concerned glance her way as Nicole was helped into the bosun's chair, winched over the side, and lowered to the waiting craft. He soon joined her when the crew who were assigned to go ashore had all boarded.

The men rowed with the silence of hard-won experience. Gordon sat in the bow and Carter crouched alongside him, directing with one upraised hand. The tide was high enough for them to make it all the way to solid footing before grounding. Instantly the oars were stowed. The men disembarked, ushered Nicole up to higher ground, then together they heaved the longboat up and under a dense cluster of trees. All with as little noise as possible.

Even so, before they had taken two dozen steps up the slope, a voice called out in French, "You're surrounded!"

Carter gripped the arm of the man nearest to him and hissed, "Don't make a move."

"Steady," Gordon agreed quietly. "I can see movement amidst the trees on either side."

Nicole looked at Gordon through the darkness, then said in French, "We come in peace!"

"If that is so," the unseen challenger asked, "why is it you come in secret and by night?"

"Because . . . because these are perilous times." Nicole kept her voice as steady as she could.

There was the rustle of numerous feet approaching. "How is it that a ship flying the British flag carries American sympathizers and a woman who speaks our tongue?"

"I am one of you," Nicole replied.

"One of us?" the man scoffed. "More likely you are a teller of tales."

"I speak the truth. My family lives in Georgetown."

"Georgetown is British. We are Acadian."

"As am I. Both British and Acadian."

A murmur of voices as they quietly conferred.

Another set of footsteps approached from the opposite side. "Cast a light here."

The voice stirred something in Nicole. But before she could think of what it was, the leader answered, "There is danger in torchlight."

"There is danger in making errors. Make a light, I say."

Flint sparked and kindling was lit; then a torch flared and hissed. In the sudden illumination, Nicole could not see farther than the hand which held the sputtering flame. But the second voice now cried, "By heaven's mercy! It is Nicole!"

She knew him then. And though she could not see him, Nicole plunged through the darkness with arms outstretched. "It is Guy! Dear, dear Uncle Guy!"

———— ✀ ————

Nicole's uncle Guy traveled with them, along with four other villagers chosen because they knew the region well enough to move without lights and because they had horses. The others were not friendly men, nor overly welcoming, even after her uncle had enfolded her and wept tears of genuine joy. They listened in silence as she explained their need to travel immediately to Georgetown. They did not object when Guy requested their help. But they only agreed when she added their willingness to pay, and pay well. Then came the swift discussion of men accustomed to acting together, deciding she and Gordon would travel on borrowed steeds, while the remaining sailors would be bedded down in the closest Acadian settlement.

Their horses were dark roans and so well trained they neither stamped nor whinnied as the unfamiliar figures approached through the shadows. As Gordon helped her into the saddle, he gave her a meaningful look and pointed at the horses' hooves. She studied them closely but did not understand. He patted her leg once, a silent warning, of what she did not know, and turned to where another man held a steed for him.

She rode with Guy to one side and Gordon on the other. There was a great deal of her Acadian father, Henri Robichaud, in her uncle, a man of great strength. When the clouds parted and night's silver lamp fell upon the way, she could see the gray in his hair and beard, reminding her with vivid clarity of how her French father was also aging, and how long it had been since they were last together. Guy's expression was that of a man who had journeyed much and endured more, yet remained throughout a person of integrity and compassion. When the way straightened and the path ahead was a wash of white moonlight and calm, she reached across and took his hand for a moment.

After some hours they halted to let the horses cool. Nicole

did not realize how exhausted she was until she slid from the horse's back. She allowed Gordon to lead her over to a log. When Guy joined them, the others moved off a few paces and stood quietly. In the glimmer of the moon, Nicole could see how their heads kept turning as they continually scouted the road ahead and behind.

Finally Gordon's earlier signals made sense to her. She looked at her horse's hooves once more and could see they had been blackened with a mixture of coal dust and oil. Their dark coats and manes reflected no light whatsoever. It was the same with the reins and stirrups, for all the metal was coated with the thick dark grease and wrapped so they did not jingle. She recalled how softly the horses had trodden upon the road, and she realized they were not shod.

She whispered to Guy, "These are smugglers?"

When Guy did not respond, Nicole translated for Gordon, who said, "We must have arrived when they were expecting a boat of their own. There is no other reason for them to have such a force out at night."

"Our friends no doubt spied your great vessel plying its way up the bay." Guy's grin so resembled her father's, she had to blink to clear her eyes. "They probably took you for a warship on patrol."

"*You* are a smuggler too?"

Guy was long in answering, and when he did he refused to meet her eye. "The roads are not safe these days. Either the British ride in force, or they do not ride at all. Same with these waters. The garrisons are depleted. Everyone is off to the south fighting the war." He then looked at her. "Brigands strike at will. Little gets through. Taxes have become absurd. We Acadian settlements have taken to 'trading.' " He shrugged meaningfully. "We survive. It is the way."

At a quiet hiss from the other smugglers, Guy turned and said, "We ride."

The closer they came to Georgetown, the faster they pushed their horses. It was only when the first faint hues appeared in the east that Nicole realized they were racing the dawn.

At her unspoken question, Guy explained over his shoulder, "We are breaking the provincial curfew. Soldiers would recognize these steeds for what they are. But for your sake, we must hold to the open road."

With the light came a morning mist, rising from the ground like lazy tendrils. Nicole realized she was growing damp when she saw the sheen of dew upon Gordon's coat. She drew her mantle closer about her and pulled the hood over her head. As they arrived at the village outskirts, the mist was draping the horses so completely the outriders became indistinct, then invisible. Houses she recognized, or wished she did, appeared with the suddenness of silent wraiths. They passed the fence lining Andrew's churchyard, but she could not make out the church itself.

She and Guy moved to the front of the group and led them through the market square and down the now-familiar lane. In spite of her exhaustion, her heart surged with joy.

The house was still shuttered for the night when they halted. Nicole slipped down from the horse unaided. Her fingers trembled as she opened the little gate and moved up the walk toward the front door. Gordon and Guy followed close behind.

But before she could knock, the door flew open and she found herself looking into Andrew's face.

Her eyes filled and overflowed as she moved into his embrace. Andrew looked so drawn, so gray. So *small*. "Hello, Father," she whispered on his shoulder.

"I heard God say my name," Andrew said. "Even before I opened my eyes and rose from bed, I knew there was joy coming to knock upon my door."

She heard him raise his voice and call out to Catherine. She heard her mother's voice rise in surprise and delight. She felt a second set of arms around her, her mother's voice in her ear. She heard their greetings to Gordon. She heard their thanks to Guy. But she could not open her eyes. Or perhaps she did, yet could not really see.

Chapter 16

Nicole sat by the fire and sipped a cup of her mother's special brew—not a black Ceylon tea, for her mother had said the last thing Nicole needed was something to keep her awake. She could feel the warmth of the hot drink seep into her bones, matching the warmth from the crackling logs. Every time her parents passed, they would lay their hands upon her shoulder.

Her uncle Guy took his own mug standing in the doorway with the other Frenchmen. They accepted thick slabs of fresh-baked bread with butter and honey, and murmured respectful thanks. In all their faces, Nicole could see the esteem in which they held both Andrew and Catherine. In between times they would glance back through the doorway, the worry etched in their faces as they watched the sun begin to shine through the mist. They could not be held much longer.

Nicole listened as Gordon addressed Guy, Catherine now serving as interpreter.

"As we told you, we have sworn our allegiance to the American cause."

"Your vessel flies the British flag," Guy noted.

"The vessel is British; we are not. Not any longer. Further explanations must wait. What you need to know now is that we are on a mission. The Americans have asked us to travel to Louisiana."

When these words were translated, the Frenchmen gathered closer, astonishment in their faces. "You travel to the second Acadia?"

"If we can. But first we must gather supplies. And in secret."

"The supplies are not a problem if you can pay."

"We can."

Guy cast a glance at his mates. "Almost every family in our village has relatives they have not heard from in years. Letters have been sent but never answered."

"We will be happy to serve as your envoy."

As Catherine translated, the mood lightened. Guy turned back and now spoke to Gordon with genuine concern. "The secrecy is another thing entirely."

Andrew broke in at this point. "The village is full of ears and eyes. Your presence is bound to come to the attention of the officials in Halifax."

"How long do we have?"

"A few days."

"Longer," Catherine pleaded.

"They cannot risk it," Andrew gently replied.

"That is not enough time."

"No. It is not. But it is all we have."

Nicole gathered her strength to stand. Here, in the first moments of greeting, their imminent departure was already being discussed. She could bear no more in her weariness. "Forgive me, I must rest," she said.

"One moment, dear Nicole." Gordon walked over to her, then guided her to where Andrew stood beside Catherine. He said, "We have a request to make of you."

Nicole could see that they were anticipating his next words. Catherine reached out to hold Nicole's hand as Gordon said to her father, "Sir, I am asking for your daughter's hand in marriage. I understand the suddenness, but the uncertainty of the times seems to require it." Then Andrew also was reaching for Gordon's hand as he finished, "We are asking that you grant us the honor of performing our wedding ceremony before we must depart."

No verbal assent to the request was required. Catherine and Nicole were embracing and weeping, and Gordon and Andrew shook hands in both solemn and hopeful agreement.

Chapter 17

Nicole awoke to birdsong and laughter. She lay and studied the room about her. Light pierced the narrow slits in the rear shutters, which was strange, for the house faced east. Which meant the time must be noon or later. Had she slept through the entire morning?

She willed herself to rise, but the muscles of her body would not respond. She lay upon her grandfather Price's bed. He had insisted, and she had been too tired to protest for long. Her pillow must have come from her parents' bed, for she could smell Catherine's fragrance.

The door opened, and Nicole knew it was her mother from the way the light silhouetted her frame. "Good morning, Mother," she managed around a yawn.

Catherine stepped inside. "How are you feeling, Nicole?"

"So much better I can hardly believe it."

"I'm glad." Catherine eased herself down on the side of Grandfather Price's bed. "You were in great need of rest."

"Gordon is awake?" Nicole asked. Her fiancé had bunked down with his men at a neighbor's house. At Catherine's nod, Nicole stretched luxuriously. "I suppose I should rise, then."

"Gordon has gone to the ship and back," Catherine told her.

"How is that possible?"

"Well, first, he needed to fetch your case and his dress uniform." She laughed openly now. "Secondly, because it has just turned four."

At Nicole's gasp, Catherine repeated, "Four o'clock—in the afternoon."

"You have let me sleep all day?" Nicole struggled to a sitting position.

"I have indeed." Catherine rose and handed Nicole the dress she had worn from the ship.

The fabric was stiff with days of salt and wear. Nicole could smell the horse, the saddle leather, the black grease from the previous night's ride. The hem was dark and rigid with mud from disembarking from the longboat and where they halted in the night. She stared at the dress and wondered if all that had happened had just been the night before. "Mama, you shouldn't have let me lie abed all day," she said, taking the frock with a small grimace.

"I would let you sleep all the coming night as well," Catherine replied. "Except for the fact that you must now hurry—wait, though, I will bring you a clean dress of mine for you to wear until . . ." But she was out the door before finishing her sentence.

Catherine was soon back with a faded but clean cotton dress to slip over Nicole's head. Her mother's hands deftly buttoned it up the back, and they moved to the door.

John Price rose from his seat by the fire and came over to beam at his granddaughter and proclaim, "Our princess has arisen!"

"Please, I'm so sorry." She was acutely aware of the late hour, of her unbrushed hair, of the short time they would have . . .

"Coming through, please. Make way!" Carter and two other sailors pushed into the room, bearing one of her trunks. "Where will you be having these now, ma'am?"

"Put them in the back room here," Catherine replied, pointing the way.

Her parents' bedroom door opened, and her father appeared. Only he was not dressed in his normal dark homespun but in his formal clergy attire. The long black robe carried crimson and gold stitching that she knew instantly was Catherine's skilled handiwork.

Andrew moved across to her and drew her into a warm embrace. "God's greetings, my Nicole. Did you rest well?"

"Yes, I . . . yes." She stepped back and looked at his robe. "Forgive me, Father. Is it the Sabbath today?"

Andrew's smile was full of love and blessing. "No, daughter. It is your wedding day."

"Oh, Mother," Nicole breathed the words as she stood in the back bedroom gazing at her trunk. Then once again their arms were around each other as she and Catherine wept and laughed together.

"My wedding day," Nicole said, looking into Catherine's face. "I cannot say I imagined it quite like this—a moment snatched out of a time of turmoil."

"Ah yes," answered Catherine, "I think I understand what you are feeling right now—joyful and a bit sad at the same time. But you must remember that the wedding ceremony itself is only the beginning of a lifetime of love and care for each other. And Gordon is the husband and the son-in-law we have prayed for. We have known him for only this short time, but your father and I believe you have chosen well."

"I too believe I have chosen well," Nicole said with a smile as they embraced again.

"But we must make preparations," Catherine said briskly, and the two women turned their attention to the trunk. After prying it open, Catherine departed to return with a tin tub. She filled it with pails of warm water from the kitchen, then helped Nicole into it. Catherine left the bedroom again and brought back a mug of tea and a piece of bread with butter and honey. Nicole was sure she wouldn't be able to eat anything, but she sipped the steaming cup and soon realized she was indeed hungry.

Nicole rose from the bath and saw her creamy white silk gown laid out upon the bed, and the shoes set alongside, and she was sure that this wedding, even in these circumstances, was right.

Catherine laced up the stays to Nicole's corset, talking all the while as she placed one hand upon the small of Nicole's back and gripped the two laces tightly in her other. The motion pulled Nicole's thoughts up sharp, and she realized Catherine had been telling how John Price's quest for his lost sibling had offered the old man not only new energy, but a new and deeper relationship with Catherine. And what had surprised her equally, she explained as she tied a double bow, was how the quest had proven such an interest to her as well. Together they had pored over John Price's father's diary. Catherine urged Nicole to ask the old man about it, to let him share this new excitement over the drama of forgotten days.

Then her mother lifted the wedding dress over Nicole's head. "Oh, my dear, you are a lovely bride," Catherine whispered as she buttoned the row of tiny pearl buttons in the back. Then Nicole carefully sat down while her mother arranged her hair and fastened it up with combs.

A knock upon the door, and a familiar voice called, "May I enter?"

Catherine rushed to the door, calling, "No, I'm sorry, Gordon, but you may not see the bride before the wedding."

"Then I shall speak my words from here, madame. Nicole, my dearest, can you hear me?"

She moved closer to the door to say, "I can. Though I can scarcely believe what is happening."

"I as well. But all is moving in its proper course, as far as I can tell. Will you trust me with this judgment?"

"I trust you with everything," she replied simply. "I trust you with my life."

There was a moment's pause, then Gordon said, "Nicole, I have something for you."

"What is it?"

"I had hoped for a more intimate moment, but this will have to do." He cleared his throat. "The evening that I met John Jackson, do you recall how I described it?"

"I believe you said it was a sign of the divine hand."

"Just so. My dearest, John's appearance resulted in a retrieval of something you had lost on my behalf."

"I . . . I don't understand."

"No. Of course not. But I thought you might like to have it for the coming ceremony."

Catherine motioned Nicole away from the door and opened it slightly.

"I shall bid you ladies farewell, for the moment," Gordon said as he passed something into Catherine's hand.

Catherine turned slowly back into the room, her gaze fastened upon a small velvet bag in her hands.

"What is it, Mama?"

As Catherine opened the bag, Nicole saw the emerald pendant and the gold chain. Catherine heard her gasp of unbelief and saw her reach out with a trembling hand. "My pendant!"

"This is yours?"

"It was."

"Never have I seen jewelry this lovely," Catherine said. "Where did you come by such a treasure?"

"Uncle Charles. He gave it to me before I left England." Nicole continued to stare at the shimmering green she held in her hand. Catherine could see the shine of her eyes caused by the tears that wished to form but were held in check. "I never thought I would ever see it again—far less call it mine."

"I don't understand. . . ."

"Nor do I. How did Gordon come upon it? It was . . ." She broke off and lifted her eyes to her mother's. She shook her head, as though to restore the present. "It's a very long story," she said and managed a forced smile.

"Then it will have to wait, I fear, as much as I'd love to hear it. But we have gentlemen waiting beyond this door who are most anxious for a wedding to take place."

Nicole's eyes took on a deeper shine. "And we will not keep them waiting longer, for I am as anxious as they." She turned and lifted her hair for Catherine to fasten the chain about her neck. "I dare not say another word, else I shall not stop weeping." She felt the weight of the pendant and attempted to look at it. "Does it suit the dress?"

Catherine moved to stand in front of Nicole. "It was made for the dress, for you, for this day." She gave Nicole a hug. "Now let me hurry and finish here so that I can ready myself as well," Catherine said as she released her.

Nicole pointed to the open trunk in the corner from which her wedding gown had come. "First there is something in the case for you."

Catherine cast her a long glance, then moved to kneel in front of it.

"Just there," Nicole said, "wrapped in the parcel."

"Oh, Nicole," Catherine breathed, lifting the white muslin wrapping and opening it. She held up the blue silk gown and laughed shakily. "I am a simple parson's wife. I cannot—"

"You can," Nicole said as she walked over and took the dress from her mother's hands. "Now it is my turn to help you."

Catherine turned slowly around as Nicole began unfastening the buttons of her mother's morning dress.

"And you must wear my pearls."

"It is too much—"

"I can't wear my pearls and Uncle Charles's pendant both. They will be fortunate to hang upon such a lovely neck," Nicole said as she fastened the clasp. "Mama, you are the mother of the bride. You are beautiful. And we both are now ready for the wedding."

———— ✿ ————

With John Price on one side and her mother on the other, Nicole walked out the door and down the garden path, through the front gate, and along the village lane. Little girls in their best frocks stood at the first crossroads, each carrying a ribbon-bedecked milk pail filled with blossoms hastily gathered from the first trees of spring—cherry, apple, tulip poplar. First they stood in the center of the lane and stared at Nicole, then at orders from their mothers dipped their hands into the pails and spread blossoms along the path.

Nicole's wedding gown was made in the latest Paris fashion. The bodice was palest cream, framed by seed pearls. The skirt was not long enough to settle upon the packed earth of the country lane but halted just above her ankles.

When the three arrived at the market square, the little girls and their mothers did not take the path Nicole expected. "We are not going to the church?"

"We have made other plans," Catherine said simply.

"But Gordon—"

"Is waiting for you up ahead."

John Price chuckled from her other side. "Couldn't fit them all into the church. Knew that from the beginning, I did."

"I don't understand."

"Your folks are loved by most everybody around these parts," he explained as together they followed the children down a side lane. The news of the wedding celebration had traveled fast, and all were invited.

It was only when she saw the forest and the path ahead that she understood. She saw how the surrounding branches had been laced with garlands of spring blossoms and tiny ribbons, and she felt the burning rise in her eyes yet again. "Oh," she whispered.

John Price laughed. "You just wait, my girl. You just wait."

Nicole found herself holding her breath. The westering light transformed the forested walk into a hall lined with green and shadows and tiny rainbow garlands.

She found herself standing on her beloved point. The perimeter was lined with large garlands of evergreen boughs, the poles set like pillars, and rows of smiling villagers turned to watch her. Burning torches upon metal pikes rose between the garlands.

Her father in his robes stood upon the fallen tree trunk, now draped in a small carpet, where she and Anne had spent so many wonderful hours. Gordon stood at the side, dressed in his formal uniform, his expression grave but his eyes smiling at her.

Nicole paused to savor the moment. The sky, the torchlight, the gathering, the sight of her father looking so strong and wise, her mother and grandfather accompanying her, and Gordon waiting for her up ahead—each vision was a jewel to capture in her memory. There to be brought out in coming days and examined more carefully, treasured more fully.

Chapter 18

Judith washed and dressed hurriedly. She had dallied longer than usual—first in John's room over the pages of his new book and then in a discussion with Charles in the library on an important matter. Breakfast would soon be served. Cook looked askance at serving food that had grown cold. Judith patted the folds of her morning gown and tucked a lace hankie in her sleeve, then quickly left her room. She stepped more briskly than normal as she passed the length of the long hall and on down the winding staircase. She was nearly out of breath as she entered the cozy breakfast room, where their morning meal was waiting to be served.

"My apologies—" she began.

"Good morning, my dear." Charles, who had risen to seat her, quickly cut in, more for the sake of the serving girl than for her own, she was sure. "Did you sleep well?"

That question had already been asked and answered earlier, but it now served to warm the atmosphere of the room. Charles nodded to the girl who stood, steaming porridge dish in hand, and she moved forward and began ladling the bowls as Judith settled herself in place and spread her napkin in her lap.

They did not speak again until the serving had been completed and the girl had been dismissed with a nod. Charles reached for Judith's hand and they bowed their heads for the morning prayer.

Charles was the first one to break the silence after their

heads were lifted. "I had a letter from Paris in this morning's post."

It could only be one thing. A report from the gentleman hired to track down the lost half sister of John Price. Judith leaned forward. "Good news?"

"I am afraid not," he said slowly, his voice conveying his disappointment. "In fact . . . little news at all. He said that, to this point, he has discovered next to nothing. He had a lead— or so he thought—that took him to the city from the coast. But it turned out to be a dead end—if you will pardon his rather crass pun. The person who was to have had some information has been dead for six or seven years. No one else seems to have shared any of her secrets."

"I am sorry," Judith said, shaking her head.

"I will write him back to keep looking," Charles responded. "Surely there is still someone—somewhere—who knows something. We will just have to dig a little deeper." He hesitated, then with a wry smile added, "There, now. I'm afraid my own sorry pun has been in poorer taste than that of my correspondent."

Judith smiled distractedly, her thoughts still on the report. She knew how desirous he was to solve this unusual puzzle for John and Catherine. But all she could do was support him and pray that somehow, someday, they would know the facts. The truth. But the past seemed so far away—so buried from view. She couldn't help but smile. *Buried from view.* Was there no end to distasteful puns this morning? She pushed the thoughts from her and became serious again. Would they ever know the truth? If only the search had begun earlier, there could have been more hope for success. But now?

Charles seemed to already have moved on from his earlier subject. "More coffee, my dear? I think I would enjoy another cup."

Judith reached for the bell near at hand and summoned the serving girl.

As soon as the coffee had been poured, Charles rose to his feet and moved behind Judith's chair. "Let's take our second

Janette Oke / T. Davis Bunn

cup in front of my library fire. It's much cozier on such a morn."

Judith was happy to comply and led the way. She always enjoyed joining Charles in the library. The fire hissed and crackled as they sipped companionably in silence. Judith pulled her eyes from the hypnotic flame to look across at her husband.

Charles rubbed his brow with his thumb and forefinger. She had come to recognize the gesture as a sign of mental agitation. The news she had carried with her to his library office was not very welcome. John's nanny had voiced her need to leave them. She would be vacating her position within a fortnight. Nursery staff were difficult to find at the best of times, but now, with Charles out of favor with so many of England's higher class, Judith feared that finding another suitable nanny might be near impossible. She was sure that Charles, restless fingers kneading his brow, was thinking the same thoughts.

"How soon?" he asked without looking up.

"She says she must care for her elderly father now that her mother is gone. She wishes to leave within two weeks, though she also expressed a desire to leave sooner if it could be arranged."

Charles lifted his head then, his expression incredulous. "Arranged?" he repeated. "I would hardly expect it to be arranged within a fortnight."

Judith nodded.

The fingers came down from Charles's forehead. "We may find ourselves caring for the needs of a young boy," he said slowly, but he did not sound particularly alarmed. Dared she hope that this privileged task might fall to her? She wondered if Charles also secretly hoped that no proper nanny could be found.

"We would make do," she said, controlling the eagerness in her voice.

He smiled then. "You would rather enjoy it, would you not?"

"Parts of it," she acknowledged with a smile of her own. "Though I do admit to feeling a bit old when he and I are out

132

in the garden and he takes it into his head to chase a butterfly, then a squirrel, then a robin—"

"Day and night," he warned softly. "You have said so yourself. Day and night—through sickness and health."

"Thank God he is a healthy child." She scarcely realized she had breathed the little prayer of thanksgiving aloud.

Charles rose from his chair and crossed to the room's long window, brushing aside the heavy drapery to look out on the day. Low clouds scudded across the sky, just beyond arm's reach, and a stout wind pulled at the bare branches of the trees along the lane. Even the birds seemed to have taken cover.

Judith moved to his side. The dreary scene made her shiver involuntarily. He seemed to sense it. "Is Howards keeping the fires well tended?"

"He just added another log in the drawing room."

"And the nursery?"

She smiled. "He has stoked that fire too. Nurse has little tolerance for cold. The bell clangs her displeasure if the fire is allowed to diminish."

"Perhaps she will not be such a loss after all." He lowered his voice. "I have never been particularly fond of her."

"Nor I," admitted Judith in a half whisper. "Still—she has cared for John well. A bit stiff and sometimes careless in her words, but she has seen well to his needs."

The frown came back. "The care of a child is of vital importance. Not just his toast and tea or his bath—his development in mind, body, and spirit depends on the way he is guided and nurtured." He reached out an arm to draw her close. "Are we up to it, my dear? Being a bachelor for so many years, I had no idea what it takes to train and care for a budding human being. It is a daunting task."

"But one we do not have to bear alone," Judith reminded him as she leaned against his substantial frame.

"No—and thank God for that. And we do need His direction now. To find another nanny. For we do need one, my dear, no matter how much we think we would love to have him all to ourselves."

Judith nodded. Wisdom told her he was right.

"I will send word to Jacobs in London." Charles's words spoke to the fact he was once again assuming responsibility. "Perhaps—with a miracle or two—he might be able to find someone for us. But in a fortnight? I think not."

"As you say—with a miracle or two, it will be done. And I am quite confident that our Lord cares more than we do about John and his future growth into a man of God."

"Of course." Charles's arm tightened for a moment before he turned them both from the window. "Now I suggest you take your place beside the fire with a cup of coffee in hand. I do not want you catching a chill."

Judith moved out of the circle of his arm and started for the door. "Do you wish me to send for Howards? It is getting a bit cold in here. Your fire looks like it could use another log."

"No need—I can tend my own fire. I get busy reading and forget it, that is all."

Charles moved to the fireplace and knelt on the hearth to balance the log on one knee and work the fire screen with his other hand.

As Judith reached for the doorknob, he spoke once more. "And try not to worry about the boy. We will pray. Surely the Almighty will direct us to one well-trained nanny somewhere out there."

She hesitated, silent for a moment. Then she smiled. "Do you know what John asked me this morning? He and I were looking out the window, and he said, 'Nana, how can the wind shake the branches when it has no hands on its arms?' "

"Hands on its arms?" Charles laughed as he rose from the hearth and brushed wood chips from his knees. "And where does he suppose its arms to be?"

"I have no idea, but that is exactly what he said." She chuckled along with her husband.

"Hands on its arms," Charles repeated, still laughing. "Where does he ever get such ideas?"

Judith smiled. "Only God knows. He is the one who gives children imaginations." She hesitated, then added, "By the time his mother gets back, I will have an entire book to share. Every day he gives me something more to add."

"Anne will treasure it. It is very good of you to record his days. Especially these little gems of unintended humor. Yes—it will be a real treasure for his mother."

"And I enjoy the doing," Judith added. She gave him a little nod and left the room. She knew he would soon be drafting the letter to Jacobs in London.

———— ✿ ————

" 'Tis a bit of a miracle at that," Charles said to Judith as he entered the morning room where she sat with handwork before the fire. "Jacobs has found us a prospect."

Judith's fingers became still in her lap. "Charles, that is indeed wonderful. I am very thankful. It has been a matter of deep concern for me. I've been—"

"Praying daily. I know."

"Please—what does your Jacobs say?"

Charles's eyes fell again to the pages of the letter in his hands. "He has discovered that a certain Mistress Lenora Paige is looking for a post. She comes from a good family that has fallen on hard times. The father died three years past in a hunting accident, and the mother more recently with a fever of some sort. There were two daughters in the family. An uncle has arranged a marriage for the older one, and her husband has taken over the management of the estate. But the younger one does not feel any longer at home there. Anyway, the younger one, who is well educated and of good breeding, so says Jacobs, needs to find some sort of employment. He thinks she would be well qualified to be a child's nurse."

Charles looked at Judith. "What do you think? Should we ask her to come for an interview?"

"I do not see that we have much choice. And it does seem like . . . like a miracle, just as you said."

He began to fold the letter as he moved toward the door.

"I will get an answer posted back to Jacobs telling him to send her out straightaway."

"Charles?"

He halted midstep and turned to her once again.

"Does . . . does the letter happen to say anything about. . . ?" She looked down at the stitchery, then lifted her head to continue. "In a world that holds so many serious needs, perhaps one is wrong to ask for such trivial things. But it did seem important to John . . . and to me. Can you tell me, does the letter say anything about her having any skills in music?"

He smiled. "You mean, can she play a pianoforte?"

Judith knew he was teasing her, and she smiled and nodded, waiting for the answer.

"Let me see," he said slowly, searching the pages with studied care. "Yes, here is something most interesting. Listen to this. 'In reply to your query, Mistress Paige has had more than a small amount of training in the arts. She sings well, sketches with some proficiency, and I understand is quite skilled on the pianoforte.' "

"Ah," breathed Judith, leaning forward. "It is the second miracle I asked Him for. I cannot wait to see John's face when he hears his first piece."

Chapter 19

Nicole's parents had given the bridal pair their home for the night. Nicole's and Gordon's objections had accomplished nothing. After a time at the village fete, with the roasting meats and the fiddler and the torchlight and the laughter, they had been cheered on their way with best wishes from all sides. Arm in arm they had walked the path down to the little cottage to discover that someone had lit a fire and prepared a tray of cider and fresh-baked bread and cheese. Fresh linens were upon her parents' bed, and rose petals spread about the sleeping chamber, upon the planked floor and the bed itself, all illuminated by candlelight.

Now it was morning, but Nicole's eyes were still closed when the bedroom door creaked open. She reached over to feel the empty pillow next to hers. She rose up on an elbow to see Gordon, already dressed, coming toward her with a steaming mug.

"Good morning, my sweet one," he said with a smile both tender and sorrowful.

Nicole pushed herself up to lean against the headboard. She knew the reason for the look on Gordon's face. He did not need to say a word.

She took a deep breath to halt a half-formed protest, but all she said was, "Is it time?"

Gordon sat down on the bedside. "I fear so, my love."

Slowly she sliced a piece of bread, cut a chunk of the

crumbling cheese, and gave it to Gordon, knowing her own smile was tremulous. "I want you to have your first meal of our married life from my hand," she told him.

He smiled in return and accepted the bread, watching her pour a mug of cider. They ate in silence for a time. Then he said, "There is something I would ask of you."

He leaned forward to kiss her, and she tasted the cider and smelled ashes and woodsmoke from the fire he must have laid in the front room. "Before we must leave, I would like us to receive communion together at your father's altar."

She set the mug down upon the tray and carefully studied his face.

"I cannot say precisely why it means so much to me," he said, stumbling slightly over the words. "I admire Andrew greatly. It came to me yesterday evening at the wedding fete. His words helped me in coming to recognize my need for faith beyond simply the outward trappings of religion. Forgive me, I do not know the proper way to explain myself."

Nicole was listening with her heart, and she thought she was understanding her husband's attempts to describe his inner journey, and she nodded for him to continue.

"I would like to think that we depart from here not merely with their blessing, but also with their heritage of faith. I can think of nothing finer than to leave here challenged by your parents to live as they have. To dedicate our life together to our Lord and seek to follow their example through all our days."

"Gordon, my dearest," she whispered and reached for his hand. "Yes, let us celebrate the sacrament with them before we must leave. . . ." Her voice nearly broke, but she willed herself to courage and to thankfulness for the blessings of this visit, brief though it needed to be.

John Price and Catherine were talking quietly in the lane beyond the garden gate when Nicole and Gordon emerged from the cottage. Her grandfather bowed a welcome of solemn good cheer, setting a proper tone for the occasion. "May God's light shine upon you, upon this day, and upon every day He grants you both."

"Thank you, Grandfather." Nicole embraced him, forcing herself not to let the sorrow overwhelm her. *Remember the joy,* she told herself, not willing to let the old man go. *Remember the bounty of these days.*

She turned to her mother. The eastern sun shone fully upon Catherine's features beneath her bonnet. Her face was far more lined than Nicole had recalled. And almost all the visible hair was gray.

"I have not had enough time here in this place," Nicole whispered, the protest spoken so lightly neither man could hear.

Catherine released her and waved at where the two men stood watching. "Walk ahead of us, if you would."

"Most certainly." Gordon offered the older gentleman an outstretched arm. "Would you care to lean upon me, sir?"

Catherine allowed them to draw several paces away before she turned to Nicole and also took her arm. "We can do this one of two ways," she said in a low voice. "We can weep and wail and mourn that you must depart far more quickly than either of us would wish. Or we can use these final moments to give thanks that you were here for your wedding, your father was able to perform the ceremony, and that you have seen him in much better health than he has been not that long ago."

Nicole nodded her assent, "I haven't really had a chance to speak of Father's health, or how you are, or—"

"We are in God's hands." Catherine held Nicole's arm closer and asked, "Do you believe this?"

"Of course, but—"

"We are His children. He has blessed us most wonderfully. What use is there in bewailing what neither of us can change?"

Nicole nodded again, but this time she found her heart also agreeing. She was truly blessed, and her spirit lifted with her inward affirmation of that fact.

Nicole picked up the conversation with, "And, Mama, you and I are going to have a bit more time together on the return to the ship." Catherine had agreed to journey with them in order to provide further introductions to any suspicious locals who might challenge their passage. Andrew, of course, was not up to such a venture.

They rounded the corner by the village market, and up ahead rose the steeple of the church. Andrew waited upon the front steps, talking with two parishioners. As soon as they came into view, he raised his hand in greeting and smiled his welcome. Nicole felt her senses reaching out in every direction. She tasted the wind and caught fragrances that defined this place—woodsmoke and verdant forest earth and animals and baking bread and the sea's chill. She heard the bleats of goats and the cries of children and a woman singing through an open window. "You are right. I know you are right."

"The question for both of us is simple. How shall we spend these final hours?"

The answer was as clear as Catherine's voice. Nicole turned to smile at her mother; then the little group walked into the church.

A treasure of memories, was how Nicole decided to describe it for Anne. After sharing the Eucharistic bread and wine with her family, after a quiet lunch, after bedding down John Price for his nap, Nicole carried quill and ink and paper out to the point, still adorned with pine garlands and rings of spring flowers.

She had only a short time before their departure, but she did not hurry in describing the events of their arrival and then their wedding. In putting the words on the page, she was able to see God's hand more clearly, and this she wrote as well.

The sun traced its way west, and she knew the time was coming for her to depart. Penning the final words to Anne was an effort, yet they rang with love.

I know that God's hand is upon me here, Nicole wrote her sister. *For were it not so, I would be weeping from all the fragments of this too-brief time. I leave my father, my mother, my grandfather, and know not when or where we shall see one another again. I leave after mere hours of wedded bliss, and this granted only because my father and mother—our father and mother—gave everything they had, even their own bed. I leave without seeing you, without even knowing if you are coming. This is as hard as anything I have ever done. Yet leave we must, as I have explained. We have responsibilities and carry charges given to us by those who are counting upon our bringing aid, and swiftly. But these reasons are not why I leave here with a sense of rightness and duty. I do so because I know we are bound by the Father of all, and that our lives shall be intertwined for eternity. I carry with me my love for this place and my wonderful family, and their love for me. I am sustained by this, and by the knowledge that a joyful reunion in heaven awaits us all. Your loving sister, Nicole.*

Chapter 20

Many of the little shipboard community became very dear to Anne and Thomas. And when Anne's own heritage was discovered—how she had been raised in Nova Scotia and knew the land well—they could not ask her enough. A dozen of the Dissenters had already settled in a burgeoning community north of Halifax. The written reports they had sent back gave helpful information, but Anne's personal experiences were another matter entirely.

In the evenings she and Thomas were surrounded by elders and their families, reviewing their plans and hopes. In many cases Anne knew no answers could be given, but she and Thomas could at least listen with compassion and grace. Having a role to fill proved a great balm during those seaborne days.

Thomas's presence proved of singular benefit as well, for there was no other person with legal background or experience among them. It seemed that every family had matters left unsettled back home or affairs that needed tending before their arrival. Marriages and dowries were brought forth. Partnerships formed. Two stores planned. A few families had been unable to sell their homes, the matters left in last-minute haste. Several had paid for land and needed their deeds studied to see if all was in order.

The days took on a disciplined routine. Mornings began with tea and Scripture. Midday meals were marked by prayers from both pastors and sometimes the elders as well. There was a full service at dusk, and more prayer and Scripture before bed. Anne found the routine a blessing and comfort, and fully involved herself in the life and worship of the little band.

The winds, strong and southerly, blew steadily. The ship heeled over at a near constant angle, drawn forward by the taut canvas. When seabirds began congregating amidst the rigging at dawn and dusk, the passengers greeted them with cries of welcome. They had learned from the sailors that the birds were both foretellers of more good weather and the first indication of land beyond the horizon.

Three weeks into the voyage, after the evening meal Anne chose a seat among the empty barrels lashed to the port railing. The curved staves offered protection from the wind that always grew chilly this time of day. She had just settled herself when she heard her husband call her name. "Here!" she answered.

Thomas appeared, bearing her heavy cloak. "I thought you might need this."

"Thank you, husband." She allowed him to settle it around her shoulders, then kept his hand from withdrawing. The Dissenters were somewhat like Quakers in their reserve, preferring no common familiarity in the sight of one another. But on this point Anne respectfully disagreed. "Sit with me, please."

Thomas eased himself down beside her, his arm about her shoulders. "This is the first moment we have had alone in days," he noted ruefully.

"I know it well."

The weeks at sea had browned his features, turning his eyes even more clear and piercing. Anne looked into his face, then said, "I have been watching another facet of your gifts coming to the fore during these weeks on board."

Gently Thomas extricated his arm and moved slightly back to look at her more fully. "What have you observed, Anne?"

"I have seen you becoming an elder to the community."

She was very glad he did not disagree.

"I have heard others speak the word when they thought I

was not listening. But it is another thing entirely to hear your perception of it."

"Elder," she repeated. "You are a man of sound judgment and impartial bearing. You seek God's will in your decisions, and you mediate with patience. Your words are a balm. You strengthen. You reassure."

"Anne, my dear, you humble me with this praise."

"Come draw closer, Thomas. I have something more to say." Their heads moved close together until they were nearly touching. "I am wondering if there is further financial help we could make available to them without the group knowing the source."

Thomas was quiet for a moment, then said, "I believe there is a way. . . . Yes, I am sure of it."

They looked at each other and smiled, then Thomas returned his arm to Anne's shoulder. They settled back to watch the stars blink into position.

The next morning a storm swept in hard and fast. The wind rose to such a pitch that lanyards hummed and snapped. The sailors raced across the decks and up the ropes, lashing the sails into the quarter-moon shapes used to weather storms.

But no one seemed to be perturbed. Other than a pair of fitful squalls, the weather had been dry, so most of the ship's water caskets were empty. And the storm was blowing from the proper quarter, such that their sail westward continued faster still. The captain, a gruff and hard-bitten man who clearly preferred to keep God in His quarter, had even come to calling their passage a blessing. He welcomed the rain, for the closer they drew to the coastline, the greater was their risk of running afoul of the Americans.

The northern colonies, now called collectively by the name of Canada, remained firmly within English hands. But the border between the revolutionaries and Canada was both fluid and very near. Sailors and officers alike kept close watch upon the horizons, casting to the four corners of the horizon for the first sign of sail. Thankfully, the only vessels they had spied the entire voyage had flown the haughty Union Jack and greeted them with flags and cannonades signaling the all clear.

And now there were great sweeping curtains of rain about them, furious torrents that heeled over the boat and doused them all. But the morning remained warm enough for most of the passengers to stay on deck and revel in the first cleansing bath they had enjoyed in days. Dry and salt-crusted faces were turned toward the heavens. Hats and bonnets were doffed, and stiffened hair was drenched with water so fresh it tasted sweet to their mouths. When one shower had passed and a trio of sailors began dancing a hornpipe upon the rain-washed deck, most of the passengers laughed and clapped in time to the communal celebration.

During the general hubbub, Anne drew close to the young pastor's wife to whisper, "We would have a quiet word with you and your husband, if you please."

The young woman nodded and moved to where her husband stood smiling at the antics.

Thomas awaited them by the far railing.

He glanced at Anne, who nodded, and he said, "We have been entrusted with quite a large sum. Charles Harrow is a man generous in purse and spirit, and he wishes for us to help those who have suffered from this conflict."

Now the pastor and his wife looked at each other, their expressions full of astonishment.

Thomas went on, "We wish to make a gift to your new community."

"In secret," Anne added.

Thomas reached into the folds of his coat and extracted a folded sheet of parchment. "I have prepared a banker's draft. At the bottom of the page is the address where we shall be residing in Georgetown. Take this to the bank in Halifax. Have them contact us if there are any questions."

The young clergyman and his wife were quite speechless.

He took the document without looking at its contents, and her eyes brimmed with tears. "We cannot tell you," the pastor finally said as he tucked the parchment into his coat, "how much your kindness and generosity means to us. I'm sure only eternity will reveal all the ways our Lord will bless our members because of your friendship and your gift."

The two women embraced while their husbands solemnly shook hands. At that moment another downpour swept over the decks, and the four could not help but laugh as they hurried to shelter.

"I believe I have had enough of bathing for one day," quipped Thomas as he wiped his face, and he and Anne ducked down the stairway below decks.

Chapter 21

Nicole gripped the reins with practiced ease. The wagon was old and creaky and very heavily laden. Prior to their departure from Georgetown, Gordon had made one final pass through the market and bought additional supplies for the voyage ahead. When it came time for them to return to their vessel, Nicole had requested that she drive. Even in this old contraption, even upon this day of painful farewells, she found pleasure in taking the reins once more.

She looked over to smile at Catherine on the seat next to her. Gordon rode nearby, keeping watchful eyes on the crew and the wagons.

Nicole flicked the reins and clicked to the team as they labored up a small rise. Trees stretched out on both sides of the lane, and the air was full of new life and the cool scent of a Nova Scotian spring. She took a deep breath. "The joys of being here, Mama, far outweigh the sorrow of the good-byes," she said to Catherine.

The departure from the small Georgetown cottage had been not as wrenching as she would have expected. Andrew and John Price had made light of their ailments, arguing good-naturedly over which one would help the other down the lane to where the wagons and their escorts waited. Nicole had held each of them a very long time, willing her strength and youth into their fragile frames. She had accepted their thanks for the visit and joined their thanks to God for keeping her safe. The little group had linked arms and hearts to pray for the mission and the voyage ahead. All of the voyages facing all of them. When Andrew had spoken those words, Nicole had been forced to swallow around the lump in her throat.

During the trip by wagon, Catherine had shared with her daughter the tale of both diaries, the letter to Anne, and how she and her father had grown closer. But mostly the two women had spoken of Nicole's grandmother's writings. Catherine had marked favorite passages to read aloud as they traveled.

"*I cannot think of being anywhere in the world but with John,*" that long-departed Mrs. Price wrote. "*He is such a kind, devoted husband. But, oh, how my heart yearns for my homeland. The winters here are so harsh and long. John does not favor me going out and about the small village alone, and there are so few women here. Those who are here seem much too busy with caring for their households to have time for visiting. Some days I fear that I will go mad with the loneliness. Perhaps if I had a child I would feel more content. I fear that when John comes home at the end of his long, busy day, I rattle on. I try to hold my tongue, but it seems I might wither away if I do not have some conversation. I think he would be content to sit by the fire and let the worrisomeness of his responsibilities slide from his shoulders in silence. I must try to be more patient.*"

Catherine read entry after entry, until it seemed the unseen lady whom neither of them had known was there with them.

"*John brought me a rose today. It was the first one of the spring. I cannot say how it touched my heart. He has always been a kind husband, but this little act of love quite overtook me. I do love him so. It pains me sorely to see him struggle with bitterness. He will not acknowledge it, but I know it is there. If only I had some way to undo what has been done. His war wound gives him sleepless nights and pain-filled days. I ache along with him. But I feel the deepest and most sorrowful injury was done to his soul. He cannot forgive those who inflicted his wounds. Daily I pray that God will aid him. His anger is much too heavy a burden to bear.*"

Nicole, in turn, told the story of her overland journey to Charles's estate in western Massachusetts, the drama of

Gordon's arrest, his coming to faith, their growing love. So much to share that the hours drummed away as swiftly as the horses' clopping hooves. Even when they stopped at midday and took a quick lunch within the forested shade, they still talked.

———— ✀ ————

They rounded the final corner far too soon for either of them. The ship appeared through a break in the trees. Too soon Carter tethered the horses and pointed the waiting sailors toward the wagon's load. Nicole found herself reluctantly releasing the reins and turning to her mother. Too soon.

"Begging your pardon, ma'am." Carter approached, holding his cap. "We're all right happy for you and the skipper. And we wish you great joy, ma'am. Great joy indeed."

"Thank you, Carter. May I introduce my mother, Madam Harrow. Mama, this is Carter, the bosun."

The two acknowledged the introduction, then Carter said, "The captain is asking that we all board this vessel. He is hoping to make the Cobequid passage and be well down Fundy before daybreak."

"Very well, Carter. Thank you." She turned toward her mother. "I must honor the captain's wishes, Mama." Her smile was tremulous.

"Of course." Catherine was already climbing down from the wagon. "Come with me for a moment, please."

She led Nicole up a gentle rise to where a point of land rose above the tree line.

"It occurred to me that I might be able to . . ." She panted as she climbed swiftly up to the ridge that pointed like a finger out into the Cobequid waters.

"Mama, what?"

"Yes! There it is! I am certain of it!"

"Certain of what?"

"Come, stand beside me." Catherine pointed out over the

waters to their right, away from the ship, farther along the narrowing bay. "Do you see where the waters curve out to the next point, just like this one?"

"Yes, but—"

"See where the earth lies bare? Where the forest has been cut back and the new fields readied for planting? Look at the big rock there at the forest's lowest edge."

"The forest rises in a series of steps."

"Exactly!" She pointed a trembling finger. "Now look at where the third step extends out."

A thrill ran through Nicole's frame.

"I do not travel this far from Georgetown very often. But my connection to the returning Acadians has brought me down this way a time or two. And I still remember the lay of the land from my early days." Catherine nodded firmly. "That is the meeting place; I am sure of it."

"Where you and Louise—?"

"You may call her Mother, my dear. I do not mind."

"Two mothers, bound by the tragedy. . . ." Nicole murmured, staring across the sweep of forest and field.

"Two friends, two daughters, four lives," Catherine added softly.

"A thousand tomorrows, and still it is not enough," Catherine said as their arms enfolded each other in a last embrace. "That is both the joy and the woe of love." She drew back and looked into Nicole's face. "The years you grew up away from me, the nights I lay a different child into your cradle, still I felt my heart connected to yours. Wherever you go, my daughter, my heart is with you."

Chapter 22

"The new governess will be arriving Thursday midday," Charles announced as he peered through his spectacles at the letter he held.

Judith already had thanked God for this answer to prayer in the days since the news of Miss Paige had come from London.

"I do not know who is anticipating this the most," she confessed, "John or me." She paused for a moment, then said, "Do you know what John asked me this morning?"

"I could never guess."

"He said, 'Nana, are you changing color for winter?'"

Charles frowned in puzzlement, then threw back his head and laughed. "When we were out riding the other morning we saw a hare."

"Yes, he told me. He said, 'Uncle Charles said that God helps the hare to change color in winter so it can hide from its 'emmamies.'"

"'Emmamies,'" repeated Charles with another chuckle. "That is more difficult to pronounce than the correct one."

"When I told him that I was not getting ready for winter, nor am I plotting a way to hide from my 'emmamies,' he said, 'Then why is your hair two colors?' I told him that it used to all be one color—just like his. We had to place our heads side by side and peek into the looking glass together. He smiled at first, but then he reached up and touched my hair. And he said, 'Why did you ask God to change it?'"

They laughed together.

"How did you answer him?"

"I am not sure. It caught me off guard. I'm afraid I did not give him a very satisfactory explanation. I said that hair changes color as one grows older, or some such thing."

"I see nothing wrong with that answer."

"Perhaps not. But I'm hopeful this new nanny will be able to help with all those ideas and thoughts and questions he has. I . . . I rather cherish his innocence. To him everything that happens, large or small, is all God's doing. I rather like him to see things that way. I trust Miss Paige can protect that innocence. It is a treasure, do you not think?"

Charles nodded, "A treasure indeed," he said with feeling.

They went to the nursery together to introduce little John to his new nanny. The young woman had arrived in midafternoon the day before, after a long and tiring journey, so after a brief welcome, she had been granted the remainder of the day to rest and get settled in her new quarters near the nursery.

Judith had decided that one would not describe Miss Paige as beautiful, but she had china blue eyes, which looked very large in her small face. And when she dared to smile, her thin features seemed to be lit from within. Judith felt almost motherly toward this tiny waif of a girl.

"She's but a child herself," she whispered to Charles after Howards, luggage in hand, had escorted the young woman to her room.

Charles merely nodded, seeming deep in thought.

"I would be tempted to send her right back to London if . . ." he began but did not finish.

"If?" prompted Judith. "If we were not desperate?"

Charles turned to her, shaking his head. "No, my dear. If *she* was not."

Judith nodded her understanding. The young woman had

no home of her own. No place to go.

"Of course we shall keep her," she said warmly. "After all, she is an answer to prayer. If she does nothing more than play the pianoforte for John, she will be worth her keep."

"She is more likely to play *with* him, I am thinking," Charles quipped.

Judith smiled. "The new nanny is not quite *that* young," she had said.

Now as the three entered John's nursery room together, Judith could see that the young woman was nervous and uncertain about this encounter. Judith whispered, "I'm sure the both of you will get on famously," and she smiled as reassuringly as she could.

"John," said Charles, and the boy lifted his head from his building blocks. "We have brought someone for you to meet. Would you stand, please?"

John stood. His small hands clasped behind his back and his head dipped shyly.

Judith moved forward to place an arm around John's shoulder. "Remember, we talked about Nurse having to leave?"

He nodded and peeked a glimpse out from under tousled hair.

"This is your new nanny, Mistress Paige. Would you greet her, please?"

Obediently John took a tentative step forward, took another peek at her, and extended a hand. "Good morning, Miss," he managed to say.

Miss Paige had also stepped forward. Judith saw her hand reach out, and as the two hands met, something extraordinary happened. The young woman's entire face lit up with her smile, the blue eyes came alive, and the cheeks suddenly flushed with a rosy color. John smiled back at her.

Judith heard a heartfelt, "Oh, I have always wanted a little brother."

"I'm not very little," John was quick to say, but his tone was matter-of-fact.

"Of course you're not. I didn't mean . . ." The new nanny

was now on her knees, pulling John into her arms. Surprisingly he did not resist.

"Oh, pardon me, ma'am," she said, quickly standing to her feet, her cheeks crimson.

But John reached out to take her hand. "Do you play the pianoforte?" he asked, looking into her face.

She merely nodded.

"Could I hear it?"

The girl looked at Judith for an answer.

"We shall have some music this evening," Judith was quick to say. "After our supper." She turned to Mistress Paige. "I will bring the former nanny in to talk with you. She is gathering her things. She will show you the rooms and give you instructions as to the workings of the nursery. Tea will be served at four. Today you will take it together here by the fire. In the future I will relieve you so you may take your tea with the staff."

She nodded in understanding and agreement. Judith had a sudden pang at the thought of all this young woman had lost and the rather daunting circumstances she now faced. She felt sure the young girl had never been sent to the kitchen to *tea* with staff in her entire young life.

"Please," Judith continued, softening her tone, "if anything confuses or troubles you, do not hesitate to speak to me. You are here to care for young John. He is a good child, so your task should not be burdensome. But we . . . we also wish you to be happy here."

It was not the speech she had intended. She wondered what Charles was thinking. He had not spoken since they had first entered the room. She felt his hand on her elbow now gently urging her toward the door.

Once in the hall, she dared to look up at him. His face was quite sober. "She is but a child," he managed, shaking his head.

"But . . . she is . . . is a sweet young thing," Judith put in.

"A child looking after a child," he said. "It will be you caring for young John." He nodded toward the nursery. "And the young miss too, I am thinking."

"I can—"

"Seems I will need to write another letter to London—to get a nanny for the nanny." But his manner didn't seem overly concerned, and Judith could not suppress a chuckle. Charles looked at her a moment, then joined in the merriment.

As promised, they all gathered in the front parlor that evening, and Charles carefully—and a bit ceremoniously, Judith thought—removed the covering drape from the instrument. She could not take her gaze from John's small face. She watched his eyes grow large in wonderment, too awed to even smile. "Can I touch it?" he whispered.

When Charles nodded, the boy moved forward, running a hand over the rich wood, then trailing his fingers lightly over the ivory keys. Charles allowed the boy time to explore, then reached down and lifted him. "I think it is time to listen to some music. Shall we let Mistress Paige play for us?"

John nodded.

Charles took his seat beside Judith, the child still in his arms. He settled John on one knee and nodded to the girl.

At first the notes came a bit haltingly, though John was captivated. He leaned forward, his eyes holding steadily to the movement of her fingers. It was not long before her nervousness was gone, and the slim fingers moved over the keyboard with confidence. Her eyes closed and her body gently swayed with the rhythm. Judith did not recognize the piece, but the music stirred her soul.

Charles too seemed lost in the music. His arms held John, but he leaned back in his chair, eyes closed, head nodding ever so slightly to match the tempo. Judith wondered if the piece was one his mother had played for him as a child.

It ended all too soon. John's hands clapped together and he cried out, "Do it again."

Charles stirred then. "Where are our manners?" he chided softly. "We request—not order. Would you like to request that

Mistress Paige play another piece?"

"Oh yes. Play another one," John called, then corrected himself. "Please, would you play another one?" he asked in a quieter tone, but his eyes were still dancing.

Two more pieces were heard before John's bedtime. He was assured that a concert would be a part of their evenings in the future.

"Please, God, bless Mama and Papa," he prayed as he knelt by his bedside that night, "and bring them back soon so they can hear the pianoforte too."

Amen, echoed in Judith's heart as she bent to tuck him in.

Chapter 23

Nicole brushed a loose strand of auburn hair back from her cheek and stared down at the large leather-bound book in her lap. Light fell over her shoulder through the cabin's rear windows onto the page. She read the text again. "Those who go down to the sea in ships, who do business on great waters, they see the works of the Lord, and His wonders in the deep. For He commands and raises the stormy wind, which lifts up the waves of the sea." She raised her head and looked out at the wind lifting up the waves. That imagery was certainly clear enough.

She could hear Gordon's voice calling instructions to the crew above on the decks, and their feet hurrying hither and yon to carry out his bidding. "He commands" also presented a mental image as she considered her husband's authority over his men and nature's obedience to its Creator. "He calms the storm, so that its waves are still" seemed particularly comforting to her heart that morning.

Their way south from the Bay of Cobequid had been sped along by a late-spring storm, to Gordon's great relief but Nicole's occasional dismay as the ship heeled far over, then righted itself, only to be repeated as waves pounded its sides. "Then they are glad because they are quiet," she read aloud. "So He guides them to their desired haven." She couldn't help but smile at the welcome sound of the last phrase, and she said it again softly. *A desired haven. That is what I am seeking,* she told herself.

Certainly her marriage to Gordon had brought her a long way toward that haven for her heart. His love and care for her were evidenced in everything he said and did. But the future still loomed uncertainly in the distance. They were now on this mission for the Americans, and it would bring them face-to-face with life-threatening danger. If the Almighty should bring them through unscathed, they would arrive in Louisiana, her childhood home, and to the family of her childhood. Is that where Gordon and she would find their ultimate home, that haven for which she yearned?

"Oh, that men would give thanks to the Lord for His goodness, and for His wonderful works to the children of men!" she read slowly. *Well, that is something I can do, I will do,* she concluded, *whether or not I know how God will guide us, or the way He will bring us to the haven.*

A knock on the cabin's door brought her to her feet. "Yes?" she called.

"Begging your pardon, Ma'am," came the voice through the door. "The captain be requesting your presence on deck."

"Very well, I will be there shortly," she told him. She set aside the book, tied her bonnet on her head, and pulled her cloak around her. Above her she heard the sound of feet stomping to attention. Ah yes, it was the Sabbath, and as was custom, the shipboard rhythm was changed for the day. The decks had been scrubbed, frayed lines replaced, sails carefully examined in preparation for the Lord's Day. She knew some vessels even carried a clergyman or occasionally a surgeon who also was a man of the cloth.

Nicole climbed the stairway and emerged into the sunlight and several rows of seamen, all in their finest togs. Gordon stood before them in his uniform, and he gave her a brief nod as Carter stepped forward to escort her to a bench. After she was seated, Gordon called the men to ease, and they found various places to seat themselves about the deck.

Gordon opened the Bible and began reading from the book

of Daniel, the story of the young man sent to his death in a lions' den but whom God saved to become a prince of Persia. Gordon's second selection was from the epistle to the Hebrews, and finally he read a Gospel text from Luke. He closed the book, and there was a long silence. Nicole thought he was finished.

"Some of you know hymns written by a pastor from London," Gordon finally began, "a gentleman named John Newton." There was a stirring of recognition around her.

"What you may not know is that John Newton once was a sailor like we are." The murmur across the deck held astonishment. "I have had occasion to study this man's life, for there is much about the man that both comforts and challenges me. He was of small beginnings, as am I. With little formal education, he served upon a merchant vessel for eight years before His Majesty's Navy demanded his services. He was press-ganged onto a man-of-war, the *Harwich*. He attempted to escape when the ship berthed at Plymouth, but he was captured and publicly flogged."

Again there was a rustle among the sailors. Many of them had been press-ganged when this ship was taken, and they still bore the scars of both lash and chain. "When his time was up," Gordon continued, "he joined another vessel bound for Africa. He took service under a slave dealer. He rose to captain of his own vessel and became known for his unbelief, his rage, his blasphemy, his merciless command of both his seamen and his slaves."

The men before him were absolutely silent, gripped by the power of the story and the fervor of its delivery. Nicole sat with her hands clasped before her, spellbound by this new facet of her husband's gifts and leadership of men.

"This slave trader made dozens of crossings from Africa to the Americas with his human cargo. He became renowned on seven seas for his strength, savvy, and wisdom. He was also vicious and spiteful, but utterly courageous and successful. Wealthy and feared, he was counted as a triumph by the entire world." Gordon gazed out over the railing for a moment, then said, "And then, in the belly of a dark sou'wester, with the storm raging and the heavens splitting, John Newton came face-to-face with his Creator."

Gordon now looked around the group. "John Newton gave up his success, his ship, his career. He returned to England to begin the study of the Scriptures and of Greek and Hebrew. In 1764 he was ordained and took a church in Olney." He hesitated a moment, this time glancing quickly at Nicole, then back to the men. "Some of you know of my own dark night of the soul, not in a storm but in British captivity. I was destined to hang as a traitor. I turned to the same Lord as Newton, asking for deliverance of my soul from eternal death. He granted my petition and also delivered me from the hangman's rope, so that I am able to stand before you and declare my allegiance to God for time and eternity."

The silence hung over the deck, and then Gordon's strong baritone took up Newton's latest hymn: "Amazing grace, how sweet the sound, that saved a wretch like me." As the men's voices joined in, tears filled Nicole's eyes at the evidence of God's grace all around her—in her husband, in these hardened men singing this song of redemption, in her own gropings for inner peace and having found a home for her heart.

She joined her voice with the rest in the last triumphant verse, "When we've been there ten thousand years . . . we've no less days to sing God's praise . . ." *And give thanks to the Lord for His goodness,* she finished in silent reprise of her earlier reading of the psalm.

Chapter 24

Although the new nanny was young, she was most conscientious about carrying out her duties with utmost care. Judith was very relieved each time she reported to Charles on the young woman's abilities.

"So you are telling me," he quipped as Judith described how Mistress Paige had quietly and firmly handled an obstinate John at breakfast, "that God did not make an error after all in bringing her our way?"

"We should have made a mistake—a dreadful mistake—had we sent her back. She is really quite mature—very bright and quick to learn."

"She has not had an easy lot, I am thinking."

Judith shook her head. "I think John is good for her. She seems really taken with the wee lad."

Charles made an abrupt change in the conversation. "I have had another letter from our man. This time he is back on the coast. He has finally located someone who knew someone who had worked for an orphanage there in France. It seems that one truly did exist."

"So at last, some good news." Judith moved closer to Charles as he sat at his desk fingering the letter.

"Not much, I am afraid. But at least a small lead that encourages me. There were records, but no one seems to know if they still exist. He is trying to locate them. If he should fail, he is not sure what the next step should be. Since this search is getting to be costly, he wonders if I wish to drop the matter."

Judith stood quietly waiting. "And do you?" she finally asked softly.

Charles finally stirred. His thumb and forefinger moved to his brow to massage his forehead. "No," he said. "Not as long as there is any shred of hope. I want to do this for John Price. For his daughter, Catherine. For Nicole. And in doing it for them, for my brother Andrew as well. It is strange. I can't really explain it, but I guess, in some way, I want to do this for myself. I think I will find pleasure in tying up this thread in their family heritage. I keep thinking, what if I had discovered that I had a sister—somewhere? A sister whom I had never had the privilege to know? I would want to find her. I truly would. And it seems—a mission of sorts to help them discover her identity."

He looked up and the fingers dropped again to the desktop. "Do you understand?"

Judith nodded. "I would want to find her too," she agreed. "With all my heart."

Days later Charles hurried into the room, waving another letter. "He has found her," he exclaimed, causing Judith to relax against the damask chairback, full of relief and excitement.

"Well—not 'found her' exactly, but he has information. An old man from the village had a sister who worked for the orphanage. He remembers her speaking of the young girl who was brought there under very unusual circumstances. It was whispered that the father was British and that he had fled the country. The young mother had died in childbirth. The date tallies with the one given by John Price."

Judith found her voice. "That is wonderful news. Does she still live?"

"We do not know. The child did not remain there. By some means, she was sent away by sea—he thinks to the New

World, as best he can tell from the fragments of information. Whether she was adopted beforehand or if she was to be adopted on the other side also is not known." He looked again at the pages he held. "There is also the possibility that she was merely transferred to another orphanage. All we know thus far is that she had been in France and she was sent out, probably to the area of Nova Scotia because of the French connections through the Acadians." His face became serious. "Nor do we yet know if she ever arrived at the destination."

Judith did not need to be reminded of the dangers of shipwreck or disease on an ocean voyage, nor of the number of young children who succumbed from one cause or another. "What do we do now?" she wondered.

"I am sending immediate orders for him to try to procure passage. If it is impossible to find a ship on which to sail, then I will urge him to discover someone in Nova Scotia or even Boston who can pick up the search over there."

"It seems so impossible," Judith acknowledged over her previous enthusiasm.

"We cannot give up now. We have found her."

Judith slowly shook her head. They had not found her.

"At least we have confirmed her existence."

"We already knew that."

"But we now know *where* she existed," Charles argued.

"You are right," Judith agreed. "It is an amazing discovery, and after all these years. Your man has done remarkably well."

"And now we need more. One more part of the mystery. We know where she has been. We must discover where she is now."

Mistress Paige soon won the hearts of the entire household. In spite of her small stature and plain features, it was not long until the kitchen chatter was only about her beautifully expressive eyes and engaging smile.

As for John, he quite adored her. She sang to him morning and night, and in between as often as he requested a song. And the evening ritual was to gather in the front parlor to listen to another short concert on the pianoforte. John was now able to recognize some of the pieces well enough to make his own requests. His aptitude for music pleased Judith to no end. "I do think he has a gift," she informed Charles on several occasions, to which Charles always smiled and nodded his agreement. He told Judith his intention was to nurture that gift to its fullest potential. They encouraged Lenora Paige in her singing and playing. The latest in music was ordered from London, with instructions for the academy there to keep them supplied in the future.

It was concert hour, and Mistress Paige and John were already gathered in the front parlor, she selecting pieces from a new music book, he touching the keyboard with his small fingers. Charles had instructed the child that he could "play" the instrument one note at a time. He would plink a key, bending his head over and to the side so that he might listen carefully. Drawing the heavy draperies before night fell, Judith smiled to herself as she watched the little boy with the serious expression.

The tinkling notes continued as Judith moved to take her customary chair. Suddenly she paused, her full attention turned to the boy and the piano. The random pressing of the keys had gradually changed. It sounded like a nursery rhyme tune coming from the keyboard. *Surely not,* she quickly dismissed the idea.

Then the melody came again.

"Mistress Paige," Judith whispered. The young woman's head lifted from the music. "Listen."

Judith saw the girl lean forward and a smile spread across her face.

"It's the little song I sing to him at bedtime," she whispered back in excitement.

John seemed totally oblivious to their presence. Over and over one tiny finger of his right hand picked out the few lines of the song. He did not stop until they were played without fumbling.

Suddenly he lifted his head and turned to his nanny. "I cannot remember what comes next. Would you sing it?"

Without a moment's hesitation, she sang the little song. A smile lit his face, and his finger went once more to the keyboard. He soon found the rest of the song.

Judith immediately went to find Charles. "You will never believe this," she said excitedly when she found him in the library. "John is playing the pianoforte. Really. He is playing all by himself."

When Charles looked dubious, Judith repeated the news and urged him to come hear it for himself. He did not require a second invitation.

Later in their bedroom, Judith said, "I can't help but think about Anne and Thomas—how much they are missing. . . ." But her voice caught.

Charles moved to put his arms around her. "They are indeed missing this, but I have an idea that they will quickly make up for lost time when they are back with their little boy."

Judith nodded against his shoulder. She would leave it all in the hands of God.

Chapter 25

The cavalry officer drew his horse nearer to where Anne and Thomas sat in a drover's wagon, one of several transporting the ship-weary band inland from Halifax Harbor. He touched a gloved hand to the polished brim of his helmet and announced, "Georgetown is beyond the next ridge, my lady. Brigands don't operate this close to a settlement. Especially not in daylight."

"You have been most kind, Captain." Anne tried to place some warmth into her words, but the British officer rode a stallion bred for combat, and neither beast nor rider elicited emotion other than fear from her. "Please convey my thanks to your master for providing an escort."

"As my lady wishes." He wheeled his horse about and shouted a command, and he and his company galloped away without a backward glance.

The drover in whose wagon they traveled was usually a taciturn man, but he now muttered through his mustache, "Them's glad to be rid o' the likes of us. Cavalry's the proudest of the lot, and this here's the governor's own men. Being sent to shepherd a bunch of pilgrims must gall them something mighty."

"That was their duty," Thomas noted shortly.

The drover's shoulder lifted in humorless mirth. "Sir, them cavalry officers would far rather be spreading havoc than keeping the peace."

The drover turned to look square at Thomas. "Don't know what clout you had with his lordship back Halifax way. But it must be something powerful, him sending the cavalry out to watch our passage like he did."

Truth be told, neither Thomas nor Anne had wanted to make their presence known to the authorities. But their arrival in Halifax had come at a time when virtually every able-bodied soldier had been sent south for the coming summer campaign. And with them had gone almost all available supplies.

Two days spent walking about the town's markets had revealed just how difficult it would be for the Dissenters to equip themselves for their westward jaunt. There were no wagons. Nor horses or mules. Foodstuffs and dry goods were priced out of reach if it hadn't been for the secret Harrow bequest through Thomas and Anne. Fortunately they were able to find seeds, farming implements, axes and nails and building supplies. Anything not required for the war was there in abundance. But tents were impossible to locate. As were cooking implements.

Anne and Thomas had finally agreed to make an appeal directly to the governor. Invoking Charles's name had resulted in instant action, for London politics had not filtered across the water. As far as the governor knew, Lord Charles Harrow, ninth earl of Sutton, remained in full royal favor, one of the richest and most powerful men in the realm. The wagon train of settlers and goods was soon on its way with Anne and Thomas riding along as far as Georgetown.

Finally, finally, they crested the ridgeline. Up ahead a white cross atop a narrow steeple hung over the surrounding forest. Anne felt her breath catch in her throat at the sight.

She slid from the lumbering wagon to walk on ahead. Thomas climbed down as well and in three strides was beside her.

"Oh, Thomas, I'm so anticipating this, but I'm so afraid—"

"Yes, I understand," Thomas said, tucking her arm in his. "But whatever we find, my dearest, the Almighty has been before us."

Anne drew a fraction closer and matched her stride to his. Light and shadow filtered through the tall pines and hardwoods onto the lane, far broader than she recalled. Georgetown's edges now reached toward the outlying farms.

Even in her uncertainty about her father's condition—or even if he was still with them—she felt her heart surge with anticipation. They turned down the central lane heading toward the market square and the town's heart. The market square was packed and bustling. A murmur began in one corner by the vegetable stall. Fingers pointed her way. A woman in black and gray broke away from the others and hurried over with a small cry, then, "Do my eyes deceive me?"

The voice sparked a memory. "Goody Newton," Anne moved quickly toward her, "it is so wonderful to see you again."

The old woman raised her hands toward the cloudless sky. "Praise be to the Lord of all," she cried. "This is indeed a miracle."

"Is something wrong?"

When the woman hesitated, Anne took a desperate hold upon Thomas's arm. "Tell me!"

"It's your dear, saintly father, child. He took a terrible turn not two nights ago." The old woman pointed a trembling finger down the lane. "Hurry now, there's not a moment to lose. May you arrive in time!"

Chapter 26

Anne had used every device in her meager stock, willing her father to regain strength and health as she bent over his bed. The herbs had been made into a series of hot infusions, and every time Andrew regained consciousness he had been urged to drink. She had prepared a strong emetic, saying the age-old words as she helped him swallow—that first it would make him feel much worse, then it would make him better. With flange and knife and bowl, she had bled him twice. When she had used the same treatments for Charles, he had improved. She had nothing else to go on, save that these were the ministrations that had helped bring her father's brother back to vigor.

Even at the worst moments, when Andrew was so weak he could barely raise his hand and her remedies were only making him feel worse, he would whisper to his beloved daughter, "I am so glad you are here."

After four endless weeks of tending Andrew's sickbed, Anne emerged from the cottage to a Sabbath morning awash in warm air and rosy hues. She walked to the gate and stood leaning upon the post, staring out at the empty lane. She lifted her face to the sky and heard the cottage door open and close behind her. The rustle of skirts signaled Catherine's approach.

"He is talking with Thomas," Catherine noted as she joined Anne at the gate.

Thomas knew nothing of nursing, but he would sit for hours beside Andrew, sometimes talking, sometimes listening patiently as Andrew attempted to converse.

"Thomas is a promise," Andrew had earlier told Catherine as she had stroked his hand, willing him to live.

"A promise of what?" Catherine asked, then wished she had not.

"A promise of tomorrow," Andrew had managed to say. "A beacon for all the morrows yet to come."

Catherine had gazed down at her husband, grasping at the hope in his words.

Now she said to her daughter, "He asked Thomas to take the pulpit today in his place."

Anne pointed out, "We have traveled here with two pastors from England. From what I've heard in the marketplace, they have preached most effectively these past three Sabbaths."

"That is what Thomas told Andrew."

"What did Father say?"

"That he would not insist, but he would consider it a great blessing if Thomas would agree."

Anne pushed hair back from her forehead. "Knowing my husband, I think I know his answer already."

The two women smiled at each other. Catherine stepped in closer. "I have been afraid to speak the words, but I think the critical corner has been turned—"

"He had no fever last night," Anne agreed. "His breathing is easier, and his pulse remains steady."

"The week after you arrived, I was seated at his side after you had gone to get some rest. I looked into my beloved husband's face," Catherine said, her whisper cracking, "and I saw death's door open before my eyes."

Anne reached for her mother's hand. "I was thinking of another illness—"

"When you lost your dear Cyril," Catherine said immediately. Her arms enfolded Anne. "My dear sweet daughter."

"All that first week, I feared you would lose your husband also." Her voice sank to barely a whisper.

They held each other and felt the sun warming their backs and necks. When the cottage door opened a third time,

Thomas called out, "Grandfather is in here burning the husks and turning the morning tea black as night."

"Good strong Sabbath brew, it is," the old man said over his shoulder.

"They also know the worst is behind us," Anne said.

"Of course they do." Catherine gave her daughter a final hug.

When Thomas walked to the church pulpit, Anne thought he looked as weary as she felt. She glanced at her mother, who also looked stretched to the limit and beyond. John Price had declined the walk to church for the morning service, saying he would stay with Andrew. Anne faced the front of the church once more and said a silent prayer for her dear Thomas, for her father, and her aging grandfather.

Almost in reply, Thomas's first words were, "Your pastor has asked me to speak for him this day. I am the first to confess that I hold neither the ability nor the insight of my father-in-law. So I ask for your prayers. I am happy to tell you that Pastor Harrow seems to be doing better this morning."

He waited through the murmur, then continued, "Though we have met over his sickbed, and though he has managed only a few words, still I feel a very intense bond with my father-in-law. I know this is partly due to all I have heard from my dear wife. I realize that it is his and Catherine's godly influence that has shaped Anne. So although I do not yet know Andrew well, still I feel his imprint upon my life."

Catherine's hand slipped into Anne's and squeezed. No word was necessary. Anne understood. She could feel it as well. Already she could sense the same spiritual anointing on her husband that she had witnessed in her father.

"I have no seminary training," Thomas continued. "My studies have been of law. And so I shall not be drawing the deep scriptural expositions and interpretations such as Pastor Harrow no doubt has granted you. Instead, I shall spend the few Sabbaths until his strength has returned to speak of other people like myself. People who were called from various walks of life to follow the Master. People like Nicodemus and Stephen and Peter, from the Gospels and from Acts. People who lived through times of great trial and distress. People who faced the upheavals of life with Christ's strength and wisdom. And we shall see what we can learn together."

Anne stole a quick glance around and noted expressions from curiosity to openness on nearby faces. As Thomas read the story of Nicodemus from the gospel of John, she sensed his audience gathering around him in spirit to listen, to explore once again the familiar story.

" . . . and this Pharisee," Thomas concluded, "a ruler of the Jews accustomed to power and prestige, came to Jesus with his honest questions. He made himself vulnerable, like a little child would come to his father. And this is our example. . . ."

A thoughtful silence followed the closing hymn, and slowly the parishioners, one by one, rose to their feet, as if pondering how closely their yearning for spiritual truth paralleled that of Nicodemus.

Catherine and Anne stood in the church's narthex as members of the congregation crowded around to greet them, welcoming Anne back into their midst and noting what a good sermon Thomas had preached.

The three finally were able to return to the cottage, their own demeanor rather silent and introspective as they walked along the lane. Anne's small pressure on Thomas's arm was quietly acknowledged with his grateful nod and smile. Anne knew he would be uncomfortable with further expressions of how proud of him she had been.

They were scarcely halfway up the front walk when the door was opened from within and John Price called to them, "I feared we would be forced to start without you!"

"I explained that you should not bother with cooking," Catherine remonstrated, hurrying ahead. "You were not even able to join us for the service. The last thing you should be doing—"

But John Price's chuckle stopped her, and he said, "We do have ourselves a very ample dinner, and I did nothing to prepare it." He swept his arm toward the kitchen and the three followed him to the doorway.

Anne and Thomas crowded in behind Catherine to stare at the table laden with a half roast, a pot of stew, and several clay jars of compote and jams and honey. There were dried bunches of winter roots and herbs. Pickled mushrooms. A bowl of sea salt. Cider.

"Several came after the service to share with us from their own meal," John explained.

"I don't know what to say," Catherine said weakly.

A voice from the back doorway replied, "Well, I most certainly do."

"Father!" Anne rushed forward and slipped an arm about Andrew's frame. Through the robe and nightdress he seemed scarcely more than skin and bones. "How are you feeling?"

"Hungry and impatient to rise from that bed." He smiled at his wife. "Did Thomas speak well?"

"He made us very proud," Catherine said softly. She moved forward and embraced him as well.

"Of course he did." Andrew allowed the two women to help him over to a chair that Thomas held for him. "Perhaps you will do us the honor of saying grace," he nodded toward his son-in-law. "It seems like years since I last ate anything that did not taste of my daughter's pungent herbs."

Chapter 27

Nicole watched as they sailed into a pale gray harbor. New Orleans at midday greeted them with scented mist and noise. After weeks of seaborne solitude, the clamor battered against her ears.

The humid heat was stifling. A strong wind had steadily borne them south around the tip of Florida and then back up the Mexican Gulf. But the breeze was nearly gone, and there was no relief from the damp and sweltering temperature.

The closer they came to the harbor docks, the more she recognized the familiar scents and odors of Louisiana—charcoal and spices and fried dough and roasting hickory coffee. Others came from oily smoke and muddy refuse exposed by the low tide and close-packed humanity.

A harbor pilot had come out by longboat to guide them in. Nicole heard him say to her husband, "With the tide as it is, Captain, I suggest you anchor out from shore and wait for the incoming sea to draw into berth."

"We have little besides ourselves to offload, sir. I'm quite happy to ride at anchor well away from the docks," Gordon replied. He paused. "Forgive me for noticing, but I fail to detect any hint of a French accent."

"Born and raised in Charleston," the pilot told Gordon. The man was a barrel-chested old salt, with long sideburns thick as fists. "The British burned me out. Made my way down here when I heard they were looking for good pilots."

"I am sorry to hear of your troubles, sir."

"That's the way of it, I suppose." He shrugged, then pointed at the flag upon the masthead. "You're flying American colors."

"That is correct."

"But you and your crew all have the sound of Limeys, if you don't mind my saying." Nicole knew the nickname had come from the new British habit of carrying the tiny fruit on all long voyages and doling them out on a weekly basis. A naval doctor, scoffed at by many, had recently suggested the fruit seemed to help prevent scurvy.

The pilot now told Gordon, "Here's as good a place as any to drop anchor."

Gordon turned to where Carter stood beside the wheel-master. "Come about into the wind."

"Aye, sir."

The ship made a graceful sweep until her nose was pointed into the sporadic easterly breeze. The sails flapped so loudly Gordon had to holler, "Release anchors and make her fast."

The crew leaped nimbly into action, almost running out along the long booms so fast it appeared they did not even require the rope-holds for balance. They gathered up the fluttering sails and tied them into place.

The pilot noted, "A well-trained crew, Captain. They move as if they were trained for battle."

Gordon understood the man's unspoken query. "My men and I came to the American cause as a unit."

"We're a fair piece removed from anyone who could confirm that. No offense intended."

"None taken. In such times a wise man always watches his back." He motioned to Carter. "Bring me the papers."

Clearly the suspicion had been anticipated, for Carter reached into the oilskin pouch slung about his shoulder and handed Gordon the packet. Gordon unfolded the letters from the American commandant of the Boston garrison and handed them over.

When the pilot saw the official seal, he murmured his

apology. "I have no right to be asking you a thing, sir," he added.

"I will be frank, sir. I would ask your lay of the land," Gordon said. "Which means I first require your confidence."

The pilot accepted the papers, studied them intently, then handed them back. "You're coming to buy?"

"We are."

"Then make yourselves ready for many hours of frustration and haggling." The pilot shook his head somberly. "A more rapacious lot than the New Orleans merchants I have never met."

Gordon looked him in the eyes, then gave a short nod of gratitude.

The morning after their arrival in New Orleans, Nicole woke up aching from head to foot. Her eyes would not focus, her body poured sweat, the slightest sound threatened to pierce through her head like a lance.

Gordon went ashore to find a practicing physician. The doctor, so rotund he had to be hauled up in the bosun's chair and then lifted bodily over the side, had the merry countenance of one who lived well.

"A flux," he declared in French after the most cursory of examinations. "Madame has come under attack from a summer flux."

Gordon hovered about her bedside. When the news was translated, he asked the doctor, "Will she be all right?"

"Oh, most certainly," he answered after Nicole's whispered interpretation. "Madame is young and evidently most strong."

"What should I do?"

"Madame must remain on board this vessel. The city air is foul this time of year."

Gordon asked her, "Would you prefer that, my dear?"

Though her head rocked painfully every time the ship

shifted at its anchors, this was a more comfortable prospect than lying in a strange bed in an airless hotel. "If it wouldn't be too much trouble," she murmured.

The doctor returned twice to check her progress, but Nicole did not learn of this for five very long days, as the fever kept her in a semiconscious state. Even when her fever abated and her strength began returning, the heat lay upon her like an oppressive coverlet.

"I have never been bothered by bayou weather before," she complained fretfully to Gordon the sixth evening after their arrival.

"This is not the bayou," he replied from his chair pulled close as possible to the cabin's open window. A constant clamor drifted in with the humid breeze. "It is the dirty, crowded harbor of a city, one that seems bent upon annoying me at every turn."

"What is the matter?"

Gordon had discarded his coat and sat with his shirtfront opened against the heat. "Nothing that cannot wait until you are better." He rose and moved to her bed to once more wet the cloth in a basin, wring it dry, and lay it on her forehead.

"I am truly feeling better already." She struggled to a sitting position, but he gently pushed her back against the pillows.

"I will tell you this much," he said, sitting down on the bed beside her. "Never did I expect to find a group of merchants more frustrating than those in Marblehead. But these Orleans gentlemen have gone those brigands one better."

"They are greedy?"

"They are the worst of pirates masquerading as gentlemen. They sit in fine parlors and serve coffee scented with roasted chicory from delicate china cups. They claim to be friends and allies both. Yet they refuse to strike a deal."

"Unless you pay," Nicole finished.

"Pay in gold," he confirmed. "At prices beyond belief. We might as well buy what we need from smugglers and privateers. At least then the money will remain within our own borders."

Nicole could not help but smile.

"You find humor in my news?"

Nicole repeated. " 'Do *us* good. *Our* borders.' That is what you said."

"Yes, I suppose I did." He sat up straighter. "I beg your pardon, my dear. I know your own loyalties cannot be as clear."

"My loyalties are to God first and then to my husband," she replied simply. She reached for his hand. "You are a man of great allegiances. It is one of your most endearing traits. When you give yourself to something, you do so totally."

Gordon gazed out the cabin window, then turned to her. "It's true, I admit. I have given myself to God, to you, and now to the American cause."

"My husband," Nicole said, her voice trembling with emotion, "I am indeed blessed."

Chapter 28

Anne carefully observed her father for another ten days before she was sure that Andrew was indeed better.

She was in the kitchen, waiting for the kettle's whistle. She poured water over the herbs knotted with string and resting in the clay mug. She used a spoon to swirl the water about, then pressed the herbs flat and set them aside. Andrew sat at the table, watching her motions with a mild frown. "Is it already time?" he complained.

Anne laughed. "I have added a touch of cinnamon and honey. Perhaps it will go down more easily." She had three different remedies she was using. The midday herbs were the ones Andrew found most objectionable. "Try this," she said, lifting the mug to his lips.

He sipped and grimaced but protested no further. Instead he patted the chair beside him. "Sit yourself down a moment. Where is Thomas?"

"I believe he is in the garden with Grandfather."

"Good." Andrew waited until Anne had moved to the chair. "I want to thank you again, daughter."

"There is no need, Father."

"There is every need." He lifted his mug. "I have no doubt these remedies of yours are doing me a world of good. But what truly saved me was your love. Seeing you again stirred my spirit so that I could not let go of life yet."

Anne reached across the table for his free hand. "I am glad," was all she could bring herself to say.

"Between the war and the distance and leaving your dear boy, I can scarcely imagine the sacrifices you and Thomas endured to come to me. How is our little John?"

"John is fine. Charles is like a second father to him. I'm sure he is fine."

"Charles. Yes, and his new wife, Judith. So many things to hear about. But not now. That is not what I wanted to speak with you about."

Andrew's hand in hers seemed so frail she was afraid to press his fingers too firmly. Only his eyes held the same fervor, the same strength of spirit.

"Anne," he said, "I wish to share something with you. Coming this close to death has permitted me a few moments of what I can only describe as a divine illumination."

Anne looked into his face and waited expectantly.

"While Thomas was seated beside me during those long hours," her father said softly, "talking about the work he shares with you and his fervor for our Lord, I am sure I heard God speak to me. It was not something I would ever have thought to say before now. But that is what happened, I am quite certain of it."

"What did He tell you?"

Andrew drew himself around. "Let me ask you this, daughter. What would be your response to Thomas studying for the ministry?"

"I would not object. How could I if . . ." Then, struck by the realization of what Andrew was saying, she whispered, "Oh, Father."

"I could not raise such a thing with him, not without first talking with you. I do not believe God gave to me an edict. He *offered* this. Do you understand?"

"I'm . . . I am not certain. Yes, yes, perhaps." Her mind was a jumble of disconnected thoughts and feelings. "I would love to return here. You know that."

"I know."

"But there is little John. And Charles now. All the responsibilities—"

"No one is asking you to decide just now. Of course there would be many considerations." He seemed to be simply musing aloud. "I wonder how Charles feels about England at this time."

"He loves his home, of course. But England?" The answer seemed to be waiting for her. "He despairs of his homeland," she went on. "It wrenches him, the course his government and his nation is to be taking."

"So his ties to England are not as strong as they once were."

"If pressed, I doubt he would feel much of any tie at all just now."

"Perhaps you might wish to discuss this with him as well." Andrew turned back to the fire. "The province of Nova Scotia is growing at an unbelievable pace. Georgetown has doubled in size just since this war began. There are problems everywhere. Having a pastor who is also trained in the law could ease the burden many of our poorer brethren carry. Not to mention the fact that here Charles would find numerous avenues for his largess, many people in need of aid, many worthy projects he could bring to fruition."

Andrew pushed himself up from the table. "I fear I can keep my eyes open no longer. Perhaps you should have a word with your husband. And with the Lord, of course. See if perhaps He will speak with you as well."

Anne watched her father move slowly toward the door, then folded her hands in front of her on the table.

Andrew slept away much of the afternoon. Anne scrubbed the kitchen, prepared the vegetables and beef stock for the evening meal, rolled out a tray of fresh biscuits, then went to seat herself on the sunlit front bench, intending to give herself over to further reflection and prayer.

In the space of several breaths, she was fast asleep.

The next thing she knew, Catherine was settling herself down beside her. Her market basket was perched on the end of the bench, full of recent purchases.

Anne straightened and pushed her dark curls away from her face. "I must have drifted off."

Catherine laughed and patted her arm. "I cannot tell you what a tonic it has been having you and Thomas here with us again."

"Of all the homecomings I have dreamed of since going to England," Anne replied, "this particular one never occurred to me."

"Who could ever have imagined such a moment?" Catherine quietly agreed. "But here we are. And at a time when I thought I should never laugh again, my darling daughters arrive. Struggling against the tides of war and man. Facing hardships I cannot imagine. Yet still they have come. And I am able to smile again. I have my husband back."

Catherine reached into the folds of her dress. "I have been carrying this around since your arrival. But you have been so busy, and the times so trying, I thought it best to wait a bit."

Anne's heart leaped at the familiar handwriting. "A letter from Nicole," she said eagerly.

Catherine was long in replying. "When was the last time you heard from your sister?"

"Ages and ages. Why?"

She handed over the letter. "She married her young officer, Gordon Goodwind, while they were here."

"Oh, Mother, I am so glad for her. And, oh, I wish I could have been here for the wedding." Anne's bittersweet emotions tugged at her heart.

"Nicole has grown into a beautiful lady," Catherine answered. "She is Gordon's wife. And her path is not yours."

"I don't understand. She has not lost her faith, I pray?"

"On the contrary. Her devotion, her love for God, is stronger than ever."

"What is it, Mother?"

Catherine pointed to the letter Anne held. "Read this, then we shall speak."

Anne hesitated, then said, "First I want to ask you something."

Catherine turned her face to the sun and closed her eyes. "Yes, please do so."

"There is no way I can put into words the anguish I have known over leaving my John behind. During the days and nights of this voyage, I have come to glimpse for the very first time what you must have suffered." Anne leaned closer and whispered, "Mama, how did you live with the loss, the wrenching uncertainty? How did you *survive*?"

Catherine was long in replying. "I survived because of my God and because of Andrew and because of you. As for enduring the unthinkable, there was no *intention* to my deeds at all." She opened her eyes and turned toward her daughter. "You, on the other hand, had the power of choice. I would imagine that was both a blessing and a curse."

The memory of days of heartache and confusion flooded back. "Yes. It was good that I had time to grow as accustomed to it as I could. But there was no way I could ever truly anticipate how it would be."

"Two loves divided by your loyalties," Catherine mused. "In some respects, yours is the harder course."

"For a season. Only for a season."

Catherine studied her daughter with wise and loving eyes. "Over the years, I have felt such a closeness to Louise through our shared distress and longing for the children we bore. Yet we both were sustained by the love we felt for the child we raised."

Anne rose to her feet and held out her hand to her mother. "Yes, love sustains us all. But we also need some dinner. It's almost ready."

The two women shared a chuckle as they moved to the kitchen.

Chapter 29

As soon as Anne had finished with the dishes, she wiped her hands on the coarse towel hanging by the corner basin, then let her fingers trail down to her apron pocket, where the letter, potent with mystery, was tucked away. The doors were open to a warm and welcoming breeze. The sunlight was strong one moment, then gone the next, as clouds chased one another off the sea and across the land. Anne stared out, debating whether she should go off by herself and break the letter's seal.

Making up her mind, she walked into the front room to tell the family she was going out for a bit of air.

They were in conversation as she entered, and her presence seemed unnoticed.

"If only Nicole could have stayed longer," Anne heard her grandfather murmur, his gaze directed to the fire.

"She remained as long as she could," Andrew replied, his own eyes averted as well.

"True, true."

The words were puzzling.

Anne changed her mind about leaving immediately and seated herself beside her husband, a frown furrowing her brow. She did not speak but waited for the next bit of conversation.

It was Thomas who finally broke the silence. "Nicole had to leave before she was ready?"

"Here and gone in three days," Catherine said, sorrow catching at the words.

Thomas looked a question at his wife. Anne shook her head in reply. This had not come up in Catherine's recounting of the wedding details.

"I certainly did not have enough time with the lass," John Price mused.

"None of us did. But we must be grateful for what we had," Andrew said.

Anne held the words in her mouth for some time, tasting the question. Her hand shifted to touch her letter through the apron's fabric. She asked, "Why was Nicole required to depart so soon?"

"Their journey did not end here," her grandfather said to the fire.

"I don't understand."

Catherine looked at her. "She is now making her way to Louisiana."

"She's going to see Papa Henri and Mama Louise? But that's wonderful news! How long has it been since she's seen them?"

"Not since they visited here," Andrew replied. "Not since before the war."

"Nonetheless," Thomas pointed out, "it seems a strange time to be making such a dangerous journey."

"They do not do it for themselves. At least, not for themselves alone." Andrew now was speaking. "The commandant of the Boston garrison has entrusted Gordon and Nicole to bear messages to the leaders of the Louisiana colony. And to bargain for some supplies—"

"Nicole is involved in the fighting?" Anne burst out in shock. "She's working for the Americans?"

"And Gordon?" Thomas had bolted upright. "A British officer has gone over to the enemy?"

Andrew's gaze drifted over, though his voice remained mild. "The Americans are not enemies. Not in this house."

"Of course not. They are not enemies in either Harrow

household. I fully concur with Charles's stand in support of the revolutionists' position." Thomas paused a moment, then continued. "But I do find myself thoroughly perplexed by Nicole's and Gordon's getting involved in the action. Surely the matter can be settled by treaty. By agreement. To actually be engaged in the war—"

"It is shocking, I agree," Andrew said. "But after the British stole Gordon's ship, press-ganged his men, imprisoned him, and threatened to hang him, I can hardly disagree with his choice."

Andrew looked directly at Thomas and Anne. "Gordon had made it clear he will not bear arms against his former countrymen."

Thomas rose and began pacing the front room. "Of course. Though I'm not sure he would be able to maintain that resolve if push came to shove. I have never met him, but I am certain Nicole's choice of husband would be a Christian and a gentleman. Even so . . ."

When her husband seemed unable to continue, Anne said for them both, "For Nicole to be directly involved in this conflict between countrymen who share the same heritage, at times the same faith, seems incomprehensible. How can they. . . ?" But Anne also drifted to a stop, looking helplessly from her parents to her husband, then to her grandfather.

John Price now cleared his throat and spoke up. "Nicole has spent her entire life searching for a home. I think she has found one to our south. In Massachusetts. In America."

Anne heard not just the words but also the calm assurance behind them. She again looked around the room. Catherine's face was serene in her inner certainty. As were her father's and grandfather's. Suddenly Anne knew she could wait no longer to read Nicole's letter.

She rose to her feet. "If you will please excuse me."

The point was empty. A few tattered wedding garlands shivering in the rising wind.

Anne seated herself upon the familiar trunk, the place from which she had watched the sea below the cliff, read favorite books, thought of the past, and dreamed of the future.

She pulled the letter from her pocket and began to read.

Before the first paragraph was completed, her sister was there beside her once again, the other half of her own life. Anne pressed the pages to her heart after reading the words, *"I am sitting here on our log in the meadow overlooking the sea. . . ."* Anne blinked away the tears and searched for the place she had stopped reading.

Anne was astonished by how matter-of-fact Nicole seemed to be about her dedication to the American cause, to their current mission. Anne halted three times during the initial read, staring out to the sea and asking herself, where did her own loyalties lie? The immediate answer was, *To the Lord above.* And certainly to Thomas and their son. But it was too simple. Too convenient. She thought about her uncle Charles declaring his support for the American Revolution, though it had cost him dearly. She had agreed with him, not so much because of strong convictions about the American cause, but because of the distress she felt over the course England and her rulers were taking, both against the colonists and against England's own poor and dispossessed. But it was also true that she and Thomas wanted peace. Peace and security for all. Freedom to live and worship God as one saw fit. A life lived in safety, children raised in lands sheltered from combat. Swords beaten into plowshares.

As Anne read on, Nicole made very clear her own abhorrence of the conflict, and Gordon's belief as a former British naval officer that he could not personally justify going into combat against England. Yet they both were acting on behalf of generals and their warriors! Anne rose and began pacing the point, as Thomas had done in the front room.

Anne halted toward the back of the meadow and reread the letter from start to finish. She did not want to argue with Nicole. She wanted to *understand.*

She looked up from the letter and found herself staring at a forgotten wedding wreath. One by one the last petals were plucked away by the strengthening wind and hurled upward to the sky. Anne stood and watched until the wreath was nothing more than a knotting of empty vines.

She lowered her head to her hands, and she wept. Though if asked, she could not have said the reason why.

Anne's days remained full with ministering to Andrew and helping about the house. At night the slightest cough from her father was enough to snatch the sleep from her. Free moments were filled with her mother and grandfather Price, repeating the news of Charles's search that Anne and Thomas had brought with them, including much speculation on what further might have turned up during the intervening months.

The diary of Catherine's mother provided quiet moments before the fire at night as they sat together and read passages aloud.

I cannot express my joy. I have been trying to do so all morning in my prayers heavenward, but there simply are no words. I am with child. I keep saying those words over and over in my heart. I am with child. I am quite sure of it now. It is a miracle. I will count the months—the weeks—the days—and then—oh, bliss—I shall have my heart and arms filled with a little someone. I know not who, but I am sure that God, in His infinite wisdom, will send me the perfect one to share my heart and feel my love. How I long to immediately share with John my hidden secret. He is so busy. So anxious. I know he feels that the frontier is no place to raise a child. Not with the French so close. So threatening. He does not trust them at all.

He is still unforgiving. I have prayed and prayed for his release from his bitterness. How I long for that day—and I pray that it will not be far in the future. But back to my wonderful secret. I will keep it tucked in my heart until I am really sure.

*There is no use causing him to fret for no good reason—and I
feel he will fret at first. He worries so about me, an adult, so I
cannot think how he will respond to our helpless baby in this
primitive settlement.*

*I talk to my little one sometimes when I am lonely. Oh,
not aloud. But she helps me through the dreariest of days. I
think my dearest John would have a difficult time understanding that, being such a no-nonsense person. He is so busy with
the matters of this new land I scarcely see him except in early
morning as I serve his porridge and again when his shoulders
already droop with weariness. I worry about him. He has so
much to bear. I am blessed to have been granted partnership
with him.*

In the hours of quiet intimacy, the fabric of Catherine's life
knit the two women more closely together. Though not by
birthright, Anne felt a connection to Catherine's mother and
to the French sister Grandfather Price had never known.

*It is getting near the time. I reminded John last evening as
we sat before the fire that we must think of names. He looked
surprised. I could not help but laugh. It was as though he thought
we were just to go on and on in our present state. I could almost
see him mentally counting the months, then nodding agreement.
I suggested the name of John if it is a boy, but he said he would
rather give the child a name of his own. He favored Reginald. It
sounds too military to me—like regiment, but I bit my tongue. If
John wishes his son to be Reginald, then Reginald he shall be. I
asked him about a name for a girl. I do not think he had ever
considered such a possibility. A girl? I think he deems our frontier
village far too rough and rustic for a girl. So he passed the need
for a girl's name off to me, saying that I should have the privilege—if perchance I gave birth to a daughter rather than a son.*

The next page brought joyous news, but the hand holding
the pen looked not as steady.

*Baby Catherine arrived an hour past midnight, five days
past. I think that John was stunned at first, but he was quick
to recover. I watched him with her today. I think she has already*

captured his heart. I should be jealous were she not so much a part of me. I have never seen such love shine from his face.

———————— ✣ ————————

Gradually the months and years they had been apart were filled with facts and thoughts and emotions. The two women discussed Nicole and Gordon's marriage in great detail, the way the villagers had gathered to celebrate with them, how the point above the cove was decorated like an outdoor chapel. Catherine's lovely gown was brought out, and of course Anne begged her to don it again. Anne reveled in the sharing, pushing away the sorrow that she had not arrived in time to share the day also.

Chapter 30

Anne emerged from the forest to find Thomas standing where the path joined the village lane. Thomas leaned toward her, questions in his eyes, but he only tucked her arm in his.

"A group of the French elders have asked for me," Thomas told her as they walked, "and Catherine is busy with Andrew, and, well—"

"You need a translator. Come, let us be off."

"Today is the time each week when the outlying French settlers visit the market," Thomas told her. "I would not have interrupted your contemplation, but with their long homeward journey, I did not want to make them wait overlong."

When they arrived at the market square, they found a large number of Frenchmen gathered by one of the last wagons. Her uncle Guy was not among them, but Anne recognized several other faces. The men all doffed their hats at their approach. Anne could not help but notice how the men seemed genuinely happy to see them.

There was no mistaking the Acadians. Most of the men were clean-shaven, with strong faces seamed by the sun and a farmer's hard life. Dark eyes normally sparkled with good cheer. Today, however, they glanced at one another before the man Anne recognized as a village elder said, "Your family is known to all as God's instrument in times of hardship."

Anne moved her head to use the bonnet's brim as a shield against the westering sun. Yet there was no sign in his expression of what lay behind the elder's strange tone. "You know I stand ready to do all I can for you and your clan," she said.

"Apologies, but not you, madame."

"My mother. Of course, she—"

"Not your mother, bless her, not this time." The elder nodded toward Thomas. "All the village tells us of the wisdom he has shown in God's house. He is also trained as a man of law and letters, is that not so?"

"Yes, that is true. But—"

"Then," the elder replied, "he may indeed be an answer to our prayers."

Thomas agreed to the meeting held three days after speaking with the French elder. For those three days people in the village spoke of little else. There was no place in the community large enough to hold everyone who wanted to attend.

John Price noticed. "Everybody who passes our house is watching and waiting."

"Apparently this issue has been building for a long time," Catherine agreed.

Thomas spent the three days studying the Scripture and praying. When Anne had wondered what he was about, he had simply told her he was making preparations.

Anne queried her mother, "You have known about this disagreement?"

"Not this one in particular. Just the fact that such a problem was bound to arise."

Thomas moved quickly to the door, saying over his shoulder, "Forgive me, but if I am to do my duty here, I must not be privy to any information in advance of the hearing."

Andrew rose to his feet and cast aside his quilt. "Do me a kindness, son, and help me out to the garden bench."

Thomas turned back to ease his arm around Andrew's

form, and Anne slipped her arm around his other side to help him to the bench.

"I am indeed proud of you, son," Andrew said as the two seated him.

"I have done nothing yet."

"You have done everything possible," Andrew countered. "You have equipped yourself with the armor of God, Scripture, and prayer, along with a fine legal mind. You are ready."

Commotion from the lane beyond the gate drew their attention. A steady stream of people were passing by the cottage, all of them headed toward the center of town. "Where are they going?" Anne wondered aloud.

"They're vying for the best seats to watch your husband wield the wisdom of Solomon," Andrew answered with a small smile directed at Thomas.

Thomas at first looked embarrassed, then sheepishly returned the smile. "Ah yes, Solomon it is," he quipped. Then he turned serious as he asked Andrew, "Do you object to holding this hearing on the church grounds? It seems to be the only area large enough—"

"Not at all," Andrew interjected. "That would make a fine place for a courtroom—the sky overhead, and all nature as witnesses."

———— ❧ ————

The grass in front of the church was covered with people, some seated on the ground, others standing around the perimeter. A murmur rose as Thomas approached with Anne at his side. Catherine had decided to stay at home with Andrew and John.

On the front steps of the church, Thomas turned to survey the crowd. A table and chairs had been positioned behind him, and an Acadian conversant in English stood nearby to translate the proceedings into French. As Thomas's eyes swept from one side to the other, the furrows upon his brow grew deeper.

It took Anne a moment to recognize what was upsetting her husband. Following his gaze, she realized the audience was firmly divided into two groups. To her left were gathered Acadian French families. To her right, the English settlers.

The gathering became absolutely silent before Thomas's obvious displeasure. "Despite different languages and cultures and histories, despite the wars and turmoil that surround us, still we are one people before our Creator. Our farms lie side by side. Our villages are so close it is hard to tell where one ends and the next begins. We shop in the same market." He paused for the interpretation, then raised his voice. "We gather in the same church. And now we shall all pray together to the same Lord." The French words flowed smoothly behind his.

"Let us stand and reach across the divide that threatens us here, and join hands as we ask the Almighty for His blessing and direction on these proceedings."

No one moved.

Thomas waited a long moment, then grasped the hand of his Acadian interpreter and held it high. "We shall join hands and hearts, or we shall disperse."

Slowly, reluctantly, people came to their feet and toward the other side.

Thomas raised his face to the heavens and prayed, "Do not let the world's thinking drive a stake through our midst, Father. Protect us from ourselves! Shield us from the temptation of anger and ire and division. Guide us, we pray. Grant us wisdom. Grant us peace." He looked out over the group, "And all God's people said . . ."

A great murmur arose from the gathering in both English and French. "Amen."

"Amen," Thomas confirmed. "Those who can, be seated."

In the slight commotion of settling once again, the central line of separation became indistinct. Families split up a bit, and hesitant smiles and cautious greetings stirred across the churchyard.

Thomas moved behind the table and motioned two groups forward. The Englishman came with four other men, the

Frenchman with five. Thomas turned to the Englishman first, since he could address this man directly. "Are all of you bringing this grievance?"

"Well, no, Your Honor. It's—"

"I am not a magistrate. I am a simple man with some training in the law, called by your village elders to act as mediator. You may refer to me as Mr. Crowley. So you all own the property in question?"

"No, sir, that is, it's my farm."

"I see. And your name is?"

"Joshua Reynolds, Your . . . Mr. Crowley."

"And these other gentlemen are. . . ?"

"Neighbors, Mr. Crowley. Friends."

"Tell me, sir. Are you afraid of standing before me and your God on your own?"

"Well, no, sir, that is—"

"Do you come here seeking to do battle? Are you coming here at the entrance to God's house seeking to make conflict?"

"It's them Frenchies there who've—"

"A simple yes or no will suffice, sir. Do you seek battle, or resolution?"

"Resolution." His head hung down.

"Fine. Then the rest of you men disperse. That's it. Go on. If Mr. Reynolds needs more strength than he can muster on his own, I will urge him to seek it from the Father of all."

Thomas waited for the four men to make their way back into the crowd, then turned to the Frenchmen. They seemed to understand what they had just observed, and the five Acadians melted back to their families.

Thomas inquired of the crowd, "You village elders, identify yourselves, please." The interpreter repeated it, and hands raised on both sides of the churchyard.

He then said, "I come here today seeking a divine answer for a thorny question. But I find a battle brewing. I will have no part in a conflict." He let that settle in a moment, then continued, "I will move forward with this task on one condition. All of you must agree that whatever decision is reached

195

here today is binding upon you all. Not just these gentlemen and their families but the entire community." He waited for the translation, then said, "Do we have agreement on this point?"

There was a long moment of muttered fumbling, then the Frenchman who had first approached Thomas called to his gathered clan, "Our only alternative is the English magistrate two days' ride from here. Should we wait for English justice?

One of the Frenchmen demanded, "What do you call this, then?"

"Look at what he has already accomplished!" The elder raised his two hands. "I have joined hands across the aisle that might as well have been a great chasm. The man to my right has been my neighbor for over ten years, but until Mr. Crowley instructed us to do so, I had never even shaken his hand."

The elder pointed at where Thomas sat. "I say, let us put our faith for justice in this man of God!"

Chapter 31

The two men, one seated on each side of Thomas, took almost three hours to each tell his story. Thomas then ordered a short recess. To Anne's astonishment, no one moved. Thankfully a gentle breeze had begun to blow in from the sea. Georgetown was close enough to the shoreline for the air to be both cool and seasoned with salt. Anne heard some children playing on the fringes of the gathering in the churchyard, but otherwise the people sat patiently waiting.

If Thomas noticed the throng at all, he gave it no mind. His attention appeared to be utterly focused upon the pages now spread over the table before him. Finally he put the top page down and rapped his knuckles upon the tabletop. "All right. I'm calling this hearing back to order."

Though the group was sitting quietly enough, Thomas's Acadian colleague repeated the announcement in French. Most of the settlers spoke enough English to make their way comfortably through a wedding or a market, as the saying went. But following something so complex as this was too taxing. Anne noted the man's careful efforts at the translation and was satisfied that he was capturing both the meaning and the spirit of the hearing and its various exchanges.

Thomas turned to the Frenchman. "Let me see if I have all the details correct here, Mr. Laroux. You have recently arrived from Louisiana, is that true?"

"Four months ago."

"And you claim that the land currently farmed by this gentleman, Joshua Reynolds, was in fact deeded to your family."

"For more than two hundred years, and seven generations of Laroux, my family has tilled this earth and tended the apple groves."

"Yet you have no actual documents to verify this claim."

"How could I, when the British soldiers forced us from our home in the middle of the night?" He was a slender man with work-hardened hands of a size for a much larger man. "The last vision I had of my beloved Acadia was of my family's farm and the farms of my neighbors burning like giant torches."

There was a stirring through the listeners, but Thomas gave it no mind. "It is vital we attempt to restrict ourselves to the facts of today, sir."

"But this *is* a matter for this day. Were it not for the expulsion, I would still be farming my land and raising my children in the home my grandfather's grandfather built!"

Thomas nodded through the interpretation. "Point taken, sir." Thomas turned in time to stifle the English farmer's protest. "Mr. Reynolds, you have had your chance to speak, and you shall have it again. For the moment allow me to concentrate upon this gentleman's words."

Thomas then inquired of the crowd, "Those of you who can verify Mr. Laroux's testimony, please make yourselves known."

Over two dozen men and women about the crowd either rose from their seats or raised their hands. Thomas said to Anne, "Do you know any of these people well?"

She pointed to one man standing midway back toward the left-hand side. "That is my uncle."

"His name?"

"Guy Robichaud."

Joshua Reynolds's obvious dismay bristled in his voice as he demanded, "How am I supposed to get a fair hearing, you being married to a Frenchie?"

Thomas did not respond immediately. Instead he first said to his wife, "Would you please translate his question for the group?" When she had done so, he countered the English farmer by pointing at Laroux and saying, "How could this French gentleman have expected a fair trial from an Englishman such as myself? The answer, sir, is that I seek not to serve one portion of this community, but rather find a solution that is acceptable and fair before God."

He then addressed the gathering with the previous translator following right after him. "Can any of the English community speak here to confirm that Mr. Robichaud is a man of honor?"

There was a long silence.

Thomas showed no ire whatsoever. "I cannot accept his testimony on something this crucial unless an English citizen is willing to confirm he is a man of honor."

"Aye, I'll do that for ye."

"And who might you be, sir?"

"Ian McDougall is the name."

"You are from Scotland, sir?"

"Arrived a year and a day hence, Your Honor."

"Could you tell us how you know this gentleman?"

"Didn't know a soul when I got here. Wife grew ill, cattle were sickly, crops weren't growing. Thought I was a goner. Robichaud here spent nigh on as much time by my homestead as tending his own holdings." The burly giant's beard quivered with fervor. "Aye, I'll stand up for Robichaud. And count it an honor to do so."

"Would you call him a man of God, sir?"

"Aye, I would. A papist, indeed. But he's bowed his head over my table more often than I care to count." He stabbed the air between them. "I'd call him kin for no other reason than the sweat he's dropped into my soil, and count myself fortunate."

"Thank you, Mr. McDougall, you may sit down." Thomas addressed the gathering. "Do any of you here know of any reason why this man's testimony should be doubted?"

When none responded, Thomas focused upon Guy himself. "Mr. Robichaud, how do you come to know about the former ownership of this disputed land?"

"Laroux's holding anchored one end of the village, ours the other."

Anne leaned forward and whispered to her husband. Thomas called over, "Is it correct that prior to the expulsion your own father was village mayor?"

"We called him the headman, leader of the council of elders." Guy remained where he was, hemmed in on all sides, fumbling with the brim of his black hat. "But it is true nonetheless."

"Would you have anything to add to the testimony you have heard?"

"Only that when Laroux arrived, he offered to buy Reynolds out."

"Is that true, Mr. Reynolds?"

The English farmer folded his arms. "I ain't selling."

"That was not the question. Did Mr. Laroux offer to buy you out?"

"Aye, he came traipsing in with some song and dance about how—"

"A simple yes or no will suffice."

"Aye. He offered. I refused."

"Thank you." Thomas returned his attention to Guy. "Mr. Robichaud, may I ask, are you currently farming your family's original homestead?"

"No, sir. I am not."

"Why not, may I ask?"

"Well, it's a bit complicated. You see, there were three families whose holdings stood where ours probably was—"

"Probably?"

"Yes, sir." Ancient shadows creased Guy's features. "You see, it was not merely our homes which the British soldiers burned. They torched our barns. They set fire to our orchards. Their plan was to wipe out every trace of our life and our heritage."

Thomas raised a hand to his brow and leaned his head on his elbow. "Go on."

"When we first arrived back, we searched and searched. But we could not be certain exactly where our farm stood. The road has been moved, new houses built, a whole new village. So as best we could figure, there are three farms sharing what once was our own land."

"Why is the situation different for Mr. Laroux here?"

"There is no mistaking where their land begins." Guy's voice turned more confident. "The Laroux family farmed a natural promontory. A rock cliff on one side, ancient woodlands on another, a steep rise climbing up behind."

"So this is definitely the same place where Mr. Reynolds lives and works."

"The new house is situated farther to the northern border, but—"

The chair to Thomas's left scraped back. Joshua Reynolds leaped to his feet and declared, "I ain't selling and I ain't moving. This is my land! Anybody come against me, I'll put them in the grave."

"You will remain seated." Thomas did not raise his voice overmuch, but his certain authority in the situation was clear to all.

"But—"

"*Sit down!*" Thomas directed a finger at the man.

Reynolds dropped like a shot. "He was the one who started it," he muttered.

"Started what?"

"Second time he came around, it was to say if I didn't take his money and move, he'd burn me out."

Thomas wheeled to his right. "Is that true?"

The Frenchman squeezed tighter in his seat. "The land has been my family's for seven generations."

"Have you people failed to learn anything from the tragedy that forced your people from your land?" Thomas was on his feet. "There is *nothing* to be gained from violence and bloodshed. Nothing!" Both hands came down upon the table. His audience was absolutely still. "You and your community elders have vowed to abide by my ruling. If you will not both retract these foolhardy threats of violence, I will order both farms and crops burned, the homesteads razed to the ground, and the earth salted!"

The gasp that followed his pronouncement was echoed after the translation had been completed. The two men's faces both were drained of color. Joshua Reynolds was the first to recover sufficiently to stammer out, "Y-you can't do that!"

"Can and will, sir. Can and will!" Thomas's iron will was unmistakable. He looked from one side of the gathering to the other, then back again. "We are surrounded by the most dire turmoil any of us have ever known. War threatens from every side. Communities like this one survive by only a fragile thread. Yet you would snap even this thread with your stubbornness and greed and hatred." His burning gaze swept the group once again.

"Your silence convicts you all." Thomas methodically gathered together his papers and deliberately stacked them. "This proceeding is concluded."

Even Anne was caught by surprise.

"I will present my decision in two weeks. Until then, I urge you all to pray for wisdom. Pray for peace." He stuffed the papers into his carryall and came around the table to stand at the top step. "Pray for us all."

Chapter 32

The journey into bayou country began with hired carriages to carry them from the New Orleans docks to the main ferry point. On the Mississippi's western side they hired boats large enough to transport both the men they would recruit and the goods they hoped to purchase. Once they actually entered bayou country, Nicole felt that time seemed to slow with the currents. The waters flowed green and inviting, and branches hung with green veils floated on the humid air above them. The air was laced with fragrances and sounds drawn from her earliest memories.

The journey into Nova Scotia, and the joy found there after a weary and difficult beginning, granted her an assurance of what was yet to come. Even so, there was no escaping how she was now feeling. *Do I belong here anymore?* she wondered. The softly scented waters of Cajun country no longer seemed like her homeland.

During the several evenings they had spent on their water-bound journey, when tents had been erected, the evening meal completed, and damp wood set upon the fires to ward off the insects, Gordon had seated himself at the fireside. He had taken to drawing out the Good Book and reading a passage aloud. The men he had chosen for this voyage were those most open to its message. His answers were often halting, as he himself sought his way forward through the questions of his men after the readings.

Nicole had reveled in the discovery of her new husband's depth of character and another aspect to his leadership of men.

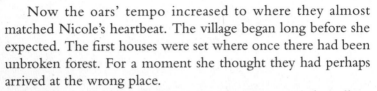

Now the oars' tempo increased to where they almost matched Nicole's heartbeat. The village began long before she expected. The first houses were set where once there had been unbroken forest. For a moment she thought they had perhaps arrived at the wrong place.

They rounded the final bend in the river, and the village she remembered was there before her. Some who seemed immediately familiar and others who were total strangers stared back at the trio of longboats.

"Alarm!" A voice cried in French from the riverbank. "Soldiers!"

"Peace!" Gordon shouted back across the water in English. "We come as friends!"

But consternation along the riverbank seemed to be heightened only further. Nicole heard French voices cry back, "British! British soldiers!"

The cry was taken up and spread like the sweep of human wildfire. More people were gathering there by the riverside. She saw glints of metal in some hands, heard the angry shouts. She opened her mouth to call out her identity but realized immediately that she would not be able to make herself heard above the tumult.

Nicole felt the tension around her as the crew grasped sword handles, but Gordon called to the men, "Hold yourselves back, lads. Keep the boats offshore and your hands out where they can be seen!"

"They've got muskets primed and aimed, Captain," murmured Carter at his elbow.

Gordon rose to his feet, turned shoreward, held out empty hands, and shouted, "Henri and Louise Robichaud!"

There was an instant's halt to the hubbub.

"Robichaud!" Gordon employed his foredeck roar to its fullest. "Henri and Louise Robichaud!"

The armed throng lining the riverbank was silent. Then a woman's voice arced high over the crowd. "*Nicole!*"

Chapter 33

Nicole's joy at the reunion with her parents was all too brief. Henri and Louise welcomed her home most lovingly. But when she introduced her husband, explaining how and where they had met, she could immediately sense their unspoken questions. *A British officer.* And she could hear again those childhood stories of their family's harrowing flight from the bloodshed and destruction at the hands of such as Gordon. They had learned to love and trust Andrew and Catherine because circumstances had placed them side by side in Acadian country. Tragedy had bonded them more closely than blood ties. But these men were not neighbors. Not friends. They were British. They spoke with strong accents, walked stiffly like soldiers, and looked far too much like a military presence, when the Robichauds and their neighbors wanted no reminders of a painful past.

Many villagers were adamantly hostile toward Gordon and his men. Their allegiance to the American cause mattered little to the Acadians, as did the fact that the Louisiana region and its Spanish and French consul-governors had declared themselves for the Americans. Here in bayou country, all who were not Cajun were suspect. The crew was forced to make camp in the farthest fields to the north. Gordon's daily walk out to their encampment was made along dusty lanes bounded by silent suspicion.

All it took was one brief glance into her father's dark eyes, and Nicole knew that similar suspicions had invaded the Robichaud home.

She came to dread the evenings. They gathered on the porch after their supper, out where they could catch whatever breeze might be blowing. Gordon would sit on the side railing in the twilight, peering intently at the pages of the Bible. She sat on a low stool at his feet, and her mother and father would settle in chairs at the porch's other side. Occasionally Gordon would lift his head to ask if he could read a passage aloud. At their silent acquiescence, he would proceed, each phrase followed by Nicole's careful interpretation.

Night after night she prayed for a miracle, even a faint shred of hope. She could not see a solution. Her parents and the other Acadians had wandered too long, too far, from the place that had been home to view Gordon and his men as anything other than their enemies.

Nicole wept as she prayed. In finding one love, she seemed to have lost another. She knew her beloved land was no longer a Louisiana bayou.

Besides the sickness in her heart, Nicole's body no longer seemed to tolerate the heat and the humid air, and she felt as ill as she had ever been. She had managed to make her way to the kitchen for breakfast. But she only nibbled at a piece of bread, and soon after she had found herself nearly overcome by dizziness and nausea. Louise helped her out to the front porch and settled her into a hammock. "I'll get a basin of water and a towel," she said.

The hand dipped into the basin, the towel was twisted dry, the cool cloth applied to Nicole's face. "You do not have a fever," her mother noted as she rose to her feet. "I am going to prepare some tea with herbs."

Nicole tried to nod, but the movement of her head made her so dizzy she thought she would fall out of the hammock.

She closed her eyes in hopes of vanquishing the nausea and waited for her mother to return.

She was lying like this when the scrape of heavier footsteps signaled the arrival of someone else. Nicole opened her eyes to find her husband leaning over her. Gordon reached out toward her brow, but then withdrew his hand quickly.

"I must go and wash. I—"

"What have you been doing?" Nicole asked, looking at his soiled shirt and pants.

"Your father has put us to work." Gordon looked over his shoulder at Henri standing on the bottom step.

"What have you been doing?" she asked again.

"Anything and everything." Gordon brushed at the dirt on his shirtfront. "The men welcomed the opportunity for some activity."

Nicole watched her father climb the steps to join them on the porch. Henri's English remained meager, but he must have been able to follow the conversation enough to add, in heavily accented words, "They good workers, these men." With a nod of approval, he added in French, "They have set to helping us raise the new barn. And this morning your husband and two other gentlemen weeded the entire north field." He nodded. "A strong back and willing hands has your husband."

"Please say his name, Papa." When he hesitated, Nicole pushed herself up on one elbow, though the porch tipped crazily at the sudden movement. "I'm asking you, Papa," she implored.

Henri's face crinkled with a smile. "But how can I get this old tongue around such an English name as this? Gor-don," he attempted slowly. The three laughed together, and Henri said it again.

Louise appeared through the door, bringing a steaming cup of fragrant tea. "You are here," she said to Gordon, motioning with her hand. "Good. You can help her sit up."

"Oh, Mama, I don't think—"

"Yes, you will feel better after you drink this." Then she

208

looked at Gordon's clothing and waved him away. "Henri can do it."

Her father eased his arm beneath her shoulders, and she couldn't help but groan as he lifted her to a sitting position in the hammock. She gripped her father's arm and waited for the world to stop spinning.

Henri's face showed deep furrows of concern. At this proximity, she could see how the winds of age and time had plowed deep fissures in the beloved features. "Oh, Papa," she murmured.

Henri must have misunderstood the emotion in her voice. "Here, let me settle you back."

Louise quickly instructed, "No, no, not yet. She must drink first." She pushed between her husband and Nicole. "Here, daughter, take a sip of this."

"I can't, Mama. Please."

"No argument, now." Louise carefully brought the mug to Nicole's lips, and she took a tentative taste.

"Again." Louise watched Nicole closely. "That's it. Drink it all."

Nicole could not help seeing how age was wrapping itself around Louise as well. She seemed to have settled into herself, growing thicker in body and shrinking in height. Silver traced its way through the dark hair and seemed reflected somehow in her mother's gaze, as though a life's worth of weariness, of strength, of hard roads and experience were imbedded there.

Nicole swallowed again, this time over the lump in her throat. "I love you, Mama," she whispered.

"There, did I not tell you?" Louise gave no acknowledgment of Nicole's bittersweet emotions. "Are you not feeling a world better?"

Nicole finished the mug, handed it back, and looked around in astonishment. "I . . . I do feel better," she said. "I think I am hungry."

Louise set the mug upon the windowsill and clapped her hands. "I knew it!"

"Louise, what is it you know?" her husband demanded.

"She is hungry! And look, see how the nausea has vanished?"

"It is a miracle, for certain."

"A miracle? Yes, a miracle." Louise laughed.

Gordon asked in English, "What is it? Are you feeling better, Nicole?"

Before Nicole could answer him, Louise reached over and hugged her daughter. "My darling Nicole." She then turned to her husband and declared, "Nicole is with child!"

Chapter 34

Gordon had looked at the three faces, obviously trying to determine the gist of Louise's joyful announcement in French from their array of expressions. When Nicole had finally found the words to tell him, his own face reflected shock, disbelief, and then joy as the truth became clear.

"We are going to have a child," he said, holding her hand in both of his. Nicole echoed his statement, not minding at all that his hands were not yet washed.

By the third day Nicole was feeling well enough to wash and pare the vegetables, a mug of the tea ever at hand. Working together with her mother at the simple chores affirmed her improving condition.

Nicole had found herself marveling at the simplest of things. The sound of her mother humming as she kneaded bread, the tread of her husband's footsteps as he left the house in the early morning, the smell of coffee brewing, the sight of a neighbor poling one of the village's flat-bottomed skiffs down the bayou across from their home—everything carried with it a special meaning and reminders of family, of memories, of the cycles of life.

In the evenings Gordon returned from the fields as weary as she had ever seen him, yet satisfied with the day. He would bathe in the shed Henri had built by the well, come in to greet her with a kiss, then kneel at her side. One work-stained hand would grip hers, the other would curve around her waist, and he would bow his head and hold himself still.

Louise finally asked in a hoarse whisper, "What is he doing?"

"You should ask him," Nicole said.

"But I speak no English."

Nicole simply looked at her mother.

Henri stepped through the doorway. Nicole held her mother's gaze for a long moment, then turned to her father.

Louise took a long breath. "Gordon," she said carefully.

He raised his head.

"What are you doing?"

When Nicole had translated, he smiled and said softly, "Praying for my wife and our child."

Henri leaned against the doorjamb and rubbed his face hard. "As should we all," he murmured. "Tell your husband—tell Gordon we welcome him to our family. We are happy for you, Nicole, and for the child who will be born." He waited while she translated, then added, "A new little Robichaud-Harrow-Goodwind"—he paused momentarily as he worked on the unfamiliar name—"to carry on the heritage of families joined by faith under the mighty hand of God."

Nicole and Gordon looked at each other as she said her father's words for him in English.

"It's a benediction," Gordon said quietly.

Louise used the corner of her apron to wipe her eyes. "Come, let us eat."

Henri sat at the head of the table, the covered dishes spread before them, and said, "Nicole, perhaps you would ask Gordon if he would bless this meal."

Henri and Louise's two sons and their families also were seated around the table, making sixteen in all. There was a faint shuffling as the two brothers shifted in their places. Each had a lifetime's collection of reasons to loathe this outsider. But

Nicole knew their respect and loyalty for their father was too great for them to protest outright.

Nicole's throat was so choked she could not speak for the longest time. The table waited silently as she collected herself and finally was able to say, "Father asks you to pray."

Gordon sat next to her, the tallest of the gathering. But it was not merely his height that set him apart. He held himself as a leader of men. Even here, at her family's dining table with the lamplight flickering and the last of summer's daylight glowing against the lace curtains, his presence was commanding. He now nodded to Henri in acknowledgment of the request.

"Father in heaven," he began, pausing so Nicole could translate his words, "we ask your blessing upon this gathering, upon this clan, upon this village, upon this nation, upon this world. We ask your peace to spread from this table out to encompass us all. We ask that the miracle which we see here, where people who have been enemies for generations can sit together and walk together, will be seen again and again until nations no longer are at war. We thank you for the divine peace. We ask that it be a blessing known by all. May your miracle come, Lord. We receive this food with thanksgiving. Amen."

Amen echoed around the table.

Though she could feel the tears in her eyes, Nicole did not make any effort to wipe them away. When she looked up, it was to see Henri's eyes also shining with unshed tears. His voice was gruff with emotion when he said, "Please thank him for his words."

There was no easy conversation at the dinner table, yet the quiet this time did not hold the strain that had marked earlier meals with the Robichaud family. Louise continued to set the mug of herbal tea at her daughter's place, saying that the more she drank at night the better her stomach would feel the next morning. Other than that, few comments broke the comfortable silence.

Toward the end of the meal, Henri cleared his throat and said, "Please tell Gordon that my sons and I are deeply grateful for the help of him and his men."

Both sons shifted again in their seats, but this time it was as though their father had opened a door for them. "None of us expected to have the barn completed in time for the midsummer harvest," the elder son put in.

"This is the most difficult part of our year," the younger son agreed. "Some fields are ready for picking, others for planting, and there is never enough help to go around."

"The barn was hit by lightning in March," Henri explained.

"We scarcely had time to get the horses out."

"All the produce we had stored in back was lost."

One of the children piped up, "The whole village smelled of roasting apples."

"They had their cider press too close to the barn. I told them that."

"The cooling cellar was under its eaves. The placing made all the sense in the world."

Nicole laughed and held up her hand. "Please, I cannot explain to Gordon so quickly—"

"Shah, shah, listen to you all," Louise admonished her family. "How can Nicole eat and talk so much?"

"I like hearing it," Nicole said, smiling around at all of them. "It sounds like family."

Gordon cleared his throat and said, "I confess there are two reasons for our help with the barn and the other things. . . ." He slowed to a stop, and Nicole quickly picked up with the translation.

Everyone around the table fell silent.

"First, because we are beholden for our keep. My men and I make it a habit of paying our own way."

"Well said," Henri replied, speaking to Gordon through his daughter but looking at him directly now. "And the second?"

"We have arrived with a problem." Gordon glanced at his wife. "Should I speak of this here?"

"If you wish."

"I don't know the proper protocol here for addressing such

a matter, and I don't wish to cause offense."

"Please," Henri said, "we don't stand on formality. Tell us of your problem."

"I represent the commandant of the Boston garrison."

"The *American* commandant."

"Yes, sir. That is correct."

"But you are a British officer."

"Papa, I have told you of this."

"I wish to hear of it from Gordon."

"You are correct, sir. I served in the British merchant navy for twelve years and two months. But more recently I have given my loyalties to the American cause. I have relinquished my British citizenship."

Henri waited until Nicole had finished translating. "So you can never go home."

"On the contrary, sir." Gordon's hand came to rest upon Nicole's. "I am home now."

All the family stared at the two hands resting upon the tabletop.

"Well spoken," Henri finally spoke, nodding slowly. "And what does the American commandant require of us?"

Swiftly Gordon outlined the problems—the lack of supplies, the blockade, the difficulties faced over pricing and shipping in New Orleans. "I confess that I accompanied Nicole here in hopes of finding another source of supply. One that would not gouge us so deeply as the merchants in New Orleans."

"The New Orleans traders are no friends of ours."

"They are pirates," the younger son muttered. "They offer pennies for our wares. Pennies!"

Gordon asked, "Would there be any chance of—"

The group turned as one toward the window and the clamor of voices.

"Not another fire." Henri leaped to his feet. "The fields—"

"I will gather my men." Gordon was already on his feet and moving to the door.

But when they reached the front porch, it was to find an

excited throng clustering in the lane separating them from the bayou.

Henri called out, "What news?"

"The English!" One voice rose above the others. "The English are leaving!"

"From the fort at Baton Rouge?"

"From everywhere!" A young man leaped into the air. "They are defeated!"

When Nicole translated, however, Gordon looked sober. "Impossible," he stated flatly. "The news is false."

Henri was watching Gordon intently. "Ask him why."

"Because the American forces do not have enough strength to bring a sudden victory. Their success is gradual, one battle at a time—"

But Henri was already turning to the joyous street scene to roar at the top of his voice, "*Hold!*"

The effect was an instant sign of Henri's authority. When the crowd's clamor died down, Henri called, "Gather the elders! We are holding a village meeting!"

Chapter 35

Henri ordered the village square readied for the meeting. Torches were lashed to poles and set in a broad circle. Benches were brought for the elders and set upon a raised canopy. Gordon's crew clustered to one side, just beyond the reach of the torchlight. Even so, as the elders climbed up on the dais, dark looks and suspicious expressions were cast their way.

Henri called to Gordon and Nicole to gather with him and the elders. He gave no indication that he heard the half-uttered protests among the crowd. He directed Gordon to one side of the dais and ushered Nicole to the platform's only chair. "How is your strength?"

"Adequate."

"We will not hold you here a moment longer than necessary." No longer the village headman, he turned to the new leader and asked, "Would you permit me to address the gathering?"

The young man seemed rather uncertain of his standing in such a moment. With evident relief he took his place at the front and announced, "Henri Robichaud is going to speak to us first." He turned and motioned for Henri to begin.

Henri paused till it was totally silent, then demanded, "Who brought the news?"

"It was I!" A lean man in sweat-stained leather riding garb stepped forward.

"You came from Baton Rouge?"

"I saw the fort with my own eyes. The British are gone!"

Henri let the hubbub resound for a moment, then lifted his hands for silence. "You heard that the British are defeated?"

"As well as. They have gone from every fort in the Louisiana territories!"

"Yes or no!" Henri's voice pounded back the hooray of the crowd. "Is there word of defeat?"

"Well, no, but it has to be true!"

"Does it?" Henri turned to his daughter. Gordon was leaning over her to hear her whispered interpretation of the proceedings. "Ask Gordon if he thinks this is defeat."

Gordon was already shaking his head before Nicole had finished speaking. "Unlikely. Nigh on impossible."

A voice from the torchlit night shouted, "You would trust an Englishman?"

"I would trust an American," Henri countered. "I would trust my son-in-law."

"He's been a traitor once. Why not again?"

Henri stiffened but did not respond directly. Instead he said to Nicole, "Ask Gordon why he thinks the English are not defeated."

"The British forces are enormous," Gordon began, speaking slowly. The crowd strained to hear Nicole's softer voice behind him. "I personally don't know the strength of their Baton Rouge contingent, but I doubt it ever numbered more than five hundred men. My guess is that they are an offshoot of the Georgia battalions. And thus the Baton Rouge outpost is relatively unimportant in the grand scheme of this conflict."

The crowd seemed to take this as a personal insult and began shouting their protests. Henri raised his voice and called out, "Let him speak!" When they were quiet, he nodded to Gordon to continue.

"I am familiar with the American strength. They cannot win at a direct assault. The British are too strong on the ground. The Americans win by attrition. A battle here, a battle there."

"Yet the British have left Baton Rouge."

"Which means the Americans are forcing them to strengthen the main regimental force. This is good news for our side. But not the ultimate good news for which we wait and pray." If Gordon was aware of the crowd's sullen hostility, he gave no sign. "My observation is that if they have withdrawn from here, it will be the same in Florida and Georgia as well. They will make their stand in the Carolinas. Or possibly Virginia."

"So the war is not over?" called someone from the crowd.

"I have no way of speaking for certain. But I think it highly unlikely."

"What would you guess is the coming course of this conflict?" Henri put in.

"The British will seek out a victory in battle on their terms," he replied without hesitation. "A massed attack of regimental proportions. And if they win, they will sue for peace. Which the Americans will refuse. Events have gone too far. The war has hardened feelings on both sides. There is only one solution to this conflict. The British must leave the colonies."

"And this has not yet happened?"

"As I said, I have no certain knowledge. But my guess is, not this summer. And probably not the next."

The original bearer of the news had held his peace up to now, but he obviously was furious at his loss of face. "But they have left Baton Rouge!" he shouted out.

Henri lifted his voice above the rising clamor. "I have led this village through both good times and bad! This has often meant defying what we would like to believe and preparing with caution. I have heard the news the same as you, and I have heard this American speak. And my heart tells me, this American speaks truth. If this is so, our troubles are not over. More distant, perhaps, and the threat is lessened. But we must proceed with caution."

He turned to Gordon. "Nicole, please thank your husband for his counsel. Tell him . . ." Henri's features seemed to flicker with the torchlight. "Tell him his coming has proven to be a godsend."

Chapter 36

Thomas had taken to long walks, sometimes lasting from after breakfast until the noon meal. He visited outlying farms. He passed through hamlets of six or seven houses clustered on every side of Georgetown. Anne occasionally accompanied him. She saw a new Georgetown, one that had grown so much she found it possible to lose direction in her own childhood hometown. In the afternoons they often took long rides by carriage, touring the surrounding countryside.

Wherever they went, either on foot or by wagon, the instant Thomas appeared, villagers would immediately acknowledge him with quiet courtesy. Anne thought they all probably understood his careful distance from them until he had announced his decision.

On the Sabbath Thomas had arranged for the younger of the two pastors who had accompanied them from England to give the sermon. The church was rather crowded, with some French families gathered among the English.

Anne's and Catherine's progress to the front pew was slowed by greetings in both French and English. Anne noticed how everything their family did was carefully observed. John Price leaned heavily upon Thomas's arm and his own cane until their little group took their places, kneeling first to pray, then seating themselves in a row.

The young English pastor, with members of his own community present as well, used his sermon as a call for peace. And the congregation became his example of God's hand at work. *Here we are,* he said, *French and English alike, newcomer and longtime settler. Together in God's house. Bound in peace.* It was a miracle, he declared, a picture of what could be if individuals and families, neighbors and acquaintances, countries and nations, put aside differences and did unto others as they would have done to them.

When the last hymn had been sung and the benediction pronounced, no one moved.

Finally Thomas stood and nodded to Anne. He helped John Price to his feet, then stepped from the pew.

The entire congregation stood with them. All waited as Thomas led his family from the church.

On the second Thursday market, Anne and Thomas walked through the village and came upon the Catholic priest who served many of the French communities. He was based in the village where Guy Robichaud lived, but traveled the distance from Truro to Georgetown, serving French parishes up and down the length of Cobequid Bay.

With the entire market frozen and watchful, Thomas doffed his hat. Through Anne he offered his greetings and asked, "You are aware of the situation we face, Father Phillipe?"

"The province speaks of nothing else," the priest replied directly. His English was heavily accented but precise. "From one end of my parish to the other, no other topic is discussed save what the magistrate will decide."

"I am not a magistrate or justice of the peace, Father."

"On the contrary," the priest replied. A slender man in his fifties, he stood a half-foot taller than Thomas. He possessed the voice of one used to addressing a congregation in the open, at times competing against the wind. The villagers around the square would easily have heard him reply, "I could think of no one who wears the title more deservedly."

Thomas fumbled with his hat for a moment, then nodded his thanks. "I am wondering if I would be able to sit down with you sometime soon—"

"Oh my, yes, I would be delighted," Father Phillipe responded quickly. "Would you care to join me for a meal?"

"Why, thank you," Thomas said, "and where should we come?"

"To the village of your wife's uncle." He smiled in Anne's direction. "The village where I believe you were born, is that not correct, Madame?"

"It is indeed, Father."

"This coming Sunday afternoon, perhaps?"

The warm handshake between the two men caused a ripple of quiet conversation around the square, Anne noticed.

The afternoon journey on the Truro road was a pleasure all its own. Sunlight fell like petals through the branches and leaves intertwined overhead. The horses clip-clopped in peaceful cadence over a largely empty road. The occupants of the few wagons they passed offered solemn Sabbath greetings. Otherwise Thomas and Anne were left alone to enjoy the warm summer afternoon, the birdsong, and the road ahead.

"I would like to ask you about something," Anne said.

Thomas took a long breath. "I'm sure you have wondered about my recent reserve, my long periods of time alone—"

"I understand, Thomas."

He turned in his seat. "You do?"

"I know you, Thomas. You seek to remind the community in their daily activities of your message. You intend for them to see you and remember. You want them to carry your warning and your demand with them. Wherever they go, whatever they do." Anne turned to look into his face. "I am your wife, Thomas. Of course I understand."

"My dear Anne." He seemed to have difficulty finding words.

"But that is not the matter I wish to discuss." Now that she had begun, her words tumbled over themselves. "I have tried twice to bring this up with Catherine. Both times she made clear, more by what she did not say than by what she said, that she simply could not discuss the subject. I cannot fault her for this. Of course I can't. How can I speak of something that divides her two daughters?"

Thomas instantly said, "Nicole's letter."

Her response was a single nod. "I have found it more distressing than I can say."

"Please try, Anne. Tell me," Thomas encouraged her.

Anne drew out the letter she had carried with her all week, yet had not been able to bring herself to read again. "I think it will be best if you hear what she has written."

Thomas listened to the entire missive without speaking. With him at her side, and knowing of his care and concern, Anne was able to complete the reading with a steady tone.

When she was finished, she refolded the letter and stowed it away. The carriage plodded on, and they traversed a small valley before Thomas finally said, "Tell me what you are wanting from me."

"I need your wisdom."

"Are you certain?"

"What can you say that will increase my distress? My sister has wed a man who was an officer in the British merchant service. He captained a ship lined with cannon and filled with swords and muskets and pistols. . . ." She stopped and swallowed hard. "I had thought he would be giving up this life as a soldier. But now I find he has elected to follow the exact same course but for the other side!"

"And he has brought Nicole with him into this new field of conflict," Thomas finished for her.

"How could he do such a thing? How could Nicole have allowed it to happen?"

Thomas spoke very slowly. "That is not all that disturbs you, is it?"

"No." She took a slow breath. "I know my sister. Nicole would not do such a thing unless she agreed with him. Unless she felt this was the right course of action. To involve herself personally in the revolution."

"That is not all, Anne," Thomas continued to prod.

"Excuse me?"

"What distresses you is that your sister has changed."

Suddenly Anne found herself choking back sobs. She clasped her hands tightly together to help regain control.

"Your sister is growing in a way that is not your own," Thomas continued, his gaze forward now upon the horses drawing their carriage. "You feel she is growing away from you."

"Yes." She swallowed hard. They were less than a half hour from the village and their visit with Father Phillipe. She would not allow herself to arrive red-eyed and tear-streaked. "That is it exactly."

"But there is something further, my dear." Thomas looked at her now and spoke with solemn conviction. "It is not only Nicole who is changing."

"What are you saying?"

"You are yourself altering course. You *both* are changing. How could you not? You are faced with impossible choices. A sick father, a child to take or leave behind, a journey through war, a village in turmoil. Of course you also are changing."

She released her grip to reach for Thomas's hand. She held it tightly as she said, "Tell me what to do!"

"Love her." He squeezed her hand gently, then said, "Pray for her. Hold her close to your heart. Ask for God's wisdom to infuse her every step. Ask for His armor to shield her from every danger, both seen and unseen. Make her safety and her peace a daily request. Bind her to your own life through your communion with God."

As the meaning of his words sank into her soul, so did a new realization. "This is what you are doing with our community, isn't it?"

Thomas looked her way without answering.

She lifted her hand and touched his cheek. It was uncommon for her to be so intimate in public. But the road was empty, and her heart was too full not to reach out. "You are binding yourself to this region and its future. You are praying as you walk, as you ride. You are making their concerns your own. You are trying with all your might to love them into wisdom, into taking the right course."

Thomas said nothing at all.

"Has my father spoken with you about his desire for you to return and take on the church and his ministry?"

"He has."

"What have you decided?"

"Little John is your son, Anne. Charles and Judith are family—"

"He is *our* son, and this is *our* shared heritage."

Thomas pulled on the reins, halting the horses. "You would return here to live?"

"I would. If that is what you decide."

"If it is God's will for us," he said quietly.

"If you decide to do this, it will be because God has directed you, has directed us," Anne replied. "Of that there is no question."

Chapter 37

They no longer spoke of the weekly mail delivery. To do so would have meant additional stress, yet the tension was always with them. For Charles, because the quest of John Price had now been taken as his own, and for Judith, because she felt deeply anything that burdened her husband.

They both knew the delivery of mail from the New World, slow in the best of times, was now in further jeopardy because of the war. Yet each week there was hope that somehow a miracle would be worked and a letter from their American contact person would manage to get through.

No report did not necessarily mean there was no news, Judith gently reminded Charles from time to time. It was difficult for her to see the disappointment in his eyes each time the mail failed to bring a letter either from France or from the New World. He would nod in acknowledgment, but she could tell he was still frustrated and impatient. Judith came to dread mail day.

She was in the back garden looking over the summer vegetables the gardener tended so carefully when she saw Charles walking quickly down the cinder path toward her, waving a sheet of paper over his head.

She knew in an instant what the letter was. She also knew what message it must contain. The look on Charles's face was enough to confirm it.

"You've heard," she said as Charles approached her.

"I have. I have."

"And it is good news."

"Wondrous. Ah yes, wondrous. Our prayers have finally been answered. He has found her. He is certain."

Judith sat down on the garden bench, and Charles joined her, spreading the sheet out on his knee with shaking fingers.

"Found her?" repeated Judith. "Really found—?"

"Well, not exactly found her," Charles said quickly. "That is, she is no longer living. But they have, with surety, located where she was taken and what happened to her. She did go to Canada, as we had been told. She was adopted there by a Huguenot family. Was raised and married there. In fact, they have also traced her descendants. She had three children, but only one lived to adulthood. I have even been given a name." He turned his eyes back to the page and scanned the written message. "It is here someplace. Ah yes. Right here. Celeste. That was the name of the child that survived." He lifted his eyes to hers again. "Pretty name, is it not? Celeste."

Before Judith could respond, he turned back to the page he held. "My man is off now to see what he can find of this Celeste. He has great hopes that she might still be living. An older woman in the village where she grew up has given him the girl's married name. She said they moved away. She was not sure just where. Moving from one place to another is common where there's not an estate to hold one to a given area. And with the war . . ." His words trailed off. It was not necessary to remind Judith that folks in troubled times often were forced to flee for safety.

"He has done well," Charles declared, looking pleased with the efforts of the man he had sent to investigate the whereabouts of John Price's missing half sister. "Remarkably well, under the circumstances."

"You will inform them?" asked Judith.

For a long moment Charles was silent. Judith could tell that he was thinking carefully before answering. At last he shook his head slowly. "I think not. Not yet. There is too much uncertainty that remains. We will see where this next lead . . ." But

Charles came to a halt while he sat thinking. "No, I think that is wrong. They should have the excitement of knowing what we have discovered to this point. We are getting close, and they should know."

He stood. "You are quite right, my dear. I should let them know immediately." He bent over and kissed the top of her head. Judith wondered just what she had said that he would credit her with being right, but she just smiled.

"You just enjoy this delightful sunshine," he said with a pat to her shoulder. "I am going in to dash off a letter to Andrew and Catherine. And John."

Judith was still smiling as she watched him go. He might dash off a letter and get it in the post, but barring a miracle, she knew it could be months and months—if ever—before it reached its intended goal. Then her smile widened and she looked up at the blue sky. "Thank you, Lord," she whispered. What was one more miracle? They already had been blessed with so many. Surely God could provide one more.

Chapter 38

Anne looked around at the family from the doorway to the kitchen. Everyone save Andrew seemed wrapped up in the meeting to come. Thomas sat rocking softly, sipping from his mug, gazing reflectively into the dark fireplace. John Price sat in the other chair and cast little glances at Thomas. Catherine was in the kitchen packing apples and cider and cheese and half a loaf of bread to take with them into town.

After breakfast Andrew had returned to his room, as he often did. He had improved greatly in the past weeks, but it was becoming clear to all that his strength would never fully return. At the time, no one had any interest in discussing a future beyond the day.

When Andrew emerged from the room a short time later, he had changed into a pair of pressed dark trousers and a starched shirt.

"Are you going to town?" Catherine asked, coming into the living room with Anne close behind her.

"That depends upon Thomas," Andrew said, easing himself onto the bench nearby.

Thomas made to rise. "Forgive me, Father. I have taken your seat."

"Remain where you are, please. I am wondering if I may come with you today."

"I would count it an honor."

Andrew was observing his son-in-law very closely. "I have

the impression that you know what decision you are to render today."

Thomas merely returned Andrew's gaze.

"In fact, I am thinking that you have known for quite a while now."

"Since the day they set the matter before me," Thomas affirmed quietly.

"I don't understand," Catherine exclaimed. "If you have known all this time, why did you require the delay in announcing it?"

"He did not require the time for himself," Andrew replied. "He did it for the village."

Thomas spoke to Catherine, yet kept his gaze upon his father-in-law. "There was a risk that if the matter had been swiftly resolved, they would see it as a simple issue."

"The problem was never the farm," Andrew said.

"Never," Thomas agreed.

Catherine looked from one man to the other. "But—"

"The elders did not request my help because they could not find the answer themselves. They asked because they needed someone who could speak to the angry and the discontented within *both* communities," Thomas replied. "They needed not an impartial judge who would speak of laws written by a distant hand. They needed someone who was both within and without."

"They heard you speak from the pulpit, and they knew they had found their go-between," Andrew said.

Slowly Thomas shook his head. "That was only part of it."

"What else, then?"

Thomas turned and looked at Anne.

"Of course," Andrew murmured.

"They know your daughter's story, the Acadian child lovingly raised by an English family. My time in the pulpit might have been my introduction to the English in the community. But the French elder approached me because of my connection to Anne, the woman they still claim as their own."

For Anne, the moment was captured in the sudden stillness.

Her grandfather in the chair, her mother near him, and her husband and her father sharing a quiet smile. She knew she would remember it for all her remaining days.

When Thomas drew out his pocket watch and rose to his feet, the little group stirred itself again.

"Yes, well," Thomas said, "we shall see what happens. It is in God's hands."

"Amen," said Andrew.

———— ✿ ————

Anne's grandfather had declared himself unable to remain at home. Such momentous events do not come but so often, he had explained. Andrew smiled his approval as John Price had slipped into his jacket. The two gentlemen said they would start out early on the way into the village so as not to slow anyone else down.

John and Andrew fell into step with Catherine and Anne and Thomas outside the churchyard gate. Together they made their way through the throng and up to the front steps. Chairs were quickly offered to Andrew and his family.

Thomas nodded to his French interpreter, and the two made their way up to the table and chairs. The Acadian farmer and the English homesteader were already there, hats held in their laps and avoiding Thomas's eye.

Anne watched her husband turn and glance at Andrew. She saw her father give a brief headshake. Instantly she understood the exchange. Thomas had asked Andrew to say the opening prayer, and Andrew had declined.

"Let us bow our heads," Thomas said, and he led them in a prayer for wisdom, for peace, each sentence repeated by the translator.

Thomas remained standing and said, "Before the proceedings may continue, we must first establish the framework. We all are part of God's community. We must not simply accept the words, we must *live* this. Our deeds—both great and small—must reflect our brotherhood." He turned to where the two farmers stood, separated by the table. "Please shake hands and apologize for words that never should have been uttered."

The two weeks must have had a profound impact on these two men. Neither of them hesitated an instant. The words they spoke were inaudible, but the expressions on their faces were clear to all.

Thomas waited until the pair had returned to their seats. He raised his hands and said, "Let us all turn and offer one another the peace of our Lord Jesus Christ."

The response was immediate. A joyful commotion filled the air as English and Acadians, farmers and merchants, shook hands and greeted one another. Anne turned and embraced her grandfather, her mother, and her smiling father. Thomas made his own way down the steps, grasping hands as they reached for his.

When he returned to the front table, he motioned for all to return to their places. "I have studied the evidence placed before me," he said, looking over the now-silent crowd. "And I have reached a finding."

He waited for the translation, then continued, "I declare that *both* men have a valid claim to the property in question."

A quiet rustling ran through the assembly. But there were no protests, not even from the two farmers seated on either side of him. Thomas continued, "It is also clear that the land in question is not large enough to support two families. Nor would their proximity promise long-term peace. And that is what we are after here. A resolution that will satisfy not just their *rights,* but guarantee their *peace.* Theirs, and that of the community at large."

He turned to the Acadian farmer. "Mr. Laroux, a question, if you please, sir."

The farmer sat up straighter.

"Cast your mind back to the time of the expulsion. It is true, is it not, that your entire holdings were burned to the ground."

"That is correct, Monsieur Crowley," he agreed through the interpreter.

"Your home was destroyed."

"Utterly, Monsieur."

"Your barns also went up in flames."

"I watched the fires light up the sky."

"Your orchards were also torched."

"The smoke was a pillar that burns still in my dreams."

"You were how old at the time?"

"Eleven."

"This is a terrible tragedy that no one should ever be forced to endure. Most especially not a young child." Thomas offered his hand. "Sir, on behalf of the British nation at large, I offer you my most sincere apologies. There is nothing I can do or say that will remove the stain of this most awful event. I, with all my countrymen, stand condemned. I humbly beg your forgiveness."

When the Acadian had finished translating, the farmer rose to his feet and took Thomas's outstretched hand.

Another tumult filled the church, subsiding only when Thomas watched the farmer seat himself and then turned to the Englishman. "Mr. Reynolds, you have been tilling this soil for how long now?" he asked the Englishman.

"This will be my twelfth planting season."

"When you arrived on the land, what did you find?"

"It had lain fallow so long the weeds and saplings stood higher than my head."

"Yet you knew it had been farmed before."

"Aye, there was no question that sometime in the distant past it had been tilled. The furrows were overgrown, but a farmer knows, sir." He looked at the Acadian and nodded soberly. "Aye, a farmer knows."

"How did you come to select this land as your own?"

"Why, it was chosen for me. I landed in Halifax and went to the land office with all the other new arrivals. This was the tract I had purchased. I signed the deed and bought my goods and loaded my family and made my way here. Simple as that."

"So you did not know if anyone else might lay claim to the land."

"Far as I knew, it was mine and mine alone. That is . . ."

"Yes, go on."

"Well, sir. The neighbors, they came to tell us of the tragedy. And that first planting, we came upon ashes in the topsoil." He lowered his head and his voice dropped. "Ashes everywhere."

The Acadian farmer covered his eyes with a work-scarred hand.

"You built a new home for yourself, did you not?"

"Aye, that I did. With the help of many gathered here today, sir."

"If I recall correctly from what Mr. Guy Robichaud reported, you chose to site your home somewhat away from where the original Laroux homestead was situated." Thomas waited through a heavy silence, then said more softly, "Was that decision taken because of the ashes as well, sir?"

The English farmer replied in a voice so soft it scarcely carried beyond the front rows. "Aye."

"You sought to remove your own family from whatever calamity had befallen those who had lived and farmed here before."

"Aye."

"You built a *new* home. You planted *new* crops. You watered the earth with your own sweat. You have established a *new* homestead."

The farmer lifted his head. "Aye, sir. I have. All that and more."

Thomas moved in a slow circle about the table.

He returned to his place behind the table and lifted a jug of fresh-pressed cider. "At our last gathering someone gave this to us to quench our thirst. Who can say whether the apples were French or English? How many different hands took part in carrying it forward?"

He walked down to the front and placed his hand upon his wife's shoulder. "My own beloved wife carries this same question each and every day of her existence upon this earth. Is she French? Is she English? Who can lay claim to her heritage?"

He turned back to the Acadian. "Mr. Laroux, it wrenches my heart to have to say this. But there is no escaping the fact. Sir, your farm is no more."

The Acadian farmer might have nodded. Or it may have simply been the shiver of a man seeking to maintain control. But his dark gaze did not waver from Thomas's face.

"I cannot order you to place the past behind you. That is your choice. But I can ask you to ponder this question: What inheritance do you seek to pass on to your children, and your children's children, and all the generations still to come? Is it a land salted with bitterness and gall? Or do you seek to leave them with a peace and security within which they might build their own hopes and aspirations?"

Thomas turned back to the congregation. "Here, then, is my decision. Mr. Laroux will have the right to choose whatever land he wishes from any that now lies fallow. He will take his time. He will search out the finest property that awaits him. He will make his selection. And then the entire community will join forces to buy this land for him."

A stirring ran through the gathering, but Thomas raised his voice to continue, "Not only that!" When the murmurs subsided, he went on, "Not only that, but all will aid him in building as fine a home as can be found here. A home, barns, corrals. *All* will give. None will rest until Mr. Laroux himself declares that he and his family are not merely grateful, but satisfied."

He then turned to the English farmer. "Mr. Reynolds, will you help?"

"I'll do more than that, sir." Joshua Reynolds was rising to his feet. "I will offer him from the best that I have."

"None here could ask more." Thomas turned to the Acadian. "Mr. Laroux, I began these proceedings with a declaration that all must abide by my decision. Sir, I hereby free you from this obligation. No one who has suffered as you and your family should have anything this momentous forced upon you. I do not order you, sir. I am simply asking you. Accept this, and with it build a future for yourself, for your family, and for the community at large."

The Acadian rose to his feet. In heavily accented English he replied, "I accept. And I thank you."

Chapter 39

Nicole had regained her normal strength and vigor by the time the produce and village wares were purchased and readied for shipment to New Orleans. An elder and a village trader were dispatched to New Orleans to contact a reputable ship-owner. With Henri's assistance, a new plan had been formulated. Everything possible was to be acquired within the bayou villages. The merchants of New Orleans were to be circumvented, except in the case that the villages could not supply the wares. And even here, the village trader and elder would act on Gordon's behalf. Thus the extra profit would come to the villages and not to the city merchants. The development of these plans had done much for Gordon's and his men's full acceptance within the Acadian community.

Gordon and Nicole were sitting in their favorite spots on the front porch, he on the railing to catch any breeze that might happen by and she moving slowly back and forth seated in the hammock.

"Have you told them yet?" Gordon was asking as Louise came through the door with a tray of tea mugs.

"Tell us what?" she said.

Nicole looked at her mother. "I thought you didn't speak English."

"I understand as much as I need to. What do you want to tell me?"

"Where is Papa?" Nicole asked.

"Out back."

"Perhaps you should fetch him."

When Louise returned with Henri, the three of them sat clustered by the side railing, their backs to the street. It was the common signal to all who passed that they were not welcoming either guests or idle talk. Gordon did not join them, as that would have required translating, and he was only too aware of the topic.

"You are seeking a way to soften ill tidings, yes?" Henri said, his voice gentle.

"How . . . how did you know?"

Henri shrugged. "It is a headman's worst duty. Go ahead, child. Speak to us."

She took a breath. "Father Andrew is ill. Very ill."

Louise tightened her grip on her apron. "You mean he was when you left Acadia."

Nicole returned her mother's gaze without speaking.

"Daughter, what are you saying?"

"It is his heart."

Henri finally asked, "Is he dying?"

"He may already . . . have passed over." Nicole could barely say the last words.

Louise was on her feet. "I must go to Catherine."

"Louise, please." Henri reached for her hand and urged her back to her chair.

"But—"

"Wait, my dear. Just one moment further." Henri called Gordon over, and indicated that he should draw up a chair.

"Daughter, ask your husband how we might travel north in safety," Henri said.

"We?" Louise stared at her husband. "You would leave the village?"

"The new headman might actually benefit from having me gone for a season," Henri replied. "Too often he turns to me for advice. He is a good man. He needs to learn to trust more in his own wisdom. As does the village."

"You have been planning this?"

"I had thought it would be better to wait until the conflict was over. But, yes, I have been searching for a reason to travel back to Acadia again."

Louise leaned back in her chair, astonishment in every feature.

Henri said, "Ask Gordon what he thinks."

When Nicole had finished translating, Gordon replied, "The voyage to Boston is not the problem."

"But from there?"

"If there have been American victories on land, my guess is the same is happening at sea. The British are determined to hold on to the northern colonies. The occupants there have always been more strongly loyalist. If the British withdraw, it will be to form a protective shield around the Nova Scotia coastline."

"This is not good," Henri mused. "Not good at all."

"There is one possibility," Gordon ventured. He turned to his wife. "Forgive me, I should have spoken with you about this in advance."

"You intend to take the ship back to her British owners."

"You knew this?"

"You have made no secret of your hopes." Nicole sighed. "To do this, you will have to purchase the vessel and request a safe passage."

Louise put in, "What are you two saying?"

Nicole did not turn from her husband. "Gordon, there is too much risk of the British imprisoning you."

Gordon began shaking his head, then stopped. "Much as I would like to return the vessel myself, I confess that you are right."

Nicole was filled with relief and leaned back in her chair.

"That leaves us, of course, with the problem of where to find a British skipper and crew."

"I have every confidence you will think of the proper course." Nicole turned back to her parents and announced in French, "We may have the beginnings of a plan."

Chapter 40

It was decided that Gordon and some of his crew would go ahead to New Orleans with two of the longboats, stuffed to the gunwales with produce, planning to use the accompanying village trader to acquire what must be bought and ready the vessel for departure. Nicole, with Henri and Louise, would travel downriver in the third longboat, accompanied by several more of the village's own flat-bottomed craft. The town threw a feast on the evening of Gordon's departure. By then the majority of the community had found reason to feel grateful for the American crew.

Two days after Gordon left, the entire village turned out to see Henri and Louise off. There were tears and a crowd of excited children who followed the boats on land far beyond the outskirts of the town. Gordon had split his crew, leaving Carter in charge of the men to guard and pilot Nicole and her parents.

Each bend in the bayou took them into swifter waters as they aimed directly for the Mississippi. The closer they came to the new nation's great artery, the stronger grew the currents. On the afternoon of the second day, with their rivulet swooping and curling around the prow, Nicole gripped the gunwale with one hand and her mother with the other, sure no one had ever traveled any faster than she did at that moment.

Though a dry summer had reduced the river by a third and more, according to the Acadian pilot guiding their craft, Nicole was amazed by the river's girth and power. The banks were two miles apart, and with each passing hour they grew broader still. By the time the river emptied into the bay fronting New Orleans, the waters had calmed to a steady, gentle flow. When the tide changed against them, the rowers had to pull hard to progress out to where the big sailing ships lay at anchor.

They saw Gordon's vessel just as the sun was setting. Eventually he spotted them and leaned over the quarterdeck's railing to call, "Your arrival could not be more providential! The customs officers have just left!" He waved to where Carter sat amidships. "Draw all the vessels around to the side away from the dock. We must make all haste in off-loading your supplies!"

As Nicole was helped onto the deck, her husband clasped her hands warmly, the promise of a more intimate embrace in his eyes.

They all worked at a feverish pace through the gathering dusk. Nicole and Louise took charge of the supplies destined for the ship's own larder, as these had to be stowed where they could easily be found. Henri remained on the river craft and supervised the Acadians. Even the pilots were enlisted to help. All had experience with the customs officials of New Orleans and counted them from the same tribe as the merchants.

After the final daylight had vanished, Gordon insisted they continue working on by moonlight. He called Nicole over and through her asked of Henri, "How much is left?"

"The last third of this skiff and another." Henri wiped the sweat streaming from his face. "With a bit more light, we could be done in another hour or two."

"We must complete the loading before dawn," Gordon said.

Henri nodded agreement, then turned to the men and called, "We must make all haste!"

Torches were lit and positioned alongside the human chain hauling the produce and wares up and over the gunwales, then stowing them in the lower holds. A second winch was fashioned and anchored farther along the railing. Even the bosun's chair was called into use, hauling up the largest of the items.

"Ho!" the lookout called down from the crow's nest, then

pointed out to shore. "A trio of shore craft are headed this way!"

"Silence!" Even the Acadians understood Gordon's tone and stopped in place. Gordon called topside, "What manner of men?"

There was a long pause, then the reply, "I can't make out much in this light . . . muskets! I see muskets, sir!"

"You are certain?"

"Aye, Skipper! A detachment of soldiers with bayonets fixed!"

"All hands!" Gordon shouted. "Make sail!"

Henri called a question, and Gordon turned quickly to Nicole.

"He says there is still the one vessel to—"

"Tell your father to climb aboard. With all haste! Carter!"

"Here, sir."

"Lash one of the skiffs to the stern for the pilot. Nicole, ask their most experienced pilot to remain and mark our way out of the channel. The rest of them are to scatter to the winds!" Gordon wheeled about. "Weigh anchor! Make course for open water and north!"

Chapter 41

When the news began to filter into Georgetown, it was mostly discounted. The reports were too farfetched, the possible results too far ranging. Besides, a place as remote as Georgetown was a hotbed of rumors. Actual news was so slow in arriving, those who hungered after word from the outside world often accepted speculation and spoke it around enough to make it fact. Thus many households, Catherine and Andrew's among them, preferred not to hear spoken reports at all. Not only was it more reliable, it kept the outside threats at bay. At least, it had worked in this fashion most of the time.

But two weeks after the hearing and Thomas's ruling, the market stirred with an undercurrent of uncertainty. Virtually all the English were also loyalists. Even the Dissenters who had recently emigrated saw themselves as subjects of the Crown, so long as the king lived up to his God-given responsibilities.

Over Friday's dinner Catherine finally ventured, "You know, Andrew, it is not my custom to bring home market rumors."

Both Thomas's and Andrew's faces took on pained expressions. Anne spoke up before they could object. "I am so glad you decided to say something, Mother. If you had not, I would."

"There has been nothing from Halifax," Andrew stated. He had resumed his monitoring of the broadsheets and papers brought in on the weekly wagons.

"That might be expected," Catherine replied, "if the news was not good."

It was as much her tone, and the guarded expression to her face, as what she said. The four sat in silence a long moment before Thomas offered, "Perhaps I should take a turn with you through the market tomorrow."

"We would be most grateful," Anne replied as Catherine nodded.

When the three set out the next morning, a chill breeze blew in off the headlands, carrying with it enough sea damp to turn Anne's cloak leaden. Even Thomas turned up his collar against the chill. The surrounding summer greens were cloaked in a windblown mist, while overhead rolled wave after wave of slate clouds.

Their arrival at the market's border caused a hush, as it had whenever Thomas had appeared since the assembly. But he took it in stride, walking among them and offering warm greetings to all he recognized. Gradually the normal bustle returned, though the group remained surrounded by a respectful quiet.

Thomas said to Catherine, "If you had to choose one person here whose word you could trust, who would that be?"

She must have anticipated the question. She answered immediately, "The greengrocer Adams. They drive their own cart to Halifax and back twice a week."

"He is an elder in the church, is he not?"

"Yes, Mr. Adams is an elder."

"Ah yes, there he is. I recognize him now." Thomas doffed his hat. "A very good morning to you, Mr. Adams."

"Why, if it isn't the magistrate himself. And his lovely wife. And Mrs. Harrow." The man's face shone bright despite the dull day. "To what do I owe this honor? I do hope no one is out for my place in the square!" he added in jest.

"No, nothing like that." Thomas paused, then said, "A reminder that I am not a magistrate."

"Magistrate or reverend, sir, you may take your pick." The man leaned over the boxes of squash and sweet potatoes. "And Georgetown is fortunate to have you as both, your honor, sir.

If you don't mind my saying. Especially in such times as these."

Anne said, "We have been hearing the most unlikely of rumors."

"Were they only rumors, Missus. Were they indeed," he answered in dark tones.

Thomas asked, "What have you heard?"

"I ain't one to be spreading tales, sir."

"Indeed so. You personally were suggested to me as a reliable source."

"I do thank you. Well, sir, I had been catching wind of this and that for several weeks now. So when I had a chance to speak to the captain of a newly arrived ship, I took it."

"What did you learn?"

The greengrocer lowered his voice. "Defeat, sir."

Thomas stepped closer while Anne and Catherine listened in shock. "Where?"

"That's the problem in a nutshell. It wasn't just one battle, nor just one place."

"You're saying the colonials have the British army in retreat?"

"I am, sir. And not just the army. There's been battles at sea as well. Off places I'd never heard of, and some I have. The blockade of New York's been broken. Charlestown has been overrun and the harbor opened to American ships."

"Impossible!"

"Aye, I'd have said the same thing. Only it's not just the one man who's told me this. Three ships now I've spoken with, and the word's all been the same. The tide's turned, sir. Turned against the Crown with all its might. Right from the Carolinas up to Boston, the British are in retreat."

Thomas pondered what he had heard. "I suppose that could explain why printed news has been so sparse these past few weeks."

"My last trip in, there was two hulks brought to Halifax harbor from the Boston blockade. I couldn't call them ships, on account of how they'd been blackened and blasted."

"The colonials are defeating the British navy?"

"Aye, it shocked me as well, that sight did. Never thought

I'd see the day when the British were anything but victorious at sea. But there it was, right before my very eyes. I spoke with one of the sailors. The man told me they barely escaped with their lives!"

When the three arrived back at the cottage, Anne announced to Andrew and John, "We have learned news, or what we think might be news."

Andrew nodded once. "The war?"

"The news is not good." Anne turned to her husband while Catherine went to sit beside Andrew.

"I would prefer to wait if I could," Thomas began, "until we can hear from at least one more witness. But matters are pressing hard and must be discussed." Swiftly Thomas outlined what they had learned from the greengrocer.

Andrew's brow creased. "I agree that matters are serious. But this news has been floating around for weeks. Months, even."

"Indeed so. Which makes the matter even more urgent."

"I don't understand," Andrew said.

Anne felt her breath catch in her throat. She moved to slip her arm through Thomas's. "Nor do I."

He turned to his wife. "My dear, it is us."

"Yes, of course," Catherine said, her tone urgent. "You are right."

"I'm sorry," Andrew said. "I am still failing to understand."

Thomas addressed the group but looked at Anne. "This is not the matter of one lost battle. It is the war itself. Not now, perhaps, but soon."

"Yes?"

"Think on this. If Britain is defeated, they do not merely lose the colonies. They have been driven from these seas." He let that sink in for a moment, then concluded, "How then should we go home?"

"My baby!" Anne breathed the words, a hand at her heart.

"Exactly," Thomas somberly agreed. "We must hasten."

Chapter 42

"Excuse me, sir. I am looking for the Reverend Collins. . . ."

The little man with bright eyes peered up at Anne intently. "I am he. And whom do I have the honor of addressing?"

Anne thought he fit Nicole's description perfectly. Just seeing him here made her sister's letters come alive, inviting both a smile and pleasant recollections. But there was no room for humor this day.

Before she could respond, the pastor gave a start. "Bless my soul."

"Pardon me?"

He set down the tray he was carrying and stepped closer. "Might you be Catherine and Andrew's daughter?"

"I am, sir. But how—"

Her words were cut off by the pastor's cry and warm embrace.

When he released her, Pastor Collins's eyes were wet with tears. "What a joy and a blessing, my child."

He took her by the elbow. "Come, my dear. Anne, that is your name, is it not?"

"Indeed, sir. Anne Crowley."

"Of course, of course. Nicole told me you had married your young man."

"Is . . . is Nicole here?"

"Oh, my dear, no. She and Gordon are off on a mission for

the commandant. Traveling by ship to the southern colonies."

"Yes. New Orleans, I know. I had hoped . . ." Anne allowed herself to be ushered to a chair by the dining room's main window. "How did you know who I was?"

"My dear, Nicole has spoken of you so often and at such length I feel I might count you among my own kin." His eyes vanished into folds as he chuckled. "That was not the first time I have held you in my arms, as a matter of fact. When you still were in your swaddling robes, your father came here to study." Pastor Collins cocked his head to the other side. "I am happy to see that you have become as lovely a woman as you were a little child."

He had such a warm smile she felt her heart aching for the inability to respond in kind. "Forgive me, sir. I wish I could be more joyful over this meeting. I have heard so much about you. Father and Mother and Nicole all think the world of you."

"They are too kind, too kind. Will you have tea?"

"Thank you, no."

He settled himself into the chair opposite her. "You are sorely distressed."

"Indeed so."

"Is there anything I can do to assist you?"

"I do not see how. But I did not know where else to turn." She could no longer hold back the tears. Anne pulled a handkerchief from her sleeve. "Forgive me."

"Perhaps if you were to tell me the trouble."

"There are so many I do not even know where to begin."

"Ah. That is the problem with problems, is it not? How they all seem to gather and press in upon one from all sides."

His sympathetic understanding only caused more tears.

"Please, begin with what lies most heavily upon your heart," he suggested.

"My son," she managed.

"From your first marriage. Cyril, that was your husband's name, yes?"

She swallowed and breathed as steadily as she could manage. "Your knowledge of my family is remarkable, sir."

"Andrew is like a son to me, and Nicole like a beloved granddaughter." He settled his hands into his lap, the portrait of a patient listener. "Where is your son now?"

"In England. And that is the problem!"

His features turned grave. "You were berthed on the vessel captured just night before last—"

"Indeed we were."

Slowly Pastor Collins shook his head. "I am so sorry, my dear."

Anne opened her mouth to recount the dreadful event, but the vivid memory was so frightening she could not speak.

"You were fired upon." The pastor shook his head. "I can scarcely imagine . . ."

One moment she had been asleep belowdecks in her bunk, lulled by the creaking timbers and the thought of sailing steadily toward her beloved son. The next, and the night was ripped asunder by flames and blasts and screams. The first cannonade took out their central mast. The wooden timbers crashed amidships with a thunder as loud as the cannons. Thomas snatched her from the bed and flung her to the floorboards, then covered her with his body. Overhead shrieked the panic and pain and fear of the world's very end.

The four American ships had laid well off and shouts across the waters told them that the British ship must strike its colors or they would sink her outright. The harsh warning was made all the more imminent by the smells of sulfur and charred wood.

Anne shuddered. "We were asleep in the central hold when it seemed as though the entire world turned to fire."

"The hold? Forgive me, I do not understand. You are the heiress to the earl of Sutton, do I not recall that correctly?"

"Actually, it is my son who has the birthright. But we traveled from England under assumed names, and my husband—"

"Thought it best to return the same way. In humble surroundings, with all the other passengers." Pastor Collins's eyes opened wide and he leaned toward her. "I don't suppose you realize that this is why we are speaking at all now."

"I don't follow you, sir."

"Were they to have known who you are, my dear, they would have imprisoned you and your husband and held you for ransom."

Anne's head dropped in defeat. "But I must return—"

"Where are you residing now?" Pastor Collins asked.

"At the Four Roses Inn."

"You would be safer here, where there is less risk of your true identity being discovered. It is modest but clean."

"Do you think—can you help us find berths?"

"Alas, my child, no ships are departing for England." The reverend pushed himself to his feet. "I shall see if one of my students can go with you and help you with your luggage."

Anne found it difficult to rise. "Whatever am I to do!" Her voice broke.

"Perhaps a miracle will arrive." But Reverend Collins's tone held out little hope. "Rest assured I shall join with you in prayer. But first let us see to you and your safety—you and your husband. Thomas, it is?"

Chapter 43

Soon after clearing the Florida Straits and entering the cooler Atlantic waters, Gordon had been accosted by a trio of American warships. He had traded two sacks of fresh mangos for a crate of laying hens and the latest news.

Over dinner that night he relayed the reports to Henri and Louise. "There have been a score of solid victories on land, and almost as many at sea. The British are in retreat from Florida and Georgia. A general by the name of Swamp Fox is harrying their attempt to hold on to the Carolinas."

"So it is as you thought," Henri responded once Nicole had translated. "There is no instant victory."

"Hardly. But the tides have shifted."

"Yet there will be more days and weeks of struggle and suffering."

"I am afraid so, sir." Gordon motioned for the seaman on duty to remove their plates. "Whoever would have thought the mighty British navy would be handed their hat. And by an upstart colonial force." Gordon shook his head, and Nicole knew his feelings were torn—admiration for the Americans, and a pang for his previous British colleagues.

During the three weeks of their voyage north, they saw no sign of the British navy. Twice more they came upon colonial forces in attack strength. They were approached and boarded, their papers carefully inspected, and then were sent upon their way. The wind remained strong and steady, first off their starboard side, then almost directly from the south. Gordon held to a run straight up the American coastline, confident now that the coastal waters were firmly held.

Nicole used the time to tell Henri and Louise of her years apart. And they talked with her about her brothers and their families, about the Acadia villagers of her childhood.

She finally brought herself to ask about Jean, who had early captured her heart but whose wildness eventually pushed her away.

Her father did not answer immediately, but then he said, "He has not come back to the bayou. There are rumors that he is still being held as a traitor. . . ."

If he said more, Nicole was not aware of it. She gazed out over the blue Atlantic and remembered the awful deception, the traitor who stole Henri's sterling name and identity to cloak his double-crossing of both the Americans and the British. . . .

"And Jean may indeed come back to us one day," she said, as if to herself.

"What has you concerned?"

Nicole gave a start as she became aware of her father's words. "Oh, Papa," she whispered, "you of all have the most to forgive."

"Ah, and if so," he responded, "I have the most blessing to receive after I've done so."

Alone in the captain's cabin, Gordon asked, "Why have you been so quiet?"

"It is difficult to explain."

"Try. Please."

"I feel as though I am learning to see the whole world anew."

"For the child, you mean."

"*Our* child."

"Yes."

"Partly that. But questions I have carried with me all my life are being answered. And in ways that I never expected."

Gordon nodded and waited.

"Questions about my home, my early years . . ."

"Yes?"

"All my life I have never felt as though I belonged. Never had a place that was truly my own."

"And now?"

"It is such a strange thing, how the home I thought I would have is burned to a husk, how the land lies fallow, how the nation is at war. Yet I feel not only settled, but that I *belong*." She struggled to put her feelings into words. "But I am discovering it is not the place that makes me feel this way. I believe God has given me the gift of a home that I take with me wherever I go. With you."

Chapter 44

Louise turned from the Boston harbor to stare at the city rising on the rocky shoreline's other side. "Such a place as this I had never expected to see in all my days."

"Some say Boston is America's grandest city," Nicole said. "Others, Philadelphia."

Henri cast a shrewd eye over his daughter. "I sense you do not share their opinion."

"I do not care overmuch for big cities," Nicole replied, but without rancor. She also looked around her. A midafternoon breeze blew in from the sea, carrying enough coolness to make even the brilliant sunshine feel pleasant. Three ships had arrived on the same incoming tide, doubling the number of vessels in the harbor. Even this number seemed dwarfed by the harbor's potential. The docks, left empty by the strictures of combat, jutted seaward.

Gordon mistook her silence for something else. He drew her to one side and murmured, "Is there something that ails you?"

"No, Gordon, I am fine. I cannot tell you all the emotions I'm feeling."

"Tell me, Nicole."

"Well, for one, I think I may have felt the baby move."

"Has this happened before?"

"Perhaps, I am not sure."

"What else?"

"I am happy the war seems to be coming to an end, that the colonists—the Americans—may have won their freedom. *Our* freedom," she repeated.

He studied her face, trying to understand. But then he lifted his head, listening.

"What is it?"

She realized that it was not only Gordon but her father who was doing the same. Both of them had turned west.

Nicole shaded her eyes and squinted against the afternoon sun. A call came high upon the wind, and then a figure, little more than a slender shadow silhouetted against the waning sunlight, ran down the dock toward them.

Nicole's cry joined instantly with the first one.

"*Anne!*"

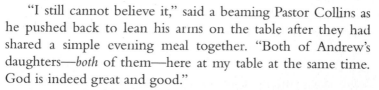

"I still cannot believe it," said a beaming Pastor Collins as he pushed back to lean his arms on the table after they had shared a simple evening meal together. "Both of Andrew's daughters—*both* of them—here at my table at the same time. God is indeed great and good."

Anne reached beneath the table to clasp Nicole's hand. She still could not believe what her eyes were seeing. Nicole was here beside her. Nicole, as full of warmth and acceptance as always. She felt such tremendous relief. She had been so frightened, so confused, even betrayed, when she had received the news about Nicole turning to side with the colonies. She had wondered how she might respond if they should ever meet again. Were they still sisters at heart? Or had they been forced by a world in conflict to an estrangement she did not want?

When the word had come to the seminary that the ship that had left for New Orleans—the ship on which she knew Nicole and her husband were to be aboard—was arriving in the harbor, Anne hesitated. Part of her wished to run to the dock to greet them, but another part of her feared what this reunion might mean. Nicole had no idea that Anne was in Boston—had likely never heard that they had come over to be with Andrew and Catherine. How would Nicole respond should they meet in such an unexpected way?

The eager side of Anne had won the momentary battle. She had donned her bonnet and short cape and hurried to the harbor. Her wildly beating heart insisted that it was her sister coming in on the arriving ship. Her sister. Not a member of the colony's combatants.

And when she had called Nicole's name and Nicole had answered with all of the love of former years, Anne had wept with relief. They were sisters still. In spite of the distance, in spite of the war, in spite of the fact that they were now on opposing sides, they were sisters. Nothing—nothing would ever change that fact. Anne could not wait until they could be excused from this table of reunion to get alone for a long, confidential chat. They had so much to say to each other.

It was Nicole who pushed back from the chatter of the table visitors. "If you will please allow me to excuse myself," she began, "it has been a very long day and I feel that a bit of rest in my room would be most welcomed."

The men at the table rose immediately to their feet, and Gordon reached to take his wife's arm. His eyes offered his apology for not thinking of her comfort sooner. She turned to him and smiled. "Why don't you stay and converse. Anne will accompany me to my room."

For a moment he looked as though he would argue, but as he caught the message in her eyes he nodded silently. "I will not be late," he assured her and let her go, Anne at her side.

"You worked that nicely," Anne whispered as they left the dining room. "You were always good at getting your desires in a most gracious way."

Nicole laughed softly. "If I had to sit there any longer and endure more male talk of war when I was aching to catch up on all your news, I would have burst," she exclaimed.

"I felt that way too. Oh, Nicole. I have missed you so terribly."

In answer Nicole reached for her hand and gave it a squeeze. But she turned the conversation in another direction. "I like your Thomas. He seems most . . . insightful."

"You don't know the half. He is so wise. So . . . in tune with God."

Then Anne brought her thoughts in check lest she go on and on regarding her husband. "I like Gordon too. He seems so in charge. Military . . . yet gentle."

Nicole smiled. Anne had summed up her husband's bearing well. "Oh, we have so much to talk about," she enthused as they reached the small room she shared with her husband. "But first of all I want a thorough report on Mother and Father. And Grandfather Price. How are they? Is Father really as ill as they say?"

Anne's face turned serious. She feared that the news she had to share was not all good.

"The commandant will see you now."

Gordon offered Nicole his arm with a wry grin when she paused to adjust the lapel of his best uniform. "Mustn't keep the general waiting, my dear," he murmured.

The commandant approached with hand outstretched. "Well met, sir. Welcome home."

Home. The word alone was enough to bring a smile to Nicole's lips.

The general gazed at her and said, "I see you are glad to be back, ma'am."

"Yes, General. More than I know how to say."

"I am most glad to hear it. Our young nation has much need of people such as yourselves." He ushered them inside, where an adjutant stood poised to pour them tea. The general waited until they were both served before asking, "You have heard the latest news?"

"So good it is scarcely believable, sir."

"Believe it, Captain. Believe it. The British are retreating on land and on sea."

"Will the war be over soon, sir?"

He took a drink from his cup, then dismissed the adjutant with a wave. "Of that we can only guess, ma'am. Guess and hope."

"Please, sir. Tell me what you think."

"They have offered several propositions to General Washington. All of them are most unacceptable."

"But for the British to discuss terms of surrender at all is rather astonishing," Gordon pointed out.

"Not surrender, sir. And that is the problem. They continue to see us as colonials. They still hold out the hope that we can be brought back into the British fold, if only the terms are agreed upon by both. And that is where they are wrong. The tides of men and war have gone too far. We seek independence from the Crown. Nothing less will do. Washington has told them that in no uncertain terms."

"What will happen?" Nicole asked with sinking heart.

"A great battle," the general replied definitely. "This year or next. A telling blow. Perhaps two. We must defeat them soundly. We must send Cornwallis packing with his tail between his legs."

Nicole set her cup to one side. She had been so in hopes of a few weeks, a few months, bringing an end to it all. . . .

Gordon said, "We come with good news and a request, sir."

"I have already seen the ship's manifest. A most remarkable haul. And extremely needed. Too much land lies fallow through this planting season. Too many farmers are far from home. Too many, I fear, shall never return."

Gordon pushed forward. "It is not merely this shipload, sir. Not at all. We may have established a new supply route that will last through the conflict and beyond."

"I say." The general set his cup aside and leaned forward. "That is good news indeed."

Swiftly Gordon described the situation they had found attempting to deal with the New Orleans traders and customs officials. He recounted their journey inland, the initial hostility of the Acadian settlers, and how things gradually altered.

"You are telling me these Acadian folk will arrange shipments north for the foreseeable future?"

"It is because of my wife and her family, General. Without them we would have returned empty-handed."

"Then I must once again express my heartfelt gratitude." But the general's shrewd gaze remained penetrating as he looked at Gordon. "Yes, I am now sufficiently prepared. Tell me the cost."

"No direct cost, General. No demands. Only a request."

"I beg your pardon?"

"My ship," Gordon continued. "It was entrusted to me by merchants in Southampton. I wish to take her home."

"You wish me to give you a vessel captured in wartime?"

"On the contrary," Gordon countered. "I am certain the merchants who entrusted me with this vessel shall willingly pay proper compensation for its return."

The general inspected them both. "Let me see if I understand this correctly. You are offering me much-needed supplies, throughout the summer and beyond. In repayment, you wish to keep this ship of yours."

"Not keep, sir—simply return it to its owners."

"Whether you agree to the return of this vessel or not," Nicole assured him, "we will endeavor to aid you. You have my father's word."

"Henri Robichaud is one of the most honorable men I have ever met, sir," Gordon added. "You can be certain that if it is humanly possible to deliver supplies, this gentleman will do so."

The general rose and crossed to the tall side windows. He stared long out at the sunlit vista, rocking up and down on his toes, his boots creaking with each motion. He clasped his hands together behind his back.

Without turning around, he declared, "Even assuming that I might relinquish the vessel, I cannot permit you to skipper her back to England. Your services are required here. And the British might not see fit to release you, no matter what offering you bring them. You have declared for their enemy."

"I am aware of this," Gordon admitted.

The general turned around. "You have thought of a solution?"

He hesitated, then asked, "Do you have British navy men in the stockade here?"

The general's eyebrows lifted in surprise. "You seek to send your vessel back with prisoners of war at the helm?"

"You said it yourself, sir. The war will be over soon enough. Demand of them their oath that they shall not engage in conflict, that they shall sail the vessel home and relinquish it to the proper owners."

"You would trust them to do so?"

"They are combatants, sir. Their allegiance is not my own. Not any longer. But I would trust them to adhere to their oath as British officers."

"And if there are not enough ready seamen?"

"They could stop by Halifax," Gordon replied quickly. "Nova Scotia must have its share of able tars looking for a working passage home. And being a British vessel, they might come and go unhindered."

"I see you have thought this through." The general nodded slowly. "You shall have my answer before dusk."

Gordon rose to his feet with Nicole. "Thank you, sir."

"One further item." The general hesitated a long moment, then moved back to his desk. "May I ask if you are a man of faith, Captain?"

Gordon immediately answered, "That I am, sir. What—?"

"I have found that a man facing the tides of war needs a strength greater than his own. Still I find myself humbled by the power of the unexpected." His fingers pushed aside papers until they came upon a small packet of bound envelopes. "As you know, our forces have had several significant victories at sea. The most recent of these only arrived in harbor yesterday evening, a merchant vessel inbound from Portsmouth. Among its papers, well . . ."

He untied the binding cord and lifted the top envelope,

then reached across the table toward Nicole. "This letter is addressed to you, ma'am. And its very existence I would count as a most astonishing miracle. One so great that I have spent the entire day wondering just what God might wish for me to do, what great and impossible task that requires such an astonishing miracle as a letter captured at sea and arriving upon my desk the same morning as we are scheduled to meet."

Nicole's heart pounded and her knees felt weak as she looked at her husband. "It is from Uncle Charles," she said through lips stiff with shock.

The general went on, "Another letter has arrived this morning. One requesting my aid in supplying a vessel to transport an envoy from General Washington to London. I cannot believe all this is mere coincidence. No, I find myself confronting a hand far wiser and surer than my own."

She accepted the letter, staring down at the envelope that bore her name in bold script. She did so hope that it was simply a greeting from her uncle, not more bad news.

But the general was still speaking. "There were other letters in the packet as well, but . . ." He sighed. "I don't suppose there is much chance that they will ever be delivered." He shook his head as he fingered the letters on his desk. "I wouldn't know how to ever get them to the addresses shown."

It was Gordon who asked the startling question that got Nicole's full attention. "Excuse me, sir, for my boldness, but does that top envelope say Georgetown?"

"Georgetown? Yes. That's not even on our shores. It's still held by the British. Not much chance . . ."

"Perhaps there is, sir. In fact, we hope to be traveling there if arrangements can be made for us to port at Halifax. My wife's kin are there."

The general looked up with widened eyes. "You don't say. You could take them with you to Georgetown? Do you think there is a way you could find the party addressed?"

"We could certainly try. It is a small village. It should not be a difficult matter."

The general looked both relieved and astounded. "I never

supposed that these letters would ever be delivered, circumstances as they are. They are all three meant for Georgetown." He lifted the letters and studied them for a moment. "In fact, it is strange, but it appears they are in the same script as the one your wife is holding."

Nicole could scarcely contain herself. She wished to grab the letters from the gentleman's hands and see for herself.

"Reverend and Mrs. Andrew Harrow," the general read absentmindedly.

"Indeed. Sir?" Gordon said, catching the excitement Nicole was feeling in his voice. "They are my wife's parents."

The general raised his eyes. It was clear from his expression that he found the words hard to comprehend. "Her parents?"

"Yes, sir. The Harrows."

The general just shook his head. When at last he seemed to have regained his tongue, he shifted the letters in his hand and said, "Is there any chance you know these other people? Mr. John Price?"

"Her grandfather."

The general extended both letters toward Gordon.

"And a Mr. and Mrs. Thomas Crowley."

"Her sister," Gordon said without hesitation, not quibbling over the fact that Nicole and Anne were not truly blood sisters.

The general was shaking his head. "Then you may deliver this too to Georgetown."

Gordon responded with a light laugh. "That will not be necessary, sir. She is here—in Boston. We can deliver that letter within the hour."

He accepted the third letter.

"This is most unbelievable," the general said. "I expected that all would lie and gather dust. And here you have been sent to me, and you are able to get them all to where they were meant to go. All I can say is that someone, somewhere, must have been in good favor with the Almighty."

Nicole could only nod, her heart echoing this truth. At the same time, her pulse beat faster. What was so important about this little packet of letters that God seemed to have arranged for a miraculous delivery to them? She prayed that it was good news.

Chapter 45

Gordon knew Nicole would find it hard to wait to find out the contents of the letter, so as soon as they had rounded the corner from the headquarters, he turned to her. "There is a low wall just over there, my dear. I am willing to spread my coat if you wish to sit."

"Oh, thank you," she said with feeling, understanding his offer. "The coat will not be necessary. My gown is already covered in dust. But I am anxious."

They crossed to the wall, and he brushed the worst of the dust from a spot for her to sit in the shade. Eagerly she tore open the envelope. Gordon sat down beside her, and she began to read aloud. He watched her as her eyes tried to scan the page ahead of her voice. They both soon knew her fears were unfounded. Charles and Judith had written a simple letter of family news, telling that they missed her and remembered her daily in their prayers. They spoke of little John and his delight with the pianoforte. They said they were both keeping well— invigorated by having a child in the home. They wondered if there was any chance at all that she might cross paths with Anne and Thomas. And they spoke of the local villagers and the individuals she had known when among them. They both ended by saying that they sent their love and trusted she was well and happy. Nicole fought back her tears. What a special gift it was to receive word from those she loved after so long a time.

She refolded the letter and slipped it back in the envelope. Then she stood hurriedly. "We must get this other letter to Anne. Quickly," she said. "She has been so anxious about news of little John."

"Are you able to walk on alone?" Gordon asked solicitously. Nicole seemed about to dash off without even giving an answer. "I must go to the stockade and select a crew—if I am that fortunate," he told her. "With what has just happened I feel much more confident. One more miracle seems easy to believe." He smiled and Nicole smiled back. She waved the letters she held in her hand. "I must share the miracle with Anne," she answered. He touched her arm and let her go, with an admonition to keep her steps to a reasonable walk.

Anne's letter proved to be much like Nicole's, only it contained much more news about small John. Judith wrote in a small script and filled four thin pages. Anne seemed to drink in each word. Nicole left her in peace until she had finished the reading and gained control of her emotions. Nicole felt her own growing child stir within her and placed a hand on her abdomen. Already she loved him—or her—dearly. She couldn't imagine what Anne must be going through parted from her beloved child.

When she felt that Anne was once again ready to talk, Nicole spoke.

"We have some other exciting news. Gordon will explain it all when he returns. It is . . . it is almost unthinkable. God has been doing some miraculous works. Miraculous. Yes, that is the only word for it."

Anne's eyes lifted. They were red and puffy, but a new light was shining there. "More exciting news?" she repeated. "I can't imagine anything more exciting than this." She lifted the letter still in her hands. "My little boy, my baby, sent me his love. He even drew a kiss on the page. And he said, through Nana, that when I come back home he will play a piece for me on the pianoforte. My baby! Just think of it. He can play the pianoforte. And he said they will be sure to have plum pudding ready for me."

She managed a trembling smile.

Nicole could only nod. Perhaps there was little in the world more exciting than that.

———— 🌿 ————

Explaining their plan to the others took the remainder of the afternoon. After a long, agonizing discussion, Nicole and Gordon decided to risk sailing to Nova Scotia with the family. Nicole so much wanted to see Andrew again, and to do so with Anne as well as Louise by her side would make the moment all the more precious. She and Gordon would remain belowdecks, of course, should their ship be detained by the British.

There were risks, to be sure, but after quiet prayer, they both felt this was the proper course. When hostilities were finally over, they would return to western Massachusetts and discover what their friend Jackson had been able to accomplish on the Harrow estate.

Henri and Louise and Anne and Thomas were most delighted with the news of their traveling companions.

"I may stay in Georgetown until the baby is born," Nicole explained to her family, "especially if Gordon is called to further duty with the American colonists."

A seminarian rapped on the doorframe to get their attention and waited for permission to speak. He brought the news that someone from the commandant's office awaited Gordon at the front door. Gordon arose and left immediately. He was not gone long. When he returned, his face was triumphant. "It is as we hoped!" he exclaimed, waving a paper. "The general has granted permission for the vessel to be sent back to Portsmouth! Not only that, but there is an experienced captain in the stockade who has offered his word as a gentleman and an officer that he will adhere to our terms. With him are enough seamen to take us as far as Nova Scotia, and then you, Anne and Thomas, across the Atlantic."

"So we have what we require." Thomas was on his feet. "And all because of you." He extended a hand toward Gordon.

"It is an answer to prayer," Anne agreed fervently.

Nicole looked at her sister, thinking of the little boy she had been missing for these many months. No wonder the news was of special significance to her. For a brief moment Nicole felt a kinship with her pain. She swallowed against her emotion.

Anne most resembled her blood parents in her gaze. Seated there between Henri and Louise, her inner feelings totally exposed upon her face, Nicole could see the power latent in those lovely dark eyes. Anne's fragile form sheathed a stalwart inner resolve and spoke of a soul that had been tested and proven to be strong.

But Anne was speaking, softly, blinking back tears that wished to form. "I cannot tell you what it means to know I shall soon see my son again."

She turned to Louise and spoke the words again in French. With a mother's understanding, Louise slipped an arm around her slim waist and drew her close.

Chapter 46

Even now, in the warmth of a perfect late summer's day, with the clouds framing a world of infinite green, Catherine could feel winter's breath. It blew not upon her face, but rather her heart.

The three of them had taken to walking together each afternoon. Though it was not stated, all knew this might well be the last summer they shared.

Catherine matched her pace to whichever of the men was moving the slowest, and yearned for those younger footsteps and stronger hearts that were, for now, much too far away.

Today Grandfather Price leaned more heavily than usual upon Catherine's arm, breathing in heavy gasps as they took the slight rise in the road leading away from the market square.

Oftentimes they would cover the entire distance without a word between them. They knew each other so well. And each was locked intently upon engraving these precious moments in deep, where they might be used to fuel the cold winter days ahead.

When the sound first came, Catherine thought it was a bird.

Andrew stopped in midstride and turned around. Squinting into the sunlight, he asked softly, "What did I just hear?"

"The wind," John Price replied. But he turned back as well.

"It can't be," Catherine agreed. Something about the

strange sound had caused her heart to surge like a bird taking flight.

Then it came again. Three voices calling so that the words seemed mixed together into angel's laughter.

"Mama!"

"Catherine!"

And a different voice, "Mama!"

And then Catherine picked up her skirts and ran toward Nicole and Anne and Louise, calling their names until the four women met in joyful tumult.

Catherine scarcely knew which pair of arms to reach for first, so she made the trip around the circle three times, holding close, weeping and rejoicing all at the same time. English and French were interchanged in a joyous jumble of words. She was vaguely aware that Henri, John Price, Andrew, Thomas, and Gordon were also greeting one another with shouts and halloos, embraces and laughter.

At last Catherine drew back, her arms still firmly around the waist of Louise. "I cannot believe it. How did you get here? Where did you come from? Nothing—no one—is getting through the enemy lines."

"Speak French, Mama," laughed Nicole, and Catherine joined the laughter, then switched to French.

In a tumbling of words, Louise poured out the unbelievable sketch of the story. The details would need to be filled in later. But they would have time for that.

"Come," said Catherine. "Come to the house. The kettle should be hot for tea. You must all be done in."

"We do not have long today," Louise explained as they walked together. "But we will have many days. Many days. But not today. We met Guy. He was in town at the market. Can you imagine that? We have not seen Guy or his family since he left the bayou. But there he was—clinging to Henri as if he would never let him go. He wants us to go home with him, and we said yes, when he is done at the market. He will bring us back when he comes in the morning. I could not believe my eyes. The market. Here it is—Frenchman beside Englishman—stall by stall. I have never seen the like of it. How can this be?"

Catherine cast a glance toward Thomas. She felt that much of the credit of the mixed market was due her son-in-law. But there wasn't time to explain all of that to Louise now. She turned to the two daughters, both of whom she claimed as her own. "Anne, could you run for some sweet cream from the spring house, and Nicole, there is fresh strawberry jam in the cellar."

From then on it was like a clamorous fete. There was so much talking and laughing that one could scarcely think. *How can so many people crowd into such a small space and share so much love and joy?* Catherine paused to wonder. Even Andrew's pale face had taken on a flush, and there was a new sparkle to his eyes. At the same time that Catherine rejoiced in the fact, she feared that his frail body might be overtaxed by all of the excitement. *God has granted this,* she reminded herself. *He knew we all needed it. Especially Andrew. Let him enjoy it to the fullest.*

It seemed far too soon when Guy arrived for Henri and Louise. Catherine vowed not to try to hold them. After all, he had more claim on them than she. She served Guy a mug of tea and some bread and jam and watched as Louise gathered her things and replaced her shawl. "I will be back soon," Louise promised as she kissed Catherine's cheek. "Until then, you have much catching up to do with our daughters."

"Yes," Catherine agreed. She was anxious for some quieter time with the two girls. As yet they had spoken very little amidst all the commotion.

After the door had closed behind their guests, Catherine began to gather the dishes for washing. Anne reached for an apron and moved for the basin, while Nicole took a towel from the wall peg. It had been a long time since the three of them had shared a kitchen.

But even the washing of the dishes was destined to be interrupted, for Gordon chose the lull in conversation to draw two letters from his satchel.

"We happened, by God's circumstances, to be at the right place at the right time. These letters were given us by the general in Boston. I promised to deliver them by hand."

Catherine came to a standstill, two mugs still held in her hands. Letters arrived so seldom that it seemed a miracle when one made it through. Gordon had handed one letter to Andrew and the other to John.

"From Charles," observed Andrew as Catherine drew near.

"Charles? He must have news."

"Not necessarily. This could simply be correspondence."

"News of what?" asked Nicole from the open kitchen doorway.

Anne joined her. "Ours was news of little John. Judith wrote also. It was so good to hear after all this time."

"News of what?" Nicole persisted. She moved into the room and Anne followed.

It was their grandfather who answered. "Charles has been searching for kin of mine. A half sister."

"I didn't know you had a half sister." Nicole's tone was one of interest but not surprise. Catherine realized there were many things about Grandfather Price Nicole did not yet know.

"No one knew for many years," John Price went on. "I never told. In fact, I was reluctant to even claim her."

The girls exchanged glances, Nicole's puzzled and Anne's pleading for patience and understanding.

"I never knew her," John Price continued, fingering the letter he held in his hand. "My father had been married before he married my mother. His first wife was never able to leave France."

"France? You mean she was French?" Nicole's voice sounded shocked.

John Price nodded.

"You think Uncle Charles might have found her?" Excitement made Nicole's words tumble over each other.

"No, not her. She has died. That much we know. But she did have one daughter who lived. We don't know if . . ."

"Open it," urged Nicole, kneeling in front of the elderly man. "Let's see if he has found the daughter."

With shaking hands, John Price tore at the flap of the envelope. Catherine noted that the tremor was more pronounced than normal. Perhaps it was tension that made him tremble so.

Anne had pressed in to join the others, easing herself to a seat on the hearth and still twisting her apron in her hands. Even Gordon and Thomas had fallen silent.

John's attention went quickly to the page, and his watery eyes scanned the first sentences.

"He has found her," he said in almost a whisper.

"Where is she?"

"Read it to us."

"What does he say?"

The questions all came at once, and John held up a hand as though commanding his troops to silence and order.

The room hushed.

"He hasn't really found her. But he does know who she is," he amended.

"Read it," Nicole urged again.

With a tremble in his voice, John began to read halfway down the page. " 'He is certain now that he has found out the identity of the woman who is your niece. I do not know if the letter I sent previously ever arrived. We have recently had a further report, and it seems to have removed all doubt about her true identity. She was born Celeste Louise Evangeline Brassard, and the records show—' "

Nicole gasped. "That is my mother's name," she exclaimed.

"What a strange coincidence. It is not a common name, is it?" Catherine queried, her heart beating fast. What did this all mean?

"I wouldn't think so. Not with three given names."

"I thought Mama was Louise," put in Anne. "I never even knew of the other names."

"She was named Celeste after her grandmother, but they

chose to call her Louise," Nicole said, her tone full of wonder.

"I never knew," said Anne again, shaking her head.

John Price had turned back to the letter. He was reading silently, but suddenly a look of pure shock registered across his face.

"Listen," he said, his voice husky. " 'She was born Celeste Louise Evangeline Brassard, but the records show that she married when she was nineteen. They lived in a village of Nova Scotia but were with the party driven out by the British. There the trail ends. The Acadians were scattered and are almost impossible to trace. We have no evidence that she is alive or dead.' "

The room was absolutely silent. Nicole half rose from her position at her grandfather's knee. Anne leaned back against the brick of the fireplace as though for support. Andrew was bent so far forward in his chair he threatened to topple from it.

Catherine sat, staring intently at her father. What was he saying? Surely she was hearing it all wrong. Surely there was some misunderstanding.

"Is this a dream?" she finally managed, shaking her head to clear it of the cobwebs.

John Price read the words aloud again, and then the room erupted.

"It's true," cried Nicole. "My mother, Louise Brassard Robichaud. She has to be the one."

Anne had risen from her seat. With tears streaming down her face she threw her arms around her grandfather's neck. "I knew it. I always knew it," she wept. "We are of one blood. We are."

Catherine sat where she was, staring at the commotion around her. It seemed so impossible. So preposterous. She and Louise—kin? It was Andrew who finally made her understand. He reached for her hand, his own eyes wet. "We British drove out our own flesh and blood," he said slowly. "What if we had never found them again?"

Nicole and Anne were now dancing around the room, waving apron and dishtowel with the hands that were not clinging to each other. And then Catherine's tears started. This was the most amazing thing she had ever heard in her lifetime. She and Louise. Kin. No wonder they had taken to each other. No wonder the tie had remained through the years. *Oh, dear God, this is too much,* she whispered. *This is too much joy to hold.*

"Oh, I must tell Mama. I must," Nicole shouted. "I can't possibly wait until morning. Is there some way to get to Guy's house?" She whirled toward Gordon. "Surely there is a cart somewhere that we can hire," she implored. "Surely someone has something."

He rose to his feet and smiled in understanding. "If you are sure—"

"Oh, I am. I am. I can't wait to tell her. I can't wait."

Gordon nodded and went for his hat.

"I'll come with you," offered Andrew. "I know most of the villagers." The two left the small cottage with the noise of merrymaking following them out the door.

Gordon and Andrew were soon back. Andrew had found a conveyance for hire, and the driver assured them that if they left right away, they would arrive before nightfall. They would need to spend the night. It was no problem for him, he maintained. He had kin in the village.

So another good-bye, thought Catherine as she watched Nicole hurriedly prepare for the trip. But her sadness was neither deep nor long-lived. They had the future before them. Nicole's stay would be much longer this time. She had even spoken of staying until after the birth of her baby. Catherine's only disappointment was that she would not be present when Louise was told the news.

They sent them on their way with a flurry of excitement, imagining the commotion that Nicole's news would create. Then Anne turned back again to the few remaining dishes to be washed, and Catherine tried to gather her thoughts enough to think about preparing the evening meal.

"I think I need a little time to catch my breath," Andrew said, turning to Thomas. "Would you give me your arm to my bed, son?"

Grandfather Price was still rereading the letter, as though his heart could not believe what his eyes were telling him. "Louise. My sister's daughter," Catherine heard him murmur. It still seemed impossible to believe.

"Halloo the house," the driver called in French, and Nicole saw many faces appear at the window. It was the first hours of nightfall, and candles had already been lit. She could see the flickering light silhouetting the figures behind the panes. But the long twilight had lingered to light the rutted track they traveled.

Nicole would have dashed from the cart had not Gordon held her arm firmly. He helped her down safely, then she rushed to the cottage.

"Mama," cried Nicole, almost before her mother opened the door.

Louise's face turned ashen. "Andrew—?"

"We have just received the most astonishing news," Nicole exclaimed, remembering to speak French. "You will not believe this. You'd best sit down."

Louise brushed the words aside with a flurry of one hand. "Since Andrew must be all right, I expect any news you could bring will be no harder to take standing than what I have heard in the past."

Nicole was vaguely aware of the little crowd that had gathered around them. Curiosity touched their faces. She put her hands on Louise's shoulders and looked deeply into her eyes.

"You and Mama Catherine are cousins."

Louise stared.

"It's true. You and Mama Catherine are first cousins."

Louise pursed her lips in stubborn unbelief. "You are saying she is French? Pawsh. I know her papa."

"No. No, it's you. You are related to her papa."

Louise's reaction was far from what Nicole had expected. Her face went white. Her jaw clamped firmly. When she did speak, her words were clipped. "Hush such foolish talk, girl. I'm French. I am not one of those British—"

"Mama!" Nicole could not believe her ears.

"I knew my mama and my papa," Louise announced firmly. "They were both French. Neither of them were kin to John Price."

Nicole felt her heart sinking with dread. She didn't know what to say or do next. "I think we need to talk," she managed quietly. "Would you join me in the garden? Papa? Gordon? Please."

The four walked into the garden and the talk lasted for an hour. Inside the cottage, Guy and his family waited impatiently. What was the meaning of the strange tale that Nicole had brought to the household? When the quartet finally did come back in to the warmth, Louise looked reasonably calm and controlled.

"It is true," she announced to her waiting family, but she sounded more resigned than excited by the fact. "I had an English grandfather on my mother's side. She never talked about it. Perhaps she didn't want me to know."

To her surprise there was no shock evidenced at the news. No shunning like there may have been in days past. No one in the household seemed even slightly disturbed.

"English blood, huh? Perhaps you can get me a little better stall location at the market," joked Guy.

"Can you teach me how to talk their words, Aunt Louise?" asked young Michel.

"He likes the English girls at the market. I think he wants to flirt with them," his younger sister put in.

Louise shook her head. No. There was nothing about the English that she understood one bit better than she had an hour ago. They still puzzled her. Confused her. Made her angry. She still carried deep wounds that they had inflicted upon both her body and her soul. She needed time. Time to think. Time to pray.

But there is Catherine, she thought. She had always claimed Catherine. Had not really thought of her as being British. Catherine was in a class all by herself. *It is an honor to be bound to Catherine by blood ties,* she concluded, her arms clutching herself as she gazed out the window.

Chapter 47

Catherine had gone to bed, worn out from the busyness and excitement of the day. She still could scarcely believe that she was not living a dream. Both daughters home. And Louise. All at the same time. It was almost more than her tired body could sustain. And it was certainly draining for Andrew. He was exhausted by the events of the day. They had needed to carry his evening meal to his bed. Even then he had to be helped with the spoon, his hands were so shaky from fatigue. Catherine could not help but worry about him. Each day a bit more of his strength seemed to drain away.

But he was happy. So happy to see his girls. So happy to have the family home. Perhaps the cost his body was paying for the pleasure was worth it.

And Louise. By now Louise would know the secret that had remained hidden for so many years. To think of it. The two young women who had met by coincidence in the meadow all those many years ago were actually first cousins. It was something beyond fairy tales.

Catherine thought back over all the years she had yearned for a friend. A sister. A woman of her own kin. And all that time she had one. And she had not known. She would treasure every minute of their time together in a new way.

What if they had known at the beginning? What if her father had known at the time of the expulsion? Would Louise's family have been spared? Poor Louise. She had suffered so much at the hands of the British.

Louise? Catherine felt her body stiffen. Would the news that Nicole carried be good news for her? Would Louise feel proud or angry to have English blood in her veins? How would she react? Perhaps she would distance herself. It was a fearful thought. She might have lost her rather than found her.

The troubling thoughts were enough to keep Catherine awake until well into the early morning. She tossed upon the bed until she feared she would disturb Andrew. She fought her pillow, fluffing it up and then punching it down to a small lump under her neck. Still she could not sleep. She began to pray. She didn't even know what words to choose. What did she want from God? A miracle. Yes—another miracle. She did not want her two daughters separated by bitterness. She did not want Louise hurt more than she already had been. She did not want to lose the woman she had just found. But at long last she ended up crying in submission, "Lord . . . Thy will be done."

Catherine heard the jingle of harness before anyone else in the house—perhaps because she had been listening for it so intently. Then she heard the low rumble of the cart wheels as they churned slowly up the lane. They were coming. But who was coming? Was it Nicole and Gordon—or would Louise and Henri be with them? She would not even let herself cross to the window and look out.

It was Anne who made the announcement. "They are here!"

"Who?" asked Catherine dumbly.

"Nicole."

"Is she alone?"

"No, of course not. I don't think Gordon would let her out of his sight." Anne laughed.

"It's just the two of them?"

Anne looked out the window again. "Oh, Papa and Mama

are there too. I thought Uncle Guy was bringing them when he came to market. They must have decided to all ride together. Don't know how they all fit in that little bit of a cart. Looks like the menfolk . . ."

But Catherine was no longer listening. Louise was there. How would Louise respond? Dared she go out to meet her, or should she wait in the cottage? She started to ask Anne how Louise looked, then realized that Anne could not possibly understand the meaning of her question. She wiped the flour from her hands on her apron and moved toward the door.

She had taken only a few steps when she saw Louise rushing toward her, arms outstretched. With a glad cry Catherine hurried to meet her.

"Oh, Catherine," Louise called and gathered her close. "We are kin. We are kin. Didn't we know it all along?"

Catherine could only weep. Her prayer for a miracle had been answered.

When she could finally speak, she pushed slightly away and smiled through her tears. "I didn't know what you might think," she admitted. "I mean, English blood! It was hardly something you could feel proud to claim."

"Let's sit," responded Louise and led the way to the rustic bench up against the house. As they seated themselves, Louise reached for Catherine's hand. "I must be honest," she began. "It was a bit of a blow at first. I had to think it through. Pray it through. But God taught me many things during my night of talking to Him. Any blood I share with you has to be a good thing. Think of it, Catherine. We are kin. Not just friends. *Kin*.

"And then I had another thought. One that caused me so much joy I nearly burst into song, waking the entire household. I had to fight to hold it back, I felt so full. To think that God had gone to such extreme lengths to place my ailing baby in the arms of *kinfolk* brought tears to my eyes and a song to my heart. Think of it. Of all of the people in Acadia, He chose you. And the precious little girl *I raised as my own*. She was. She really was. She shares my blood as well as my heart. Now, who but God could have arranged such a miraculous thing as that?"

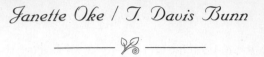
"Would you walk out to the point with me?"

Anne asked the question of Thomas. They had been to the point many times since their arrival in Georgetown, so the request was not an unusual one. But as Thomas looked at his wife's face, he felt there was more to this little excursion than a mere walk. Anne seemed distracted. Deep in thought. He knew that the point was her thinking place. The spot she sought when she needed time to work through a dilemma or sort out an emotion. He nodded and reached for her light shawl, spreading it over her shoulders.

The day was a glorious one. Neither too warm, nor chilly. The wind blew just enough to stir the leaves of the trees. Nearby a bird sang to its mate high in the branches above. Thomas found it hard not to express his thoughts about the perfection of the morning, but he held his tongue. He would not speak until Anne was ready.

She settled herself on the familiar log, and her gaze swept out over the scene before them. He watched her slim shoulders rise and fall. Then she settled back, eyes upon a small fishing boat gently rocking on the waters beyond. A strange calm seemed to relax her face.

"I always used to come here," she began without looking at him. He nodded.

"There was so much to think about. To try to sort out."

He reached for her hand and held it, his thumb rubbing gently back and forth against the smoothness of the skin.

"Was I English? Was I French? Just who was I, anyway?"

Still he remained silent.

She turned to him then. "You know—I've never told anyone this—but there was a time in my early life when I childishly imagined that it might be discovered there had been a mistake. That I was not the child who they said I was. That the switch had been made back—or not at all—and that I was *really* the daughter of Andrew and Catherine. My parents. I wanted to be their daughter. I didn't want parents I didn't even know. I even felt . . ." She hesitated, then blurted out as though saying it would rid her mind of the pollution, the anger. "I even felt anger toward Louise for bearing me. A sickly French child. I wanted—I longed to be English like the parents I loved. All of my evil thoughts made me feel . . . spiteful, sinful. And guilty. I felt so guilty I feared God might strike me down.

"Then I turned absolutely opposite in my thinking. I wanted to be French. I was angry with my mother Catherine for what she had done. If I couldn't be French and with my own family, then she should have let me die, not taken me away from my family to that English doctor. I longed to know my birth mother. My real mother. I ached to be a part of my French culture. My heritage. I couldn't understand why God had let it happen. I felt angry with Him too. It frightened me at times . . . the intensity of my feelings . . . the swings back and forth from one side to the other. I could never sort out who I was. What I was. It took me many years of struggling until I was honestly able to accept what had happened to me. It was not the fault of my parents Louise and Henri, nor the fault of my parents Catherine and Andrew. Nor was it because God was trying to punish me. It was just a fact of life."

Thomas held her hand and watched her face as she obviously struggled to find words for her emotions.

"Life can hand out some extremely painful things," she finally said, looking out over the water below them. "Once I realized that, I knew I had to stop blaming all those involved and let God direct my life. 'Submit,' I kept telling myself. 'Submit to God. One day He will make it plain. Make it right.' And I was finally able to accept things as they were. To find an inner peace. But I still felt . . . unsettled . . . whenever the thoughts came. Like a little piece of me was missing."

She turned to look at Thomas. He nodded silently, fearing that the struggle was still going on, wondering how he could help her.

But there was no anguish in Anne's eyes. There was calm. The hand he was holding was not trembling but returning his warm grasp. She smiled, ever so slightly, and her voice held a triumphant note.

"And now this! I still can scarcely believe it. I am both. French and English. I am connected to both families. Imagine! Just imagine. I finally feel that I have found myself. God has settled the issue for me through this discovery of my parentage. Imagine it!"

Thomas could feel the tears hot behind his eyelids. Why was he weeping? Seldom did he respond with tears. This was a joyous occasion. An answer to many years of prayer on the part of his beloved wife. Perhaps there really was no other way to express his deep emotion than through tears.

He slipped his arm around her and drew her close. He felt Anne's own tears as she pressed her cheek to his. His arm tightened and they sat in silence, drinking in the wonder and closeness of the moment together.

At length Anne drew back and settled against him. He had never seen her so at peace.

"You love it here, don't you?" He wouldn't have needed to make it a question. He knew the answer.

She sighed and looked out over the waters. "I think it is the most beautiful place in the world."

"Yet it brought so much pain," he reminded her.

"It was not the land that betrayed us," Anne said thoughtfully. "It was greed and lust for power . . . and fear. I think fear most of all. England and France had been at war for such a long time. I think they had forgotten how to live at peace. They raised their children to think of the other nation as the enemy. When the British came here, to a land settled by French, who outnumbered them by far, they sought to make British subjects of them. When that failed, they became fearful. Afraid that France would strike first and the Acadians would join them. They knew they could never win if it came to that. So they did what they thought they had to do. They drove them out. Like animals . . ."

Thomas waited a moment, then said, "Fear makes people do dreadful things—unreasonable things. It becomes a vicious frenzy of who will strike first to save themselves from the other. And neither side stops to reason that the other might not be considering striking at all. The enemy of our souls takes full advantage of mankind's fears. It is one of his most powerful weapons of deceit and destruction. For fear invariably turns to hate. And the hidden message is, 'Lash out. Destroy. Subdue.' Hate is a dreadful thing. God help us to never let hatred become a cancer to our soul."

Thomas paused again, then added with a smile, "My apologies for the lecture, my dear."

They both laughed, then she said softly, "Every day I thank God that He did not allow me to be engulfed in bitterness and hatred. For giving me the grace—His grace—to forgive what was done to both of my families. Bitterness and hatred are too heavy a load for even the strongest to carry. No matter what the sin against us, we only compound the pain if we cannot forgive."

She hesitated, her eyes returning to the vast land and seascape that stretched out for miles. A gull cried and was answered by another that confidently rode the gentle waves beneath the cliffside.

"It's not the land," she said again, snuggling in against him. "The land is beautiful. God created every part of this"—she waved a hand out over the scene before them—"and pronounced it good. It still is good. It still bears His mark. His touch. I can sense it whenever I watch the waves, or hear the call of the gulls, or feel the breeze touch my cheek. I can feel it whenever I am here. And I will take this feeling—this morning's solace—with me wherever God leads me. And if He should ever decide to bring me back—us back—then I will accept this . . . this very spot, as a special gift from Him."

Gordon stirred with the consciousness that the bed beside him was empty. Nicole should have been there getting much-needed rest after the emotional turmoil of the day. Was she ill? Had Andrew taken a bad turn in the night? Grandfather Price?

He pushed himself up on one elbow and let his eyes seek out the darkened room. She was there. At the open window, staring out into the emptiness of the night.

"Is something wrong?" he asked quietly. "Are you all right?"

She half turned to him. Even in the semidarkness he could sense it was neither pain nor anxiety that had taken her from bed.

"No, it's fine," she replied in a whispery voice. "In fact, I have never felt better. Never."

He could see her outline more clearly now and saw that her hand moved to rest on the spot where her unborn baby lay. He pushed back the covers and left the bed to join her.

"It's a beautiful night," she whispered as he gathered her close. One arm lifted to encircle his neck. "I couldn't sleep. I was too full of . . . of peace." She laughed softly. In the light from the full moon that was bright enough to cast shadows in the garden, Gordon could see her wrinkle her nose playfully. "That sounds silly, doesn't it? But it's true. I am just so . . . so full of thankfulness and . . . and love and peace that I couldn't sleep. I felt I needed to be up, enjoying God's world. His blessings. Oh, Gordon . . ." Her arm tightened about his neck. "I have been so blessed. I am so blessed. Do you know, the thing that bothered me most when I discovered I was English instead of French was that I couldn't really claim kinship to my mother Louise. And here we are—related. I can't believe it. And our baby—he or she—can also claim that heritage. Oh, I know, not directly. He will not have French blood flowing through his little veins, but he will have French kinfolk. I can teach him French for a perfectly legitimate reason."

She stopped for a moment and brushed back the curtain with her free hand. "But it's more than that. In a way, I think of all of this as a promise. A blending of two cultures. Perhaps we can help to show the world that it does work. Show others that man *can* live with respect for those of another nation. That hate and war and pain do not need to be. Oh, I pray that for my son—our son. And I see him as a place to start. We can teach him that, Gordon. To love his neighbor, no matter who that neighbor might be. To seek for peace. And perhaps he can share it with others and it can just grow and grow until there is no longer hate and strife in our world. Wouldn't that be wonderful?"

"Wonderful indeed." He brushed back her long hair and placed a kiss on her brow. "And you sound rather sure about a son," he teased.

She smiled. "Or a daughter," she said with a lift of her chin.

"A promise," Nicole said after a moment. "Love is a promise of all good things, and the circle of love just keeps growing larger if we allow it. But we—you and I and all of the others—we need to nurture it, like a garden, and tend it with care."

"And keep out the weeds," mused Gordon, taking up her analogy as he rubbed his chin against the softness of her hair.

"Keep out the weeds," she echoed. "Weeds of bitterness and envy and hatred and greed."

"And water it with prayer," Gordon added.

"Yes, that is the secret we must never forget."

They turned to the window together and looked out across the garden. A rabbit eased out of the shadows to nibble on a remaining turnip leaf. The breeze stirred the heads of the fall asters until they nodded to one another as though in silent conversation. In the serenity of the soft flush of moonlight, the world looked whole. At peace. And in spite of the unrest, the conflict of the world beyond, the future before them held nothing but promise.